The Quiet Heart

by
Mrs. Oliphant

The Quiet Heart
by Mrs. Oliphant

Copyright © 2024

All Rights reserved.

No part of this publication may be reproduced, stored in a retrieval system, or transmitted in any form or by any means, electronic, mechanical, photocopying or Otherwise, without the written permission of the publisher.
The author/editor asserts the moral right to be identified as the author/editor of this work.

ISBN: 978-93-64283-27-4

Published by

DOUBLE 9 BOOKS
2/13-B, Ansari Road
Daryaganj, New Delhi – 110002
info@double9books.com
www.double9books.com
Tel. 011-40042856

This book is under public domain

ABOUT THE AUTHOR

Mrs Oliphant was a prolific Scottish author, known for her extensive contributions to Victorian literature. Throughout her career, she wrote over 120 works, including novels, biographies, histories, and literary criticism. Her writing often explored themes of domestic life, societal norms, and personal morality, reflecting the complexities of Victorian society. Mrs. Oliphant's most notable works are Chronicles of Carlingford: A series of novels set in a fictional English town, examining the lives and relationships of its inhabitants, **Hester:** A novel exploring themes of business, family loyalty, and the role of women in society and **The Rector** A novella that delves into the conflicts and duties of a parish rector. Margaret Oliphant's work remains significant for its detailed portrayal of Victorian society and its focus on the inner lives of women. Her ability to capture the nuances of domestic life and the struggles of her characters has earned her a lasting place in literary history. Her writings provide valuable insights into the social and cultural dynamics of her time, making her an important figure in the study of 19th-century literature. Oliphant's writing is marked by vivid and precise descriptions of settings and characters. She meticulously depicts domestic interiors, social environments, and the minutiae of everyday life, bringing the Victorian era to life for her readers.

CONTENTS

CHAPTER I	7
CHAPTER II	12
CHAPTER III	16
CHAPTER IV	23
CHAPTER V	27
CHAPTER VI	31
CHAPTER VII	36
CHAPTER VIII	43
CHAPTER IX	47
CHAPTER X	53
CHAPTER XI	59
CHAPTER XII	63
CHAPTER XIII	68
CHAPTER XIV	72
CHAPTER XV	77
CHAPTER XVI	81
CHAPTER XVII	84
CHAPTER XVIII	89
CHAPTER XIX	93
CHAPTER XX	97
CHAPTER XXI	102

CHAPTER XXII 107
CHAPTER XXIII 110
CHAPTER XXIV 114
CHAPTER XXV 119
CHAPTER XXVI 123
CHAPTER XXVII 126
CHAPTER XXVIII 129
CHAPTER XXIX 133
CHAPTER XXX 137
CHAPTER XXXI 142
CHAPTER XXXII 145
CHAPTER XXXIII 149
CHAPTER XXXIV 153
CHAPTER XXXV 159
CHAPTER XXXVI 163
CHAPTER XXXVII 167

CHAPTER I

"Ye'll no ken, Jenny, if Miss Menie's in?"

"And what for should I no ken?" exclaimed the hot and impatient Jenny Durward, sole servant, housekeeper, and self-constituted guardian of Mrs. Laurie of Burnside, and her young fatherless daughter. "Do ye think ony ane comes or gangs in the house out of my knowledge? And where should Miss Menie be but in, sitting at her seam in the mistress's parlour, at this hour of the day?"

"I was meaning nae offence," said meek Nelly Panton: "I'm sure ye ken, Jenny woman, I wouldna disturb the very cat by the fire if it was just me; but my mother, you see, has ta'en an ill turn, and there's nae peace wi' her, day or night, a' for naething but because she's anxious in her mind — and if you would just let me get a word o' Miss Menie —"

"Am I hindering ye?" cried the indignant Jenny; "she's no ill to be seen, in her wilful way, even on wandering about the garden, damp roads or dry; but for a' the whims I've kent in her head, ae time and anither, I never heard of her setting up for either skill or wisdom past the common. I reckon she never had a sair head hersel — what kind of a helper could she be to your mother? and if she's heard of a sair heart, that's a' the length her knowledge gangs — what good is Miss Menie to do to you?"

"I'm sure I'm no meaning ony ill," said Nelly, disconsolately, sitting down on a wooden stool with passive resignation; "and it's aye kent o' me that I never provokit onybody a' my born days. I'm just wanting to speak a word to the young leddy, that's a'."

Now Nelly Panton, meekly passive as she was, had an eminent gift in the way of provocation, and kept in a perpetual fever the warmer tempers in her neighbourhood. Jenny, virtuously resolved to command herself, went out with sufficient abruptness to her kitchen door, to "fuff," as she herself called it, her incipient passion away. The visitor took no notice of Jenny's withdrawal from the field. Slow pertinacity, certain of ultimate success, calmed away all excitement from Nelly. She had taken her place with perfect composure, to wait, though it might be for hours, till the person she wished to see came to her call.

It was a day of early spring, and had rained plentifully in the morning. Light white clouds, tossed and blown about by a fantastic wind, threw their soft shadow on a clear deep sky of blue; and raindrops, glittering in the sunshine, hung upon flowers and branches, and fell now and then in a gleam from the shaken hedge or garden fruit-trees. The garden paths were wet—the road without had a flowing rivulet of accumulated rain, which almost made as much ringing with its hasty footsteps as did the burn itself under the little bridge which crossed the way—and the blue-slated roof of this house of Burnside blazed like a slanted mirror in the eyes of the full sun.

Not the faintest shade of architectural pretensions dignified this house of Burnside. Four substantial walls of rough grey stone, a slated roof, with but one projecting attic window to break its slope—a door in the gable where one would least have expected a door to be—and windows breaking the wall just where the builder found it convenient that the wall should be broken. The house stood upon a little knoll, the ground on all sides sloping downward,—at one hand to the course of the burn—at the other, to the edge of the plantation which benevolently threw up a line of tall firs to screen its human neighbours from the unfriendly east. Close upon the very edge of the walls pressed the soft grass of the lawn; some spring-flowers looked out from little bits of border soil here and there; and a fairy larch stood half-way up the ascent on the sunniest side, shaking itself free of the encumbering rain with a pretty, coquettish grace, and throwing a glistening flash of little diamonds, now and then, as if in sport, over the fluttering hair and sunny face, which seem to have a natural sisterhood and companionship with the free and graceful tree.

Hair that was smoothly shaded this morning over the young, clear, youthful brow—the wind has found out scores of little curls hidden in the braids, and turns them out with a child's laughter, full of sweet triumph and delight—a face that looks up full and clearly to answer the brave smile upon the sky. Twenty years old, with warm blood flashing in her cheeks, a fearless, innocent courage gleaming from her eyes, and never a cloud over her all her life long, save some such soft, white, rounded shadow as floats yonder in our sight over the undiscouraged heavens—for it is very true that neither headache nor heartache has yet been known to Menie Laurie by any surer knowledge than the hearing of the ear.

Maiden meditation—No: there is little of this in the stir of life that makes an unconscious atmosphere about her, here where she stands in the fearless safety of her natural home. Not that Menie is notably thoughtless either, or poor in the qualities of mind which produce thought—but her mind lies still, like a charmed sea under the sunshine. There has never a ship of hope gone down yet under those dazzling waters, never a storm arisen upon them to chafe the waves against the rocks; nothing but flecks of summer clouds, quiet shadows of summer nights, darkness all lit and glorified with mellow moonbeams—and how her heart would be if some strange ghost of tempest rose upon the sky, her heart neither knows nor fears.

The window is open behind you, Menie; Mrs Laurie fears no draughts, and it is well; but our mother's patience, like other good things, has a limit, and having called you vainly three times over, she closes behind you this mode of return. No great matter. See what a little sparkling shower this poor brown-coated sparrow has shaken from the thorny branch he has just perched upon; and as your eyes wander in this direction, your ear becomes aware of a certain sound, a quick impatient breath sent hard through the expanded nostrils, which is the well-known token in the house of Burnside of Jenny's "fuff;" and straightway your eyes brighten, Menie Laurie—one could not have fancied it was possible a minute ago—and smiles half hidden break over all your face, flushing here and there in such a kindly suffusion of playfulness and mirth, that even Jenny herself is not angry when she sees how this fuff of hers makes excellent sport for you.

"What ails our Jenny now?" said Menie, turning the angle of the wall to enter by the kitchen door.

"Lassie, dinna drive folk doited," answered Jenny. "I'm thrang at my wark—gang in yonder and speak to her yoursel."

Nelly Panton sits mournfully upon the wooden stool. If you take her own word for it, no one is more contemptuous of "fyking" and "making a wark" than Jenny of Burnside; but the kitchen—woe be to the hapless stranger who ventures to commend it!—is quite resplendent with brightness and good order. The fire, cheerfully burning in the grate, finds a whole array of brilliant surfaces to dance in, and dances to its heart's content. Glittering metal and earthenware, Jenny's looking-glass at one side, and the dark polish of Jenny's oak table with its folding leaf at the other, line all the walls with warmth and light; and the fire, repulsed and defeated only by this one obstinately opaque body before it, besets the dark outline of Nelly Panton with a very tremble of eagerness, seeking in vain for something, if it were but the pin of her shawl, or the lifting of her eye, to repeat its kindly glimmer in. There is no pin visible in Nelly's doleful shawl, so closely wrapped about her person, and Nelly's pensive glances seek the floor, and the light falls off from her figure foiled and baffled, finding nothing congenial there. Come you hither, Menie Laurie, that the friendly fireside spirit may be consoled—playing in warm rays upon your hair, which the wind has blown about so pleasantly that the bright threads hang a hundred different ways, and catch a various glow of reflection in every curl—leaping up triumphantly under the raised lids of these sunny eyes—catching a little ring upon your finger, a little golden clasp at your white neck. No wonder Nelly draws her shawl closer, and turns her back upon the light, as she rises to speak to you.

"My mother's ill and anxious in her mind, Miss Menie; and no to say *that* its lane, but thrawn and perverse as onybody could conceive. I'm sure ye'll hear nae character of me in the haill countryside for onything but being as harmless a person as could gang about quiet wark in ony house; but she's ta'en a turn that she canna bide even me; and aye for ever, night and morning, keeping up a constant wark about her son. I like Johnnie weel enough mysel—but what's the guid o' seeking letters as lang as we ken he's weel?—and that's what I'm aye saying, but she'll no hearken to me."

"Does Johnnie write so seldom?—but I'm sure nothing ails him, or we should have heard," said Menie. "Tell her she's to keep up her heart—he'll do very well yonder. You should make her cheery, Nelly, now when you're at home the whole day."

"I do what I can, Miss Menie," said Nelly, shaking her head mournfully. "I tell her a lad's just as safe in the toun as in the country, and that it's a real unbelieving-like thing to be aye groaning even on about Johnnie, and her has mair bairns. But someway she gets nae satisfaction, and I think she would be mair pleased if you could get a line from Mr Randall saying when he saw him, and whether he's doing well or no, than a' the reason I could gie her if I was preaching frae this to Martinmas. I came away from my wark anes errant to bid ye. Will you ask Mr Randall about Johnnie, Miss Menie, that I may get some peace wi' my mother?"

The breath comes quickly over Menie Laurie's lip—a little flutter of added colour—a momentary falling of the eyelids—a shy, conscious smile hovering about the mouth—and then Menie nods her head assentingly and says, "Yes, Nelly, I will."

"Yes, Nelly, I will," repeated Menie, after a little pause of blushing self-communion. "Tell her I'll come and let her hear as soon as there is any news; and say I think she should be cheery, Nelly, now she has you at home."

Making a meek inclination of her person, neither a bow nor a curtsy, but something half-way between them, in answer to this speech, Nelly goes away; and almost encountering her on her outward passage over the threshold, enters Jenny fuffing at a furious rate, and casting her head up into the air with wrathful contempt, like some little shaggy Highland pony whose pride has been wounded. For Jenny's wrath has nothing of the dignity conferred by superior stature or commanding person, and it is hard to restrain a smile at the vigour of her "fuff."

"Twenty years auld, and nae mair sense than that!—the lassie's daft! I would like to ken how it's possible for mortal woman to be cheery with Nelly Panton within half a mile o' her! If they flit to the Brigend at the next term, as they're aye threatening, I'll gie the mistress her leave mysel."

"I think I'll run away if you're aye so crabbed, Jenny," said her young mistress. "What has everybody done?"

"Everybody's done just a' the mischief they could do," said Jenny, pathetically: "there's no an article ever happens in this house that mightna be mended if some ither body had the guiding o't. There's a' the gangrels o' the countryside coming and gaun with their stories—there's the mistress hersel, that might have mair sense, ta'en a cauld in her head, and a hoast fit to waken a' the toun, standing at the door hearing Bessy Edgar's clavers about a no-weel wean—and there's yoursel the warst of a'. Do you think if onybody had ever askit me, that *I* would have gien my consent to let a lassie o' your years plight her troth to a wandering lad away to seek his fortune, like Randall Home? But you'll never ken the guid friend you've lost in Jenny till the puir body's out o' the gate, and in her grave; and I wouldna say how soon that might be if there's nae end o' on-gauns like thir."

And with a loud long sigh Jenny sallied out through the paved passage, from which you could catch a gleam of sunshine playing in chequers on the strip of coloured matting and the margin of stones, to deliver just such another lecture to the mistress in the parlour.

While Menie stands alone, her head thrown forward a little, her hair playing lightly on her cheek, in a pause of pleasant fancy—yes, it is true, Menie is betrothed. Calm as her heart lies in her pure girl's breast, Menie has seen the sky flush out of its natural summer beauty with the warmer passionate hues of this new love; and many a tint of joyous changeful colour plays about the bright horizon of Menie's fancy, and throws a charm of speculation into the future, which never spectre has risen yet to obscure. It would need a sermon heavier than Jenny's to throw a single vapour of doubt or distrust upon Menie Laurie's quiet heart.

CHAPTER II

Mrs Laurie of Burnside sits alone in her sunny parlour. The fire in the grate, quite discountenanced and overborne by the light which pours in from the west window, keeps up a persevering crackle, intent to catch the ear, and keep itself in notice by that means if by no other. It is the only sound you can hear, except the hum of the eight-day clock in the passage without, and Jenny's distant step upon the kitchen floor;—Menie is out again on some further explorations about the garden—Mrs Laurie sits and works alone.

You might call this room a drawing-room if you were ambitiously disposed—it is only the parlour in Burnside. Every piece of wood about it is dark with age and careful preservation; rich ancient mahogany glimmering clear in the polish of many a year's labour—little tables with twisted spiral legs and fantastic ornaments almost as black as ebony—and here in the corner a fine old cabinet of oak, with its carved projections of flower and berry burnished bright, and standing out in clear relief from the dark background. On the table lies some "fancy-work," which it irks the soul of Mrs Laurie to see her daughter employed on; but what is to be done with Menie's fingers, when our mother feels the household necessities of sewing scarcely enough to supply herself?

Go lightly over the rich colours of this well-preserved carpet, which is older than yourself most probably, though it wears its age so well, and we can look out and see what lies beyond the Burnside garden before Mrs Laurie is aware. The west window is all fringed and glittering with raindrops lying lightly on the pale green buds of these honeysuckle boughs, and now and then one of them falls pattering down upon the grass like a sigh. Do not believe in it—it is but a mock of nature—the counterfeit wherewithal a light heart enhances to itself its own calm joy; for in reality and truth there is no such thing as sighing here.

Some thatched houses in a cluster, just where the green-mossed wall of the bridge breaks out of the shelter of these guarding fir-trees—one triumphant slated roof lifting itself a story higher than the gossipry of those good neighbours who lay their brown heads together in a perpetual quiet discussion of what goes on below. The light lies quietly, half caressing, upon the thatch roofs, but gleams off the wet slates, and flashes from the tiles yonder, in a sudden glow. There are some loitering firs about, to thrust their outline on the enclosing sky, and a hazy background of bare trees fluttering and glistering in the light, all conscious of the new-budded leaves, which at this distance we cannot see. Beyond the Brigend your eye loses itself on a line of road travelling away towards the hills, with two great heavy ash-trees holding their gaunt arms over it for a portal and gateway—on a level line of fields, broken hedges, scattered trees, with the blue tints of distance, and here and there the abrupt brown dash of a new-ploughed field to diversify the soft universal green—and on the hills themselves, a bold semi-circular sweep stealing off faintly to the sky on one hand—while at the other, Criffel, bluff and burly, slopes his great shoulder down upon the unseen sea.

Nearer at hand the burn itself looks through the garden's thorny boundary with glints and sunny glances, interchanging merrily with Menie on the lawn, who pays its smiles with interest. This is almost all we have to look at from the west window of Burnside.

And now, if you turn within to our mother in her easy-chair. It is not quite what you call benign, this broad, full, well-developed brow; and the eyes under it so brown, and liquid, and dewy, one fancies they could flash with impatience now and then, and laugh out the warmest mirth, as well as smile that smile of kindness, which few eyes express so well; and it is best to say at the beginning that our mother is not benign, and that it is no abstract being of a superior class lifted on the height of patience, experience, and years, who sits before us in this cushioned chair, bending her brow a little over the letter in her hand. Sorrow and experience she has had in her day; but still our mother, with warm human hands, and breast as full of hope and energy as it was twenty years ago, takes a full grasp of life.

The linen she has been mending lies on the table beside her, more than half concealing Menie's lighter occupation; and, with her elbow leant upon it, Mrs Laurie holds a letter with a half-puzzle of amusement, a half-abstraction of thought. Strangely adverse to all her moods and habits is the proposal it makes, yet Mrs Laurie lingers over it, hesitates, almost thinks she will accept. Such a multitude of things are possible to be done when one does them "for Menie's sake."

For Menie's sake—but, in the mean time, it is best that Menie should be called in to share the deliberation; and here she comes accordingly, with such an odour of fresh air about her as makes the parlour fragrant. Menie has a restless way of wandering about on sunny afternoons; there is something in her that will not compose into quietness; and very poor speed, when it is sunshine, comes Menie's "fancy-work;" so that there is nothing more common than this fragrance of fresh air in the parlour when Menie's presence is needed there.

"Your father's aunt has written me a letter. I want your wisest thought about it. Read it, Menie," said Mrs Laurie, leaning back in her chair, with an air of exhaustion. Menie read—

"My dear Mrs Laurie,—I find I really have forgotten your Christian name; and whether I have quite a right to call you my dear niece, or whether you might not think it an uncalled-for thing in me who have not the privilege of years, or if, one way or another, you would be pleased, I cannot tell, having so little acquaintance with your mental habits or ways of thinking. Indeed I confess I had nearly forgotten, my dear, that John Laurie had a wife and a little girl in Kirklands still, till just a chance recalled it to me: and I really have no means of finding out whether I should condole with you for living so much out of the world, or wish you joy of a pretty little house like Burnside, with its nice neighbourhood and good air. I am sometimes a little dull myself, living alone; and as I have positively made up my mind never to marry, and am so particular in my society that I never have above half-a-dozen friends whom I care to visit, it has occurred to me, since you were recalled to my recollection, that we might do worse than join our incomes together, and live as one household. I have pretty reception-rooms in my house, and a sleeping-room more than I need—a very good apartment; and the advantage of being near London is very great for a little girl, for masters, and all that: besides that, I flatter myself the attention I should make a point of paying her would be of great importance to your child; and out of what we could put together of our joint savings, we might make a very pretty marriage-portion for her when her time comes; for I have no other relations, as I fancy you know, and have very decidedly made up my mind, whatever persecution I may be exposed to on the subject, never to marry. I have one tolerably good servant, who is my own maid, and another very bad one, who has charge of all the household matters: the grief and annoyance this woman is to me are beyond description; and if you should happen to have an attached and faithful person in your house, I advise you to bring her with you;—of course you will require an attendant of your own.

"I shall be glad to have a letter from you soon, letting me know what you will do. You would have a cheerful life with me, I think. I am myself a person of uncommonly lively disposition, though I have known so many of the more refined sorrows of life; and the freshness of youth is a delightful study. I feel I shall grow quite a child in sympathy with your little girl. Pray come—Hampstead is a delightful locality; so near London, too, and within reach of society so very excellent—and I am sure you would find the change greatly for your daughter's good.

"With much regard and kind feeling to both her and you, I am affectionately yours,

"Annie Laurie."

"To Hampstead! to London!" Menie says nothing more, but her eyes shine upon her mother's with a restless glow of appeal. London holds many a wonder to the young curious heart which yet knows nothing of the world, and London holds Randall Home.

"You would like to go, Menie? But how we should like this aunt of yours is a different story," said Mrs Laurie; "and for my part, I am very well content with Burnside."

"It is true she calls me a little girl," said Menie, turning to her own particular grievance; "but I should think she means everything very kindly, for all that."

"Fantastic old wife!" said Mrs Laurie, with a little impatient derision, not unlike Jenny's fuff. "She was older than your father, Menie—a woman near sixty, I'll warrant; and *she* has made up her mind never to marry—did ever anybody hear the like! But you need not look so disappointed either. Put away the letter—we'll take a night's rest on it, and then we'll decide."

But Menie read it over once more before she laid it aside, and Menie betrayed her anxiety about the decision in a hundred questions which her mother could not answer. Mrs Laurie had only once been in London, and could tell nothing of Hampstead, the only reminiscence remaining with her being of a verdant stretch of turf, all dinted over with little mounds and hollows rich in green fern and furze, which the benighted natives called a heath. Born within sight of Lochar Moss, Mrs Laurie laughed the pretensions of this metropolitan heath to scorn.

CHAPTER III

The wind sweeps freshly down from among the hills, a busy knave, drying up the gleaming pools along the road as he hurries forward for a moment's pause and boisterous gossip with these two ash-trees. Very solemn and abstracted as they stand, these elders of the wood, looking as if session or synod were the least convention they could stoop to, it is wonderful how tolerant they are of every breath of gossip, and with what ready interest they rustle over all their twigs to see a new unwonted stranger face pass under them. Menie Laurie, pausing to look up through the hoar branches to the full blue sky, is too well known and familiar to receive more than the friendly wave of recognition accorded to every cottar neighbour nigh.

And clear and fresh as your own life, Menie, is the blue bright sky which stoops above you. White clouds all streaked and broken fly over it at a headlong pace, now and then throwing from their hasty hands a sprinkling of rain that flashes in the sunshine. April is on the fields, moving in that quiet stir with which you can hear the young green corn-blades rustle, as they strike through the softened soil. April sits throned upon the hills, weeping as she smiles in the blue distance, and trying on her veil of misty sunshine, after a hundred fantastic fashions, like a spoiled child; and April, Menie Laurie—April, restless, fearless, springing forward on the future, gladdening all this bright to-day with a breath of rippling sweet commotion, which dimples all the surface over, but never disturbs the deeper waters at their fountain-head—is in your youthful heart.

Hurrying to many a bright conclusion are the speculations that possess it now—not extremely reasonable, or owning any curb of logic—not even very consequent, full of joyous irrelevancies—digressions at which yourself would laugh aloud if this running stream of fancy were but audible and expressed—notwithstanding, full of interest, full of pleasure, and keeping time with their rapid pace to the flying progress of the clouds.

And the road glides away merrily under these straying footsteps; now hastening, now loitering, as the momentary mood suggests. Old hawthorns, doddered and crabbed, stand here and there forlorn upon the edges of the way; and where the hedge is younger and less broken, there are warm banks of turf, and clear bits of gleaming water, which it would be an insult to call ditches, looking up through tangled grass, and a wilderness of delicate stem and leaf, half weeds, half flowers. But now we have a stile to cross, mounting up from the high-road; and now it is a sunny hillside path, narrow and hemmed in between a low stone-wall, from which all manner of mosses and tufts of waving herbage have taken away the rudeness, and a field of young green corn: innocent enough just now are these soft plants low upon the fragrant soil in the blade; but you shall see how the bearded spikes will push you to the wall, and the red poppies mock you, lying safe under shelter of the tall corn-forest, if you try to pass in September where you can pass so easily in Spring.

A soft incline, at first sloping smoothly under the full sunshine—by-and-by more rugged and broken, with something that looks half like the ancient channel of a hill-spring, breaking all the soft pasture-grass into a rough projecting outline, like a miniature coast—and now a low hedge rough with thorns and brambles, instead of the dyke; for, after all, this is no gentle southland hill, but one of the warders of the Scottish Border, waving his plumed cap proudly in the fresh spring air, as he looks over the low-lying debatable moors on the other side, and defies the fells of Cumberland. If this were June, as it is April, you would see foliage clustering richly about the bold brow which he lifts to the clouds; just now the branches hang down, like long light brown ringlets, half unravelled with the spring rain and morning dew, and droop upon his falling shoulders as low as this green nest here, so sheltered and solitary, which he holds in his expanded arms.

It is no easy task to come at the state entrance and principal gate of the farmhouse of Crofthill. But now that you have caught sight of its white walls and slated roof, hold on stoutly—fear no gap in the hedge, no rude stone-stair projecting out of the grey limestone dyke—and two or three leaps and stumbles will bring you to the mossy paling, and to some possible entrance-door. If there is no one about—a very improbable circumstance, seeing that some curious eye at a window must have ere now found out a passenger on the ascent, or some quick ear heard the dry hedgerow branches crash under the coming foot—it is impossible to describe the strange feeling of isolation which falls upon you, here at the door of as friendly a little home as is on all the Border. At your right hand those warder hills, in many a diverse tint of long-worn livery, hold the vigilant line as far as Criffel, whose post is on the sea; on the other side they disappear like a file of grey-headed marshal-men, into the cloudy distance; underneath, remote, and still, breaking softly into the fresh daylight, mapped out with gleaming burns and long lines of winding road, lies the level country we have left; and Burnside yonder, with its thin silvery glimmer of attendant water, its dark background of trees, and the Brigend hamlet of which it is patrician and superior, lies quiet and silent under the full sun.

The farmhouse of Crofthill is but two storeys high, and, with a strange triangular slope of garden before it, fronts sideways, indifferent to the landscape, though there is one glorious gable-window which makes amends. Menie Laurie, bound for the Crofthill farmhouse, knows the view so well that she does not pause for even a momentary glance, but, lightly stepping over the last stile, is ready to meet this welcoming figure which already calls to her, running down the garden to the little mossy wicket in the paling of the lower end.

"July! July! you might have come to meet me," said Menie. The air is so quiet that her soft girl's voice rings over all the hill.

July—but you must not look for anything like the gorgeous summer month, in this little timid slight figure running down the sloping way with her light brown hair so soft and silky that it is almost impossible to retain it either in braid or curl, floating on the air behind her, and her gentle pale face faintly glowing with a little flush of pleasure. If there had been anything symbolic in the name, they had better have called her February, this poor little July Home; but there is nothing symbolic in the name—only John Home of Crofthill, many a long year ago, had the hap to find somewhere, and bring triumphantly to his house on the hill, a pretty little sentimental wife, with some real refinement in her soft nature, and a good deal of the fantastic girl-romance, which passes muster for it among the unlearned. Mrs Home, who called her son Randall, called her little daughter Julia— Mrs Home's husband, who knew of nothing better than Johns or Janets, being quiescent, and kindly submissive. But by-and-by, gentle Mrs Home drooped like the pale little flower she was, and fell with the cold spring showers into her grave. Then came big Miss Janet Home from Mid-Lothian, where she had spent her younger days, to be mistress of her brother's southland farm; and Miss Janet's one name for the flush of summer, and for her brother's little motherless petted girl, was Juley; so July came to be the child's acknowledged name.

But July springs half into Menie Laurie's arms, and they go up through the garden together, to where Miss Janet stands waiting on the threshold. In simple stature, Miss Janet would make two of her little niece; and though there is no other superfluous bulk about her, her strong and massive framework would not misbecome a man; though a verier woman's heart never beat within the daintiest boddice, than this one which sometimes "thuds" rather tumultuously, under the large printed dark cotton gown of Miss Janet Home.

"Eh, bairn, I'm glad to see you," said Miss Janet, holding in her own large brown hand the soft fingers of Menie. "Come in-by, and get yoursel rested. You see there's a letter frae Randy this morning—"

With many a fit of indignation had Menie resented this Randy, which contracted so unceremoniously her hero's name; but the penitent Miss Janet perpetually forgot, and immediately attributed the little cloud on her favourite's brow to some jealousy of this same letter of Randy's—and pique that it should come to Randy's humble home instead of to his lady-love.

"I'm aye sae uplifted about a letter," continued Miss Janet, as she led her visitor in, "though you that gets them every day mayna think—Eh, Miss Menie, my dear! I mind noo it's a' me; but you needna gloom at what was just a forget. I'll never ca' him Randy again; but, you see, I mind him so weel in his wee coatie—a bit smout o' a bairn."

This did not exactly mend matters; but Menie had taken off her bonnet by this time, and found her usual seat in the dim farm-parlour, with its small windows and low-roofed green-stained walls. It was one of the articles of Miss Janet's creed, that blinds looked well from without; so, although there could never a mortal look in through the thick panes to spy the household economics of Crofthill, only one narrow strip of the unveiled casement appeared between the little muslin curtain and the blind. The gable window, commanding as it did half the level country of Dumfriesshire, was less protected; but the front one cast a positive shadow upon the dark thrifty coloured carpet, the hair-cloth chairs, the mahogany table with its sombre cover, and gave to the room such an atmosphere of shrouded shadowed quiet, that the little bouquet of daffodils and wallflowers on the side-table hung their heads with languid melancholy, and an unaccustomed spectator scarcely ventured with more than a whisper to break the calm.

But Menie Laurie was not unaccustomed, and knew very well where was the brightest corner, nor had much hesitation in drawing up the blind. But Menie had grown very busy with the "fancy" work she had brought with her, when Miss Janet approached with Randall's letter in her hand. Scandal said that Menie Laurie's pretty fingers were never so industrious at home as they found it agreeable to be abroad, and Menie was coy and occupied, and put Randall's letter aside.

"My dear, if you're busy I'll read it to you, mysel," said Miss Janet, who had no appreciation of coyness, "and you can tell your faither, July, that Miss Menie's come, and that the tea's just ready; and ye can gie a look ben to the kitchen as you're passing, and see that Tibbie's no forgetting the time; and now gang about quiet, like a good bairn, and dinna disturb me. I'm gaun to read the letter."

And Miss Janet smoothed down her apron, to lay this prized epistle safely on her knee, and wiped her glasses with affectionate eagerness. "My dear, I'm no a grand reader of Randall's write mysel," said Miss Janet, clearing her voice, "and he's getting an awfu' crabbed hand, as you ken; but I've good-will, and you'll just put up with me."

It would have been hard for any one gifted with a heart to fail of putting up with Miss Janet as she conned her nephew's letter. True, she had to pause now and then for a word—true, that she did not much assist Randall's punctuation; but it was worth even a better letter than Randall's to see the absorbed face, the affectionate care upon her brow, the anxiety that pondered over all these crabbed corners, and would not lose a word. Menie Laurie had soul enough not to be impatient—even to look up at the abstracted Miss Janet with a little dew in her eye, though her process of reading was very slow.

But now came Tibbie, the household servant of Crofthill, with the tea; and now a little stir in the passage intimated that the maister, fresh from his hillside fields, was hanging up his broad-brimmed hat in the passage. Miss Janet seated herself at the tray—Menie drew her chair away from the window, and a little nearer to the table, and, heralded by July, who came in again like a quiet shadow, her little pale face appearing in the midst of a stream of soft hair once more blown out of its fastenings by the wind—John Home of Crofthill made his appearance, stooping under his low parlour-door.

And perhaps it was these low portals which gave to the lofty figure of the hillside farmer its habitual stoop; but John Home might have been a moss-trooping chieftain for his strength—a baron of romance, for the unconscious dignity and even grace of his bearing. He was older than you would have expected July's father to be, and had a magnificent mass of white hair, towering into a natural crest of curls over his forehead. The eyes were blue, something cold by natural colour, but warm and kindly in their shining—the face full of shrewd intelligence, humour, and good judgment. He had been nothing all his life but the farmer of Crofthill—and Crofthill was anything but a considerable farm; nevertheless John Home stood in the countryside distinct as his own hill—and not unlike. A genius son does not fall to the lot of every southland farmer, and Randall's aspirations had elevated, unawares, the whole tone of the family. Randall's engagement, too, and the magic which made Mrs Laurie of Burnside's young lady-daughter, and not any farmhouse beauty near, so kindly and intimate a visitor in Crofthill, was not without its additional influence; but the house lost nothing of its perfectly unpretending simplicity in the higher aims to which it unconsciously opened its breast.

"And what is this I hear, of going to London?" said John Home, as he took his seat at table. Self-respect hinders familiarity—the good farmer did not like to call his daughter-in-law elect by her own simple Christian name; so half in joke, and half to cover the shy, constitutional hesitation, of which even age had not recovered him, Menie bore in Crofthill, in contrast with the other name of July habitual there, the pretty nickname of May—"Is it true that Burnside is to flit bodily, as July says? I ken ane that will like the change; but I must say that I ken some mair that will not be quite so thankful."

"Ye may say that, John," said Miss Janet, with a sigh. "I'm sure, for his ain part, Miss Menie, he'll no think the place is like itsel, and you away; for if ever I saw a man"——

"Whisht," said Crofthill hurriedly. The good man did not like his partiality spoken of in presence of its object. "But I would like to hear when this terrible flitting is to be."

"My mother has not made up her mind yet," said Menie. "It was yesterday the letter came, and I left her still as undecided as ever—for she is only half inclined to go, Mr Home; and as for Jenny"——

"It will be worth while to hear what Jenny says of London," said John Home with a smile; "but the countryside will gather a cloud when we think May's gone from Burnside. Well, July, speak out, woman; what is't you're whispering now?"

"I was saying that Randall would be glad," said July softly. July had a fashion of whispering her share of the conversation to her next neighbour, to be repeated for the general benefit.

"Eh, puir laddie!" exclaimed Miss Janet, with glistening eye. "I could find it in my heart to be glad too, Miss Menie, though we are to lose you, for his sake. I think I see the glint in his eye when he hears the good news."

And Miss Janet's own eyes shone with loving, unselfish sympathy, as she repeated, "Randy, puir callant! and no a creature heeding about him, mair than he was a common young man, in a' yon muckle toun!"

"We'll let Randall say his pleasure himsel," said his father, who was more delicately careful of embarrassing Menie than either sister or daughter—perhaps more, indeed, than the occasion required. "For my part, I'm no glad, and never would pretend to be; and if Mrs Laurie makes up her mind to stay"——

"What then?" said Menie, looking up quickly, with a flush of displeasure.

"I'll say she's a very sensible woman," said the farmer. "Ay, May, my lassie, truly will I, for a' that bonnie gloom of yours—or whatever my son Randall may have to say."

CHAPTER IV

"I've been hearing something from Miss Menie, mem," said Jenny, entering the parlour of Burnside with a determined air, and planting herself firmly behind the door. Jenny was very short, very much of one thickness from the shoulders to the edge of the full round skirts under which pattered her hasty feet—and had a slight deformity, variously estimated by herself and her rustic equals according to the humour of the moment—being no more than "a high shouther" in Jenny's sunshiny weather, but reaching the length of a desperate "thraw" when Jenny's temper had come to be as "thrawn" as her frame. A full circle, bunchy, substantial, and comfortable, were Jenny's woollen skirts, striped in cheerful colours; and you had no warrant for supposing that any slovenly superfluous bulk increased the natural dimensions of the round, considerable waist, or stiff, well-tightened boddice, of which Jenny's clean short gown and firmly tied apron-strings defined the shape so well. Very scanty was Jenny's hair, and very little of it appeared under her white muslin cap; and Jenny's complexion was nothing to boast of, though some withered bloom remained upon her cheeks. Her lips closed upon each other firmly; her brow was marked with sundry horizontal lines, which it was by no means difficult to deepen into a frown; and Jenny's eyes, grey, keen, and active, were at this present moment set in fierce steadiness and gravity; while the little snort of her "fuff," and the little nod of her cap, with its full, well-ironed borders, gave timely intimation of the mood in which Jenny came.

"Yes, Jenny," said Mrs Laurie, laying down her work on her knee, and sitting back into her chair. Mrs Laurie knew the signs and premonitions well, and lost no time in setting her back against the rock, and taking up her weapons of defence.

"I say I've been hearing something from Miss Menie, mem," repeated Jenny still more emphatically; "things are come a gey length, to my puir thought, when it's the youngest of the house that brings word of a great change to me!—and I'm thinking the best thing we can do is to part friends as lang as we can keep up decent appearances; so maybe ye'll take the trouble, mem, if it's no owre muckle freedom of me asking you, to look out for a new lass afore the term."

"Indeed, Jenny, I'll do no such thing," said Mrs Laurie quietly. Jenny heeded not, but went on with a little nervous motion of her head, half shake, half nod, and many a snort and half-drawn breath interposed between.

"There's been waur folk than Jenny serving in this house, I reckon. I've kent women mysel that did less wark with mair slaistry—and aye as muckle concerned for the credit of the house; but I'm no gaun to sound my ain praise; and I would like to ken whether I'm to be held to the six months' warning, or if I may put up my kist and make my flitting like other folk at the term?"

"You can make your flitting, Jenny, when we make ours; that is soon enough, surely," said Mrs Laurie with a half smile. Jenny had not roused her mistress yet to anything but defence, so with a louder fuff than ever she rushed to the attack again.

"For a smooth-spoken lass—believe hersel, she wouldna raise the stour without pardon craved—I would recommend Nelly Panton. There's no muckle love lost atween her and me—but she'll say ony ill of Jenny—and aye have a curtsy ready for a lady's ca', and her een on the grund, and neither mind nor heart o' her ain, if the mistress says no. Na, I wouldna say but Nelly Panton's the very ane to answer, for she'll never take twa thoughts about casting off father and mother, kin and country, whenever ye like to bid—though ye'll mind, mem, it's for sake of the wage, and no for sake of you."

"Dear me, Jenny," said Mrs Laurie impatiently, "when did I ask for such a sacrifice? What makes ye such a crabbed body, woman? Did I ever bid a servant of mine give up father or mother for me? You have been about Burnside ten years now, Jenny—when did you know me do anything like that?"

"A lady mayna mean ony ill—I'm no saying't," said Jenny; "but ane may make a bonnie lock of mischief without kenning. I've been ten years about Burnside—ay, and mair siller!—and to think the mistress should be laying her odds and ends thegither—a woman at her time of life—to flit away to a strange country, and never letting on a word to Jenny, till the puir body's either forced into a ship upon the sea, or thrown on the cauld world to find her drap parritch at ony doorstep where there's charity! Eh, sirs, what's the favour of this world to trust to! But I'm no gaun to break my heart about it, for Jenny has twa guid hands o' her ain—nae thanks to some folk—to make her bread by yet!"

"Jenny's an unreasonable body," said her mistress, with half-amused annoyance: "and if you were not spoken to before, it was just because my mind was unsettled, and it's only since yesterday I have thought of it at all.

If I make up my mind to go, it's for anything but pleasure to myself—so you have no occasion to upbraid me, Jenny, for doing this at my time of life."

"Me!" exclaimed Jenny, lifting her hands in appeal, "me upbraid the mistress! Eh, sirs, the like of that! But, mem, will you tell me, if it's no for your ain pleasure, you that's an independent lady, what for would you leave Burnside?"

Mrs Laurie hesitated; but Mrs Laurie knew very well that nothing could be more unprofitable than any resentment of Jenny's fuff—and her own transitory displeasure had already died away.

"You may say we're independent at this present time," she said with a little sigh; "but did it never occur to you, Jenny—if anything happened to me—my poor lassie!—what's to become of Menie then?"

"Havers!" cried Jenny loudly. "I mean—I ask your pardon—but what's gaun to happen to you this twenty years and mair?"

"Twenty years is a lifetime of itself," said her mistress; "it might not be twenty days nor twenty hours. The like of us have no right to reckon our time."

"It's time for me to buckle my shoon to my feet, and my cloak to my shouthers, if you're thinking upon your call," said Jenny. "But, no to be ill-mannered, putting my forbears in ae word with yours, we're baith come of a lang-lived race—and you're just in your prime, as weel as ever ye was; and 'deed, I canna think it onything but a reflection upon myself, that maybe might get to the kirk mair constant if I was to try, when I hear ye speaking like that to puir auld wizened Jenny, that's six and fifty guid, no to speak of the thraw she's had a' her days."

And a single hot tear of petulant distress fell upon Jenny's arm.

"Well, Jenny," said Mrs Laurie, "one thing we'll agree in, I know—you could not wish so ill a wish to Menie, poor thing, as that she might leave this world before her mother. You would think it in the course of nature that Menie should see both you and me in our graves. Now, if I was taken away next week, or next year,—what is my poor bairn to do?"

And Jenny vainly fuffed to conceal the little fit of sobbing which this idea brought upon her. "Do! She'll be married upon her ain gudeman lang years afore that time comes; and Randall Home's a decent lad, though I'll no say he would have just taken *my* fancy, if onybody had askit me; and she'll hae a hunder pound or twa to keep her pocket, of what you're aye saving for her; and I have twa-three bawbees laid up in the bank mysel."

"Ay, Jenny, so have I," said her mistress; "but two or three hundred pounds is a poor provision for a young friendless thing like Menie; and I have nothing but a liferent in Burnside; and my annuity, you know, ends with me. No doubt there's Randall Home to take into consideration; but the two of them are very young, Jenny, and many a thing may come in the way. I would like Menie to have something else to depend on than Randall Home."

"Bless me, mem, you've a mote in your een the day," said Jenny impatiently. "What's the puir callant done now? They tell me he's as weel-doing a lad as can be, and what would onybody have mair?"

"Hush, Jenny," said Mrs Laurie, "and hear me to an end. This lady has a better income than I have, and she says we may lay our savings together for Menie—a very good offer; and Menie can get better education, whatever may happen to her; and we can see with our own eyes how Randall Home is coming on in the world; for you see, Jenny, I have a kind of right to be selfish on Menie's account. I've tried poverty myself in my day; and Menie is my only bairn."

The tears came into the mother's eyes. Menie had not always been her only bairn; and visions of a bold brother, two years older than her little girl, and natural protector and champion of Menie, flashed up before her in the bright air of this home room, where ten years ago her first-born paled and sickened to his early death.

"I wouldna gang—no a fit," exclaimed Jenny, breaking into a little passion of anger and tears. "Wha's trusting in Providence now—wha's leaving the ane out of the question that has a' in His hands—and making plans like as if He didna remain when we were a' away? I didna think there had been sae little mense—I couldna have believed there was sae little grace in a house like this—and I wouldna gang a fit—no me—as if I thought Providence was owre puir an inheritance for the bairn!"

And Jenny hurried away to her kitchen, to expend both tears and anger; but Jenny's opposition to the London "flitting," in spite of her indignant protest, died from that hour.

CHAPTER V

The sun is dipping low into the burning sea far away, which Criffel's envious shoulder hides from us; and the last sheaf of rays, like a handful of golden arrows, strikes down into the plain, grazing this same strong shoulder with ineffectual fire as they pass. Touches as of rosy fingers are on all the clouds, and here and there one hangs upon the sky in an ecstacy, suspended not upon the common air, but on some special atmosphere of light. The long attendant shadows have faded from the trees, the roadside pools have lost their brilliant glimmer, and a wakeful whispering hush about the hedgerows and old hawthorns stir all those curious budded watchers, to hear the slow lounging steps of rustic labourers on the road, and wait for the delicate gleam out of the east which shall herald the new-risen moon.

And light are your home-going steps, May Marion, upon this quiet road, which breathes out fresh evening odours from all its dewy neighbour fields—not slow, but lingering—arrested by a hundred fanciful delays. Before you is no great range of prospect—the two ash-trees, holding up their united arms, very much as the children of the Brigend, playing under them, hold up *their* small clasped hands arched over the merry troop who are rushing yonder "through the needle ee"—the hamlet's meditative houses, standing about the road here and there, in the pleasant vacancy of the slow-falling gloaming—the burn rumbling drowsily under the bridge—the kye coming home along the further way—and farthest off of all, the grave plantation firs, making a dark background for your own pleasant home. The purple shadows are fading into palmer grey upon the hills behind, and the hills themselves you could almost fancy contract their circle, and grasp each other's hands in closer rank, with a manful tenderness for this still country, child-like and unfearing, which by-and-by will fall asleep at their feet. Your heart scarcely sings in the hush, though you carry it so lightly; its day's song is over, Menie Laurie—and the quiet heart comes down with a little flutter of sweet thought into the calm of its kindly nest.

The light is fading when Menie reaches the Brigend; and by the door of one of the cottages, Nelly Panton, in her close bonnet and humble enveloping shawl, stands beside the stone seat on which an older woman, who holds her head away with pertinacity, has seated herself to rest.

"She'll no take heart, whatever I can do," says the slow steady voice of Nelly, from which the elastic evening air seems to droop away, throwing it down heavily upon the darkening earth. "I'm sure I couldna say mair, auntie, nor do mair to please her than I aye try, in my quiet way; but morning and night she mourns after Johnnie, making nae mair account of me than if I was a stranger in the house. And what should ail Johnnie?—for I'm sure I dinna ken what would come o' folk in our condition if we were aye write-writing from ae hand to anither, like them that have naething else to do. If onything was wrang, we would hear fast enough. I'm saying, mother!"

"If you would but let me be!" groaned the older woman; "I'm no complaining to you. If I *am* anxious in my mind, I'm no wanting to publish't afore a' the parish. I'm meaning nae offence to you, Marget—but I think this lassie's tongue will drive me out of my wits."

"That's just her way," said Nelly, with mournful complacency. "Instead of taking it kind when I try to ease her, ye would think I was doing somebody an injury; and I'm sure it's a fashious temper indeed that canna put up with me—for I've aye been counted as quiet a lass as there is in the haill countryside, and never did ill to onybody a' my days. From morning to night I'm aye doing my endeavour to get comfort to her—hearing of the lads that have done weel in London, and aye standing up for Johnnie that he's no sae ill as he's ca'ed, though he mayna write as often as some do; and just yesterday I gaed myself to Burnside, a guid mile o' gate from our house, to ask Miss Menie Laurie to write to Randall Home for word about Johnnie,—and I'm sure what ony mortal could do mair, I canna tell."

"What business has Miss Menie Laurie, or Randall Home either, with my trouble?" exclaimed the mother indignantly. "Am I no to daur shed a tear in my ain house, but a' the toun's to hear o't? Yes, Miss Menie, I see it's you, but I canna help it. I'm no meaning disrespect either to you or ony of your friends; but naebody could thole to have their private thoughts turned out for a' the world to see—and she'll put me daft if she gets encouragement to gang on at this rate."

"Must I not ask about Johnnie, Mrs. Lithgow?" said Menie; "Nelly said it would comfort you."

"Nelly's aye saying something to aggravate a puir woman out of baith life and patience," said Nelly's mother; "and he's just her half-brother, you see, and she hasna the interest in him she might have. I'm sure I canna tell how she came to be a daughter of mine," continued the poor woman, rising and turning away to address herself, rapidly and low, to Menie's particular ear. "I would do mony a thing afore I would have my ain troubled thoughts, or so muckle as a breath on Johnnie's credit, kent in the countryside; and I'm no sae anxious—no near sae anxious as that cuttie says; but, Miss Menie, you're an innocent lassie—I'll trust you. I have a tremble in my heart for my young son, away yonder his lane. No that Johnnie has ony ill ways— far from that, far from that—and a better son to his mother never was the world owre; but an innocent thing like you disna ken how a puir laddie's tempted—and there's no a creature near hand to mind him of his duty, and naething but a wheen careless English, that disna ken our kirk nor our ways, at every side of him—and I charged him he was to gang to nae kirk but our ain. I'm sure I dinna ken—whiles things that folk mean for guid counsel turn out snares—and I'm sair bewildered in my mind. If you'll just write, Miss Menie—just like as it was out of your ain head, and bid the young gentleman—I hear he's turned a grand scholar, and awfu' clever—take the pains to ask how Johnnie's winning on—but no to say you have heard ony ill of him. I wouldna have him think his mother was doubtful of him, no for a' Kirklands parish—and he's aye in the office of that muckle paper that a'body's heard about—at least as far as I ken. Eh, Miss Menie, it's a sair thing to have so mony weary miles of land and water, and sae muckle uncertainty, between ane's ain heart and them that ane likes best."

With gravity and concern Menie received this confidence, and gave her promise; but Menie did not know how "sair" and terrible this uncertainty was—could not comprehend the wavering paleness of terror, the sickly gleams of anxiety which shot over the poor mother's face—and a wistful murmur of inquiry, a pity which was almost awe, were all the echoes this voice of real human suffering awoke in Menie's quiet heart.

And when she had soothed, and comforted, and promised, this gentle heart went on its way—its flutter of sweet thoughts subdued, but only into a fresh reposing calm, like the stillness all bedewed and starry which gathered on the dim home-country round. Wisdom of the world—Experience chill and sober—Knowledge of human kind—grim sisterhood, avoid your twilight way—and by yourself all fearless and undaunted, hoping all things, believing all things, thinking no evil, you are brave enough to go forth, Menie Laurie, upon the world without a tremble; by-and-by will come the time to go forth—and Heaver send the lion to guard this quiet heart upon its way.

In her own chamber, when the night had fully fallen, Menie wrote her letter. Many a mile of land and water, many a new-developed thought on one side, lay between Menie Laurie and Randall Home; but uncertainty had never sickened the blithe child's hope within her; an ample country, full of mountain-peaks and rocks of danger—burning with hidden breaks of desert, with wells of Marah treacherous and insecure, was the soul which fate had linked so early to Menie Laurie's soul. She knew the sunny plains that were in it—the mounts of vision, the glens of dreamy sweet romance; but all besides, and all that lay deepest in her own unexplored mind, remained to be discovered. But what she did not know she could not fear.

CHAPTER VI

"Jenny, Jenny, canna ye open the door—it's just me."

"It's just you, mischief and mischief-maker as ye are," muttered Jenny, in answer to Nelly Panton's soft appeal; "and what are you wanting here?"

But Jenny could not be so inhospitable as to shut out with a closed door the applicant for admission, especially as a rapid April shower was just then flashing out of the morning skies. Nelly came in breathless, shaking some bright raindrops off her dingy shawl; but neither the rain upon her cheeks, nor the fresh wind that carried it, nor even the haste of her own errand, sufficed to bring any animating colour to Nelly Panton's face.

"I'm no to stay a minute," she said breathlessly. "No a creature kens I'm here; and you're no to bid me stay, but just gie me your advice and let me rin—I maun be hame before my mother kens."

"*I* have nae will to keep ye; ye needna be feared," retorted Jenny. "And what's your pleasure now, that you've got so early out to Burnside?"

"Nane of the ladies 'll be stirring yet," said Nelly, looking round cautiously. "It was just a thing I wanted to ask you, Jenny—I ken you're aye a guid friend."

"Sorrow!" muttered Jenny between her teeth—but the end of the sentence died away; and whether the word was used as an epithet, or whether it was "Sorrow take you!" Jenny's favourite ban, Nelly, innocently confiding, did not pause to inquire.

"For I heard in the Brigend that you had been kent to say that you wouldna gang a' the gate to London if the mistress ga'e you triple your wage," said Nelly, "and that you would recommend her to a younger lass. My auntie, Marget Panton, even gaed the length to say that ye had been heard to mention my name; but I wouldna have the face to believe that, though mony thanks to ye for the thought; and I just ran out whenever I rose this morning, to say, do ye think I might put in an application, Jenny, aye counting on you as a guid friend?"

"Wha ever gave ye warrant to believe that I was a guid friend?" exclaimed Jenny. "My patience! you taking upon you to offer yoursel for my place. *My* place! And wha daured to say I wanted to leave the mistress? Do ye think wage, or triple wage, counts wi' me? Do ye think I'm just like yoursel, you pitiful self-seeking creature? Do ye think ony mortal would ever be the better of you in ony strait, frae a sair finger to a family misfortune? Gae way wi' ye! My place, my certy! Would naething serve ye but that?"

"Ye see I'm no taking weel wi' hame," said the undismayed Nelly. "My mother and me canna put up right, and me being sae lang away before, she's got out of the use of my attentions, and canna understand them. But I'm real attentive for a' that, Jenny, and handy in mony a thing that wouldna be expected frae the like o' you; and I could wait on Miss Menie, ye ken, being mair like her ain years, and fleech up the mistress grand. I ken I could—besides greeing wi' the stranger servants, which it's no to be expected you would do, being aye used to your ain way. But for my part, I'm real quiet and inoffensive—folk never ken me in a house; and I have my ain reasons for wanting to gang to London, baith to look after Johnnie, and ither concerns o' my ain—and I would aye stand your friend constant, and be thankful to you for recommending me—and I'm sure afore the year was done the mistress would be thankful too for a guid lass—and I could recommend you to a real fine wee cottage atween Kirklands and the Brigend, with a very cheery window looking to the road, that would do grand for a single woman; or my mother would be blithe to take you in for a lodger, and she's guid company when she's no thrawn—and Jenny, woman——"

"Gang out of this house," said Jenny, with quiet fury, holding the door wide open in her hand, and setting down her right foot upon the floor of her own domain, with a stamp of absolute supremacy. "No anither word—gang out of this door, and let me see your face again if ye daur! Gang to London—fleech up the mistress—wait upon Miss Menie! My patience!—and you'll ca' a decent woman thrawn to me! Gang out o' this house, ye shadow!—the sight o' you's enough to thraw ony mortal temper. Your mother, honest woman!—but I canna forgive her for being art or part in bringing the like of you to this world. Are ye gaun away peaceably—or I'll put ye out by the shouthers wi' my ain twa hands!"

"Eh, sic a temper!" said Nelly Panton, vanishing from the threshold as Jenny made one rapid step forward. "I'm sure I forgive you, Jenny, though I'm sure as weel, that if the rain hadna laid a' the stour, mony a ane has shaken the dust off their feet for a testimony against less ill usage than you've gien me; but I'm thankful for my guid disposition—I'm thankful that there's nae crook in me, and I leave you to your ain thoughts, Jenny Durward; it's weel kent what a life thae twa puir ladies lead wi' ye, through a' the countryside."

The kitchen door violently shut, by good fortune drowned for Jenny this last vindictive utterance, and Nelly Panton, unexcited, drew her shawl again close over her elbows, and went with her stealthy steps upon her way—a veritable shadow falling dark across the sunshine, and without a spot of brightness in her, within or without, to throw back reflection, or answer to the sunny morning light which flashed upon all the glistening way.

But no such quietness possessed the soul of Jenny of Burnside; over the fresh sanded floor of her bright kitchen her short vigorous steps pattered like hail. Cups and saucers came ringing down from her hands upon the tray, which she was crowding with breakfast "things." The bread-basket quivered upon the table where her excited hand had set it down. She turned to the hearth, and the poor little copper kettle rang upon the grate—the poker assaulted the startled fire—the very chain quaked and trembled, hanging from the old-fashioned crook far back in the abyss of the chimney. Very conspicuous in this state of the mental atmosphere became Jenny's high shoulder. It seemed to develop and increase with every additional fuff, and the most liberal and kindly commentator could not have denied this morning the existence of the "thraw."

And not without audible expression, over and above the hard-drawn breath of the "fuff," was Jenny's indignation. "My place, my certy! less wouldna serve her!"—"Handier than could be expected frae the like o' me!"—"Stand my friend constant!"—"A cot-house atween Kirklands and the Brigend!" A snort of rage punctuated and separated every successive quotation, till, as Jenny cooled down a little, there came to her relief a variety of extremely complimentary titles, all very eloquent and expressive, conveying in the clearest language Jenny's opinion of the good qualities of Nelly Panton, which last, by-and-by, however, softened still further into the milder chorus of "a bonnie ane!" with which Jenny's wrath gradually wore itself away.

All this time the sunshine lay silent and unbroken upon the paved passage, with its strip of matting, and the light shone quiet in Mrs Laurie's parlour. The petulant rain had ceased to ring upon the panes, though some large drops hung there still, clinging to the framework of the window, and gradually shrinking and drying up before the light. The branches without made a sheen through the air, almost as dazzling as if every tree were a Highland dancer with a drawn claymore in his right hand; and the larch flung its spray of rain upon Menie Laurie's chamber window, bidding her down to the new life and the new day which brightened all the watching hills.

And now comes Mrs Laurie steadily down the stairs with her little shawl in her hand, and traces of a mind made up and determined in her face; and now comes Menie, with a half song on her lips, and a little light of amusement and expectation in her eyes, for Menie has heard afar off the sound of Jenny's excitement. But Jenny, too decorous to invade the dignity of the breakfast-table, says nothing when she brings in the kettle, and does not even add to its fuff the sound of her own, and Menie has time to grow composed and grave, and to hear with a more serious emotion Mrs Laurie's decision. Not without a sigh Mrs Laurie intimates it, though her daughter knows nothing of the one reason which has overweighed all others. But the ruling mind of the household, having decided, loses no time in secondary hesitations. "We will try to let Burnside as it is, Menie," said Mrs Laurie, looking round upon the familiar room. "If we can get a careful tenant, it will be far better not to remove the furniture. If we make it known at once, the house may be taken before the term; and I will write to your aunt and say that we accept her offer. It is a long journey by land, and expensive. I think we will go to Edinburgh first, Menie. The weather is settled, and should be fine at Whitsunday; and then to London by sea."

Menie did not trust herself to express in words the excitement of hope and pleasure with which she heard this great and momentous change brought down into a matter of sober everyday arrangement; but it was not difficult to understand and translate the varying colour on her cheek, and the sudden gleam of her sunny eyes. As it happened, however, with a natural caprice, the one objection which her mother's will could not set aside suddenly suggested itself to Menie. She looked up with a slight alarm — "But Jenny, mother?" Menie Laurie could not realise the possibility of leaving Jenny behind.

Mrs Laurie's hand had not left the bell. Jenny, at the door, caught the words with satisfaction. But Jenny did not choose to acknowledge herself subject to any influence exercised by the "youngest of the house;" and Jenny, moreover, had come prepared, and had no time to lose in preliminaries.

"There's twa or three things to be done about the house before onybody can stir out o' this," said Jenny emphatically, pausing when she had half cleared the breakfast-table. "I want to ken, mem, if it's your pleasure, what time we're to gang away."

"I have just been thinking—about the term, Jenny," said her mistress, accepting Jenny's adhesion quietly and without remark—"if we can get a tenant to Burnside."

"I thought you would be wanting a tenant to Burnside," muttered Jenny, "to make every table and chair in the house a shame to be seen, and the place no fit to live in when we come back; but it's nane o' Jenny's business if the things maun be spoiled. I have had a woman at me this morning wi' an offer to gang in my place. I've nae business to keep it out o' your knowledge, so you may get Nelly Panton yet, if it's your pleasure, instead o' me. I'm speaking to your mother, Miss Menie; the like o' you has nae call to put in your word. Am I to tell Nelly you would like to speak to her, mem—or what am I to say?"

And Jenny again planted her right foot firmly before her, again expanded her irascible nostril, and, with comic perversity and defiance, stood and waited for her mistress's answer.

"Away you go, Jenny, and put your work in order," said Mrs Laurie; "get somebody in from the Brigend to help you, and let everything be ready for the flitting—you know I don't want Nelly Panton—no, you need not interrupt me—nor anybody else. We'll all go to London together, and we'll all come back again some time, if we're spared. I don't know how you would manage without *us*, Jenny; but see, there's Menie with open eyes wondering what we should do without you."

"Na, the bairn has discrimination," said Jenny steadily; "that's just what I say to mysel. Nae doubt it's a great change to a woman at my time o' life, but I just say what could the two ladies do, mair especially a young lassie like Miss Menie, and that's enough to reconcile ane to mony a thing. Weel, I'll see the wark putten in hands; but if you take my advice, mem, ye'll see baith mistress and maid afore ye let fremd folk into Burnside. It's no ilka hand that can keep up a room like this; for I ken mysel the things were nae mair like what they are now, when I came first, than fir wood's like oak; and what's the matter of twa or three pounds, by the month, for rent, in comparison wi' ruining a haill house o' furniture?—though, to be sure, it's nae business o' mine; and if folk winna take guid counsel when it's offered, naebody can blame Jenny."

So saying, Jenny went briskly to her kitchen, to set on foot immediate preparations for the removal, leaving her "guid counsel" for Mrs Laurie's consideration. Mrs Laurie found little time to deliberate. She had few distant friends, and no great range of correspondents at any time, and another perusal of Miss Annie Laurie's epistle set her down to answer it with a puzzled face. A little amusement, a little impatience, a little annoyance, drew together the incipient curve on Mrs Laurie's brow, and Jenny's advice got no such justice at her hands as would have satisfied Jenny, and was summarily dismissed when its time of consideration came.

CHAPTER VII

"Johnnie Lithgow exists no longer." The words chased the colour from Menie Laurie's cheek, and drew a pitying exclamation from her lips. Alas, for Johnnie Lithgow's mourning mother! But Menie read on and laughed, and was consoled. "There is no such person known about the office of the great paper; but Mr Lythgoe, the rising critic, the leader of popular judgments, and writer of popular articles, is fast growing into fame and notice. The days of the compositor are over, and I fear the author must be a little troubled about the plebeian family who once rejoiced the poor young printer's heart. Yet the heart remains a very good heart, my dear Menie — vain, perhaps, and a little fickle and wavering, not quite knowing its own mind, but a very simple kindly heart in the main, and sure to come back to all the natural duties and loves. I give you full warrant to comfort the mother. Johnnie has been somewhat *fêted* and lionised of late, and is not, perhaps, at present exactly what our sober unexcitable friends call *steady*. His head is turned with the unusual attention he has been receiving, and perhaps a little salutary humiliation may be necessary to bring him down again; but I have no fear of him in the end. He is very clever, writes extremely well, and is one of the most wise and sensible of men — in print. I almost wonder that I have not mentioned him to you sooner, for he and I have seen a good deal of each other of late, and Johnnie is a very good fellow, I assure you — not without natural refinement, and very fresh, and hearty, and genial; moreover, a rising man, as the common slang goes, and one who has made a wonderful leap in a very short time; so we must pardon him in his first elation if he seems a little negligent of his friends."

A slight flush of colour ran wavering over Menie's cheek as "a little salutary humiliation may be necessary" she repeated under her breath, and, starting at the sound of her own voice, looked round guiltily, as if in terror lest she had been overheard. But there was no one to overhear — no one but her own heart, which, suddenly startled out of its quiet, looks round too with a timid, troubled glance, as if a ghost had crossed its line of vision, and hears these words echoing softly among all the trees. Well, there is no harm in the words, but Menie feels as if, in whispering them, she had betrayed some secret of her betrothed, and with an uneasy step and clouded face she turns away.

Why?—or what has Randall done to call this shadow up on Menie Laurie's way? But Menie Laurie neither could or would tell, and only feels a cloud of vague vexation and unexplainable displeasure rise slowly up upon her heart.

Yet it is no very long time till Mrs Laurie hears the news, unshadowed by any dissatisfaction, and very soon after Menie is speeding along the Kirklands road restored to all her usual cloudlessness, though it happens somehow, that, after a second bold plunge at it in the stillness of her own room, which reddened Menie's cheek again with involuntary anger, she skips this objectionable paragraph in Randall's letter, and, asking herself half audibly, what Johnnie Lithgow is to her, solaces herself out of her uneasiness by Randall's exultation over her own last letter. For Randall is most heartily and cordially rejoiced to think of having his betrothed so near him—there can be no doubt of that.

And here upon the hillside path, almost like one of those same delicate beechen boughs which wave over its summit, July Home comes fluttering down before the wind—her soft uncertain feet scarcely touching the ground, as you can think—her brown dress waving—her silky hair betraying itself as usual, astray upon her shoulders. Down comes July, not without a stumble now and then, over boulder or bramble, but looking very much as if she floated on the sweet atmosphere which streams down fresh and full from the top of the hill, and the elastic spring air could bear her well enough upon its sunny current for all the weight she has. Very simple are the girlish salutations exchanged when the friends meet. "Eh, Menie, where are you going?" and "Is that you, July?—you can come with me."

And now the road has two shadows upon it instead of one, and a murmur of low-toned voices running like a hidden tinkle of water along the hedgerow's side. "Johnnie Lithgow! eh, I'm glad he's turned clever," said little July; "he used to come up the hill at nights when nobody ever played with me; and I think, Menie—you'll no be angry?—he had more patience than Randall, for I mind him once carrying me, when I was just a little thing, all the way round the wood to the Resting Stane, to see the sunset, and minding what I said too, though I was so wee. I'm glad, Menie—I'm sure I'm very glad; but Randall, being clever himself, might have told us about Johnnie Lithgow before."

"You never can think that Johnnie Lithgow is as clever as Randall," said Menie, indignantly. "That's not what I mean either. Randall's not clever, July. You need not look so strange at me. Clever! Jenny's clever; I'm clever myself at some things; but Randall—I call Randall a genius, July."

And Menie raised loftily the face which was now glowing with a flash of affectionate pride. With a little awe July assented; but July still in her inmost heart asserted Randall to be clever, and rather avoided a discussion of this perplexing word genius, which July did not feel herself quite competent to define or understand.

And now the road begins to slope upwards, the hedgerow breaks and opens upon braes of close grass, marked here and there by bars and streaks of brown, like stationary shadows, and rich with little nests of low-growing heather and hillside flowers. An amphitheatre of low hills opens now from the summit of this one, which the road mounts. Bare unwooded slopes, falling away at their base into cultivated fields, and rising upward in stretches of close-cropped pasture land; soft luxurious grass, sweet with its thyme and heather, with small eyes of flowers piercing up from under its close-woven blades—soft as summer couch need be, and elastic as ever repelled the foot of passing herdsman; but looking somewhat bare in its piebald livery, as it breaks upon the bright spring sky above.

And the road dives down—down into the hollows of the circle, where gleams a winding burn, and rises a village, its roofs of tile and thatch basking serenely in the sun. A little church, holding up a little open belfry against the hillside, as if entreating to be lifted higher, stands at the entrance of the village; and you can already see the little span-broad bridges that cross the burn, and the signboards which hang above the doors of the cottage shops in the main street. Here, too, keeping the road almost like an official of equal authority, the smithy glows with its fiery eye upon the kirk; for the kirk, you will perceive, is almost a new one, and has little pretensions to the hereditary reverence of its small dependency, standing there bare and alone, without a single grave to keep watch upon; whereas the smiddy's antique roof is heavy with lichens; and ploughs and harrows, resplendent in primitive red and blue, obtrude themselves a little way beyond its door, with the satisfaction of conscious wealth.

And here is a cottage turning its back upon the burn, and modestly setting down its white doorstep upon the rude causeway; the door is open, and some one sits at work by the fireside within; but in a corner stands a sack of meal, and a little humble counter interposes sideways between the fire and the threshold. Some humble goods lie on the window-shelves, and the counter itself has a small miscellany—dim glasses, full of "sweeties;" dimmer still with balls of cotton, blue and white, with stiffly-twisted sticks of sampler worsted, and red and yellow stalks of barley-sugar, scarcely to be distinguished from the thread. Altogether the counter, with its dangling scales, the half-filled shelves that break the light from the window, and the few drawers behind, fit out the village shop where Mrs Lithgow does a little daily business, enough to keep herself, alone and widowed, in daily bread.

For Nelly Panton, sitting behind at the fire, is a mantua-maker, and maintains herself. By good fortune, this maintenance is very cheaply accomplished; and Nelly's "drap parritch" and cup of tea are by much the smallest burden which her society entails upon her mother. Decent lass as Nelly is, she has come through no small number of vicissitudes, and swayed between household service and this same disconsolate mantua-making of hers, like the discontented pendulum—not to speak of two or three occasions past, when Nelly has been just on the eve of being married, a consummation which even the devout desire of Mrs Lithgow has not yet succeeded in bringing peacefully to pass—for Nelly and her lovers, as Mrs Lithgow laments pathetically, "can never gree lang enough," and some kind fairy always interposes in time to prevent any young man of Kirklands from accomplishing to himself such a fate.

Mrs Lithgow's dress is scarcely less doleful than her daughter: a petticoat of some dark woollen stuff, and a clean white short-gown, are scarcely enlivened by the check apron, bright blue and white as it is, which girds in the upper garment; but the close cap which marks her second widowhood encloses a face fresh, though care-worn, with lines of anxious thought something too clearly defined about the brow and cheeks. A little perplexity adds just now to the care upon the widow's face; for upon her counter stands a square wooden box, strongly corded and sealed, over which, with much bewilderment, the good woman ponders. Very true, it is directed to Mrs Lithgow, Kirklands, and Kirklands knows no Mrs Lithgow but herself; but with a knife in her hand to cut the cord, and a little broken hammer beside her on the counter, with which she proposes to "prise" open the securely nailed lid, the widow still hangs marvelling over the address, and the broad red office-seal, and wonders once again who it can be that sends this mystery to her.

"I've heard of folk getting what lookit like a grand present, and it turning out naething but a wisp o' straw, or a wecht o' stanes," said the perplexed Mrs Lithgow, as her young visitors saluted her; "but this is neither to ca' very heavy nor very licht; and it's no directed in a hand o write that ane might have kenned, but in muckle printed letters like a book; and I'm sure I canna divine, if I was thinking on a'body I ever kent a' my days, wha could send such a thing to me."

"But if you open the box you'll see," cried July Home. "Eh! I wish you would open it the time we're here; for I think I ken it's from Johnnie, and Menie Laurie has grand news of Johnnie in her letter. I was as glad as if it was me. He's turned clever, Mrs Lithgow; he's growing to be a great man, like our Randall. Eh! Menie, what ails her?"

Something ailed her that July did not know;—a trembling thrill of apprehensive joy, an intense realisation for the moment of all her terrors and sorrows, suddenly inspired, and flooded over with the light of a new hope. The colour fled from Mrs Lithgow's very lips; the little broken hammer fell with a heavy clang upon the floor at her feet. Her eyes turned wistfully, eagerly, upon Menie; the light swam in them, and yet they could read so clearly the expression of this face.

And Menie, conquering her blush and hesitation, took out her letter, and read bravely so much of it as was suitable for the mother's ear. The mother forgot all about the mysterious box, even though it seemed so likely now to come from Johnnie. She sat down abruptly on the wooden chair behind the counter; she lifted up her checked apron, and pressed it with both hands into the corners of her eyes. "My puir laddie! my puir laddie!"— You could almost have fancied it was some misfortune to Johnnie which caused this swelling of his mother's heart.

"And he's in among grand folk, and turning a muckle man himsel," said Mrs Lithgow softly, after a considerable pause. "Was that what the letter said?—was that what the folk telled me?—and he's my son for a' that—Johnnie Lithgow, my ain little young bairn."

"I think, mother, ye may just as weel let me open the box," said Nelly, coming forward with her noiseless step. "We'll ken by what's in't if he's keeping thought of us; though I'm sure it's no muckle like as if he was, keeping folk anxious sae lang, and him prospering. I'll just open the box. I wouldna be ane to hang at his tails if Johnnie thought shame of his poor friends; but still a considerate lad would mind that there's mony a little thing might be useful at Kirklands. I'll open the box and see."

The mother rose to thrust her away angrily. "Is it what he sends *I'm* heeding about, think ye?" she exclaimed, with momentary passion, "I'm his mother! I'm seeking naething but his ain welfare and well-doing. Was't gifts I wanted, or profit by my son? But ane needna speak to you."

"Eh! but there's maybe a letter," said July Home, with a little natural artifice. "Mrs Lithgow, I would open it and see."

And Mrs Lithgow, with this hope, cut the cords vigorously, though with a trembling hand—rejecting, not without anger, the offered assistance of Nelly, who now crossed her hands demurely on her apron, and stood, virtuous and resigned, looking on. Little July, very eager and curious, could not restrain her restless fingers, but helped to loose the knots involuntarily with a zealous aid, which the widow did not refuse; and Menie, not quite sure that it was right to intrude upon the mother's joy, but very certain that she would greatly like to see what Johnnie Lithgow sent home, lingered, with shyer and less visible curiosity, between the counter and the door.

But Mrs Lithgow's hands, trembling with anxiety, and the excitement of great joy, and the little thin fingers of July, never very nervous at any time, made but slow progress in their work; and poor July even achieved a scratch here and there from refractory nails before it was concluded. When the lid had been fairly lifted off, a solemn pause ensued. No letter appeared; but a brilliant gown-piece of printed cotton lay uppermost, the cover and wrapper of various grandeurs below. Mrs Lithgow pulled out these hidden glories hurriedly, laying them aside with only a passing glance; a piece of silk, too grand by far for anybody within a mile of Kirklands; ribbons which even Menie Laurie beheld with a flutter of admiration; and a host of other articles of feminine adornment, so indisputably put together by masculine hands, that the more indifferent spectators were tempted to laughter at last. But Mrs Lithgow had no leisure to laugh—no time to admire the somewhat coarse shawl which she could wear, nor the gay gowns which she could not. Down to the very depths and conclusion of all, to the white paper lying in the bottom of the box; but not a scrap of written paper bade his mother receive all these from Johnnie. The gift came unaccompanied by a single word to identify the giver. Mrs Lithgow sat down again in her chair, subdued and silent, and Menie had discernment enough to see the bitter tears of disappointed hope that gathered in the mother's eyes; but she said nothing, either of comment or complaint, till the slow business-like examination with which Nelly began to turn over these anonymous gifts, startled into sudden provocation and anger the excitement which, but for pride and jealous regard that no one should have a word to say against her son, would fain have found another channel.

"Eh! Mrs Lithgow, isn't it bonnie?" cried simple little July Home, as she smoothed down with her hand the glistening folds of silk. Mrs Lithgow had laid violent hands upon it, to thrust it back into the box out of Nelly's way; but as July spoke, her own womanish interest was roused, and now, when the first shock had passed, the tears in the widow's eyes grew less salt and bitter; she looked at the beautiful fabric glistening in the light—she looked at the little pile of bright ribbons—at the warm comfortable shawl, and her heart returned to its first flush of thankfulness and content.

"It's farowre grand for the like o' me," she said at last; "it would be mair becoming some o' you young ladies; but a young lad's no to be expected to ken about such things; and he's bought it for the finest he could get, and spent a lock o' siller on't, to pleasure his mother. I'm no surprised mysel—

it's just like his kind heart; but there's few folk fit to judge my Johnnie; he was never like other callants a' his days."

But still Mrs Lithgow could not bear Nelly's slow matter-of-fact perusal, and comment on her new treasures. She put them up one by one, restored them to the box, and carried it away to her own room in her own arms, to be privately wept and rejoiced over there.

"Randall never sent home anything like yon," said July softly to herself, as they returned to Burnside, "and Randall was clever before Johnnie Lithgow. I wonder he never had the thought."

"Randall knows better," said Menie. "When Randall sends things, he sends becoming things; it's only you, July, that have not the thought: if Johnnie Lithgow had been wise, he would not have sent such presents to Kirklands."

But just then a line of a certain favourite song crossed Menie's mind against her will—"Wisdom's sae cauld;" and July looked down upon her own printed frock, and thought a silken gown, like Johnnie Lithgow's present, might be a very becoming thing. At seventeen—even at twenty—one appreciates a piece of kindly folly fully better than an act of wisdom.

CHAPTER VIII

But Menie Laurie was by no means satisfied that even simple little July should make comparison so frequent between Randall, her own hero, and the altogether new and sudden elevation of Johnnie Lithgow. Johnnie Lithgow might be very clever, might be a newspaper conductor, and a rising man; but Randall—Randall, in spite of the little chillness of that assumed superiority which could think humiliation necessary to bring his youthful countryman down—in spite of Menie's consciousness that there lacked something of the frank and generous tone with which one high spirit should acknowledge the excellence of another—Randall was still the ideal genius, the something so far above "clever," that Menie felt him insulted by praise so mean as this word implied.

There was little time for speculation on the subject, yet many a mood of Menie's was tinged by its passing gleam, for Menie sometimes thought her betrothed unappreciated, and was lofty and scornful, and disposed in his behalf to defy all the world. Sometimes impatient of the estimation, which, great though it was, was not great enough, Menie felt not without a consoling self-satisfaction that she alone did Randall perfect justice. Johnnie Lithgow!—what though he did write articles! Menie was very glad to believe, condescendingly, that he might be clever, but he never could be Randall Home.

"You'll hae heard the news," said Miss Janet, sitting very upright in one of the Burnside easy-chairs, with her hands crossed on her knee; "they say that you and our Randall, Miss Menie, my dear, were the first, between you, to carry word of it to his mother, and her breaking her heart about her son. But Mrs Lithgow's gotten a letter frae Johnnie now, a' about how grand he is—and I hear he's paying a haill guinea by the week for his twa rooms, and seeing a' the great folk in the land—no to say that he's writing now the paper he ance printed, and is great friends with our Randy. Randy was aye awfu' particular o' his company. I was saying mysel, it was the best sign I heard of Johnnie Lithgow that Randall Home was taking him by the hand; I'm no meaning pride, Mrs Laurie. I'm sure I ken sae weel it's a' his ain doing, and the fine nature his Maker gave him, that I aye say we've nae right to be proud; but it would be sinning folks' mercies no to ken—and I never saw a lad like Randall Home a' my days."

Menie said nothing in this presence. Shy at all times to speak of Randall—before her own mother and his aunt it was a thing impossible; but she glanced up hastily with glowing eyes, and a flush of sudden colour, to meet Miss Janet's look. Miss Janet's face was full of affectionate pride and tenderness, but the good simple features had always a little cloud of humility and deprecation hovering over them. Miss Janet knew herself liable to attack on many points, knew herself very homely, and not at all worthy of the honour of being Randall's aunt, and had been snubbed and put down a great many times in the course of her kindly life—so Miss Janet was wont to deliver her modest sentiments with a little air of half-troubled propitiatory fear.

Mrs Laurie made little response. She was busy with her work at the moment, and, not without little angles of temper for her own share, did not always quite join in this devout admiration of Randall Home. Menie, "thinking shame," said nothing either, and, in the momentary silence which ensued, Miss Janet's heart rose with a flutter of apprehension; she feared she had said something amiss—too much or too little; and Miss Janet's cheeks grew red under the abashed eyes which she bent so anxiously over the well-known pattern of Mrs Laurie's carpet.

"I'm feared you're thinking it's a' vain-glory that gars me speak," said Miss Janet, tracing the outline with her large foot; "and it's very true that ane deceives ane's-sel in a thing like this; but it's no just because he's our Randall, Mrs Laurie; and it's no that I'm grudging at Johnnie Lithgow for being clever—but I canna think he's like my ain bairn."

"A merry little white-headed fellow, with a wisp of curls," said Mrs Laurie, good-humouredly—"No, he's not like Randall, Miss Janet—I think I'll answer for that as well as you; but we'll see them both, very likely, when we get to London. Strange things happen in this world," continued Menie's mother, drawing herself up with a little conscious pride and pique, which the accompanying smile showed her own half amusement with. "There's young Walter Wellwood of Kirkland will never be anything but a dull country gentleman, though he comes of a clever family, and has had every advantage; and here is a boy out of Kirklands parish-school taking up literature and learning at his own hand!"

Miss Janet was slightly disturbed, and looked uneasy. Randall too had begun his career in the parish-school of Kirklands: there was a suspicion in this speech of something derogatory to him.

"But the maister in Kirklands is very clever, Mrs Laurie," said Miss Janet, anxiously; "he makes grand scholars. When our Randall gaed to the grammar-school in Dumfries, the gentlemen a' made a wonder o' him; and for a' his natural parts, he couldna hae gotten on sae fast without a guid teacher; and it's no every man *could* maister Randy. I mind at the time the gentlemen couldna say enough to commend the Dominie. I warrant they a' think weel o' him still, on account of his guid success, and the like o' him deserves to get credit wi' his laddies. I'm sure Johnnie Lithgow, having had nae other instruction, should be very grateful to the maister."

"The maister will be very proud of him," said Menie; "though they say in Kirklands that ever so many ministers have been brought up in the school. But never mind Johnnie Lithgow—everybody speaks of him now; and, mother, you were to tell Miss Janet about when we are going away."

"I think John will never look out of the end window mair," said Miss Janet. "I can see he's shifting his chair already—him that used to be sae fond o' the view; and I'm sure I'll be very dreary mysel, thinking there's naebody I ken in Burnside. But what if you dinna like London, Mrs Laurie? It's very grand, I believe, and you've lived in great touns before, and ken the ways o' the world better than the like o' me; but after a country life, I would think ane would weary o' the toun; and if you do, will you come hame?"

Mrs Laurie shook her head. "I was very well content in Burnside," she said. "With my own will I never would have left it, Miss Janet; but I go for good reasons, and not for pleasure; and my reasons will last, whether I weary or no. There's Menie must get masters, you know, and learn to be accomplished—or Miss Annie Laurie will put her to shame."

"I dinna ken what she could learn, for my part," said Miss Janet, affectionately, "nor how she could weel be better or bonnier, for a'body can see the genty lady-breeding Miss Menie's got; and there's naebody atween this and the hills needs to be telt o' the kind heart and the pleasant tongue, and the face that every creature's blithe to see; and I'm sure I never heard a voice like her for singing; and a' the grand tunes she can play, and draw landscapes, and work ony kind o' bonnie thing you like to mention. Didna you draw a likeness o' Jenny, Miss Menie, my dear? And I'm sure yon view you took frae the tap o' our hill is just the very place itsel—as natural as can be; and, for my part, Mrs Laurie, I dinna ken what mortal could desire for her mair."

Mrs Laurie smiled; but the mother was not displeased, though she did think it possible still to add to Menie's acquirements, if not to her excellence; and Menie herself went off laughing and blushing, fully resolved in her own mind to destroy forthwith that likeness wherein poor Jenny's "high shouther" figured with an emphasis and distinctness extremely annoying to the baffled artist, whose pencil ran away with her very often in these same much-commended drawings, and who was sadly puzzled in most cases how to make two sides of anything alike. And Menie knew her tunes were anything but grand, her landscapes not at all remarkable for truth—yet Menie was by no means distressed by Miss Janet's simple-hearted praise.

The evening was spent in much talk of the departure. July Home had followed her aunt, and sat in reverential silence listening to the conversation, and making a hundred little confidential communications of her own opinion to Menie, which Menie had some trouble in reporting for the general good. It was nine o'clock of the moonlight April night when the farmer of Crofthill came to escort his "womankind" home. The clear silent radiance darkened the distant hills, even while it lent a silver outline to their wakeful guardian range, and Menie came in a little saddened from the gate, where the father of her betrothed had grasped her hand so closely in his good-night. "No mony mair good-nights now," said John Home. "I'll no get up my heart the morn, though it is the first day of summer. You should have slipped up the hill the night to gather the dew in the morning, May; but I'll learn to think the May mornings darker than they used to be, when your ain month takes my bonnie lassie from Burnside. Weel, weel, ane's loss is anither's gain; but I grudge you to London smoke, and London crowds. You must mind, May, my woman, and kept your hame heart."

Your home heart, Menie—your heart of simple trust and untried quiet. Is it a good wish, think you, kind and loving though the wisher be? But Menie looks up at the sky, with something trembling faintly in her mind, like the quiver of this charmed air under the flood of light—and has note of unknown voices, faces, visions, coming in upon the calm of her fair youth, unknown, unfeared; and so she turns to the home lights again, with nothing but the sweet thrill of innocent expectation to rouse her, secure in the peace and tranquil serenity of this home heart of hers, which goes away softly, through the moonlight and the shadow, through the familiar gloom of the little hall, and into the comforts of the mother's parlour, singing its song of conscious happiness under its breath.

CHAPTER IX

Left behind! July Home has dried her eyes at last; and out of many a childish fit of tears and sobbing, suddenly becomes silent like a child, and, standing on the road, looks wistfully after them, with her lips apart, and her breast now and then trembling with the swell of her half-subsided grief. The gentle May wind has taken out of its braid July's brown silky hair, and toys with it upon July's neck with a half-derisive sympathy, as a big brother plays with the transitory sorrow of a child. But the faint colour has fled from July's cheek, except just on this one flushed spot where it has been resting on her hand; and with a wistful longing, her young innocent eyes travel along the vacant road. No one is there to catch this lingering look; and even the far-off sound, which she bends forward to hear, has died away in the distance. Another sob comes trembling up—another faint swell of her breast, and quiver of her lip—and July turns sadly away into the forsaken house, to which such a sudden air of emptiness and desolation has come; and, sitting down on the carpet by the window, once more bends down her face into her hands, and cries to her heart's content.

There is no change in the parlour of Burnside—not a little table, not a single chair, has been moved out of its place; yet it is strange to see the forlorn deserted look which everything has already learned to wear. Mrs Laurie's chair gapes with its open empty arms—Menie's stool turns drearily towards the wall—and the centre table stands out chill and prominent, cleared of all kindly litter, idle and presumptuous, the principal object in the room, no longer submitting to be drawn about here and there, to be covered or uncovered for anybody's pleasure. And, seated close into the window which commands the road, very silent and upright, shawled and bonneted, sits Miss Janet Home, who, perchance, since she neither rebukes nor comforts poor little weeping July, may possibly be crying too.

And Jenny's busy feet waken no home-like echoes now in the bright kitchen, where no scrutiny, however keen, could find speck or spot to discredit Jenny. Instead of the usual genius of the place, a "strange woman" rests with some apparent fatigue upon the chair by the wall which flanks Jenny's oaken table, and, wiping her forehead as she takes off her bonnet, eyes at a respectful distance the fire, which is just now making a valorous attempt to keep up some heartiness and spirit in the bereaved domain which misses Jenny. The strange bonnet, with its gay ribbons, makes a dull reflection in the dark polish of the oak, but the warm moist hand of its owner leaves such a mark as no one ever saw there during the reign of Jenny; and Jenny would know all her forebodings of destruction to the furniture in a fair way for accomplishment, could she see how the new tenant's maid, sent forward before her mistress to take possession, spends her first hour in Burnside.

But Jenny, far off and unwitting, full of a child's simplicity of wonder and admiration—yet sometimes remembering, with her natural impatience, that this delight and interest does not quite become her dignity—travels away—to Dumfries—to Edinburgh—to the new world, of which she knows as little as any child. And Menie Laurie, full of vigorous youthful spirits, and natural excitement, forgets, in half an hour, the heaviness of the leave-taking, and manages, with many a laugh and wreathed smile, to veil much wonder and curiosity of her own, under the unveilable exuberance of Jenny's. Mrs Laurie herself, clouded and careworn though she looks, and dreary as are her backward glances to the familiar hills of her own country, clears into amusement by-and-by; and the fresh Mayday has done its work upon them all, and brightened the little party into universal smiles and cheerfulness, before the journey draws towards its end, and weariness comes in to restore the quiet, if not to restore the tears and sadness, with which they took their leave of home.

"And this is the main street, I'll warrant," said Jenny, as Menie led her on the following morning over the bright pavement of Princes Street; "and I would just like to ken, Miss Menie, what a' thae folk's doing out-by at this time o' the day? Business? havers! I'm no that great a bairn that I dinna ken the odds between a decent woman gaun an errand, and idle folk wandering about the street. Eh! but they are even-down temptations thae windows! The like of that now for a grand gown to gang to parties! And I reckon ye'll be seeing big folk yonder-away—and the Englishers are awfu' hands for grand claes. I dinna think ye've onything now ye could see great company in, but that blue thing you got a twelvemonth since, and twa-three bits o' muslin. Eh! Miss Menie, bairn, just you look at that!"

And Menie paused, well pleased to look, and admired, if not so loudly, at least with admiration quite as genuine as Jenny's own. But as they passed on, Jenny's captivated eyes found every shop more glorious than the other, and Jenny's eager hands had fished out of the narrow little basket she carried, a long narrow purse of chamois leather, in which lay safe a little bundle of one-pound notes, prisoned in the extreme corners at either end. Jenny's fingers grew nervous as they fumbled at the strait enclosure wherein her humble treasure was almost too secure, and Jenny was tremulously anxious to ascertain which of all these splendours Menie liked best, a sublime purpose dawning upon her own mind the while. And now it is extremely difficult to draw Jenny up the steep ascent of the Calton Hill, and fix her wandering thoughts upon the scene below. It is very fine, Jenny fancies; but after all, Jenny, who has been on terms of daily intimacy with Criffel, sees nothing startling about Arthur's Seat—which is only, like its southland brother, "a muckle hill"—whereas not even the High Street of Dumfries holds any faintest shadowing of the glory of these Princes Street shops; and Jenny's mind is absorbed in elaborate calculations, and her lips move in the deep abstraction of mental arithmetic, while still her fingers pinch the straitened corners of the chamois-leather purse.

"I'll can find the house grand mysel. I ken the street, and I ken the stair, as weel as if I had lived in't a' my days," says Jenny eagerly. "Touts, bairn! canna ye let folk abee? I would like to hear wha would fash their heads wi' Jenny—and I saw a thing I liked grand in ane o' thae muckle shops. Just you gang your ways hame to your mamma, Miss Menie; there's nae fears o' me."

"But, Jenny, I'll go with you and help you to buy," said Menie. "I would like to see into that great shop myself."

"Ye'll see't another time," said Jenny, coaxingly. "Just you gang your ain gate, like a guid bairn, and let Jenny gang hers ance in her life. I'll let you see what it is after I have bought it—but I'm gaun my lane the now. Now, Miss Menie, I'm just as positive as you. My patience!—as if folk couldna be trusted to ware their ain siller—and the mistress waiting on you, and me kens the house better than you! Now you'll just be a guid bairn, and I'll take my ain time, and be in in half an hour."

Thus dismissed, Menie had no resource but to betake herself with some laughing wonder to the lodging where Mrs Laurie rested after the journey of yesterday; while Jenny, looking jealously behind her to make sure that she was not observed, returned to a long and loving contemplation of the brilliant silk gown which had caught her fancy first.

"I never bought her onything a' her days, if it wasna ance that bit wee coral necklace, that she wore when she was a little bairn—and she aye has it in her drawer yet, for puir auld Jenny's sake," mused Jenny at the shop window; "and I'm no like to need muckle siller mysel, unless there's some sair downcome at hand. I wouldna say but I'll be feared at the price, wi' a' this grand shop to keep up—but I think I never saw onything sae bonnie, and I'll just get up a stout heart, and gang in and try."

But many difficulties beset this daring enterprise of Jenny's. First, the impossibility of having brought to her the one magnificent gown of gowns—then a fainting of horror at the price—then a sudden bewilderment and wavering, consequent upon the sight of a hundred others as glorious as the first. While Jenny mused and pondered with curved brow and closed lips, two or three very fine gentlemen, looking on with unrestrained amusement, awoke her out of her deliberations, and out of her first awe of themselves, into a very distinct and emphatic fuff of resentment, and Jenny's decision was made at last somewhat abruptly, in the midst of a smothered explosion of laughter, which sent her hasty short steps pattering out of the shop, in intense wrath. But in spite of Jenny's expanded nostrils, and scarcely restrainable vituperation, Jenny carried off triumphantly, in her arms, the gown of gowns; and Jenny's indignation did not lessen the swell of admiring pride with which she contemplated, pressed to her bosom tenderly, the white paper parcel wherein her gift lay hid.

"Ye'll let me ken how you like this, Miss Menie," said Jenny, peremptorily, thrusting the parcel into Menie's hand, at the door of her mother's room; "and see if some o' your grand London mantua-makers canna make such a gown out o't as ye might wear ony place. Take it ben—I'm no wanting ye to look at it here."

"But what is it?" asked Menie, wonderingly.

"You have naething ado but open it and see," was the answer; "and ye can put it on on your birthday if you like—that's the 10th o' next month—there's plenty o' time to get it made—and I'll gang and ask thae strange folk about the dinner mysel."

But neither message nor voice could reach Jenny for a full hour thereafter. Jenny was a little afraid of thanks, and could not be discovered in parlour or kitchen, though the whole "flat" grew vocal with her name. Penetrating at last into the depths of the dark closet where Jenny slept, Menie found her seated on her trunk, with her fingers in her ears; but this precaution had evidently been quite ineffectual so far as Jenny's sharp sense of hearing was concerned. Menie Laurie put her own arms within the projected arm of the follower of the family, and drew her away to her mother's room. Like a culprit, faintly resisting, Jenny went.

"I'm sure if I had kent ye would have been as pleased," said Jenny, when she had in some degree recovered herself, "ye might have gotten ane long ago; but ye'll mind Jenny when ye put it on, and I'm sure it's my heart's wish baith it and you may be lang to the fore, when Jenny's gane and forgotten out o' mind. 'Deed ay, it's very bonnie. I kent I was a gey guid judge mysel, and it was the first ane I lighted on, afore we had been out o' the house ten minutes—it's been rinning in my head ever since then."

"But, Jenny, it must have been very expensive," said Mrs Laurie, quickly.

"I warrant it was nae cheaper than they could help," said Jenny. "Eh! mem, the manners o' them—and a' dressed out like gentlemen, too. I thought the first ane that came to me was a placed minister, at the very least; and to see the breeding o' them, nae better than as mony hinds! Na, I would like to see the cottar lad in a' Kirklands that would have daured to make his laugh o' me!"

A few days' delay in Edinburgh gave Mrs Laurie space and opportunity of settling various little matters of business, which were necessary for the comfort of their removal; and then the little family embarked in the new steamer, which had but lately superseded the smack, with some such feelings of forlornness and excitement as Australian emigrants might have in these days. Jenny set herself down firmly in a corner of the deck, with her back against the bulwark of the ship, and her eyes tenaciously fixed upon a coil of rope near at hand. Jenny had a vague idea that this might be something serviceable in case of shipwreck, and with jealous care she watched it; a boat, too, swayed gently in its place above her—there was a certain security in being near it; but Jenny's soul was troubled to see Menie wandering hither and thither upon the sunny deck, and her mother quietly reading by the cabin door. Jenny thought it something like a tempting of Providence to read a book securely in this frail ark, which a sudden caprice of uncertain wind and sea might throw in a moment into mortal peril.

But calm and fair as ever Mayday shone, this quiet morning brightened into noon, and their vessel rustled bravely through the Firth, skirting the southern shore. Past every lingering suburban roof—past the sea-bathing houses, quiet on the sands—gliding by the foot of green North-Berwick Law—passing like a shadow across the gloomy Bass, where it broods upon the sea, like a cairn of memorial stones over its martyrs dead—past the mouldering might of old Tantallon, sending a roll of white foam up upon those little coves of Berwickshire, which here and there open up a momentary glimpse of red-roofed fisher-houses, and fisher cobbles resting on the beach under shelter of the high braes and fretted rocks of the coast. Menie Laurie, leaning over the side, looks almost wistfully sometimes at those rude little houses, lying serene among the rocks like a sea-bird's nest. Many a smuggler's romance—many a story of shipwreck and daring bravery, must dwell about this shore; the young traveller only sees how the tiled roof glows against the rock which lends its friendly support behind—how the stony path leads downward to the boat—how the wife at the cottage door looks out, shading her eyes with her hands, and the fisher bairns shout along the sea margin, where only feet amphibious could find footing, and clap their hands in honour of the new wonder, still unfamiliar to their coast. Something chill comes over Menie as her eye lingers on these wild rock-cradled hamlets, so far apart from all the world. Stronger waves of the ocean are breaking here upon the beach, and scarcely a house among them has not lost a father or son at sea; yet there steals a thrill of envy upon the young voyager as one by one they disappear out of her sight. So many homes, rude though their kind is, and wild their place—but as for Menie Laurie, and Menie Laurie's mother, they are leaving home behind.

And now the wide sea sweeps into the sky before them—the northern line of hills receding far away among the clouds, and fishing-boats and passing vessels speck the great breadth of water faintly, with long distances between, and an air of forlorn solitude upon the whole. And the day wanes, and darkness steals apace over the sky and sea. Landward born and landward bred, Jenny sets her back more firmly against the bulwark, and will not be persuaded to descend, though the night air is chill upon her face. Jenny feels some security in her own vigilant unwavering watch upon those great folds of sea-water—those dark cliffs of Northumberland—those fierce castles glooming here and there out from the gathering night. If sudden squall or tempest should fall upon this quiet sea, Jenny at least will have earliest note of it, and with an intense concentration of watchfulness she maintains her outlook; while Mrs Laurie and Menie, reluctantly leaving her, lie down, not without some kindred misgivings, to their first night's rest at sea.

CHAPTER X

A second night upon these untrusted waters found the travellers a little less nervous and timid, but the hearts of all lightened when the early sunshine showed them the green flat river-banks on either side of their cabin windows. Menie, hurrying on deck, was the first to see over the flat margin and glimmering reach the towers of Greenwich rising against its verdant hill. The sun was dancing on the busy Thames; wherries, which Menie's eyes followed with wonder—so slight and frail they looked—shot across the river like so many flying arrows; great hay barges, heavy with their fragrant freight, and gay with brilliant colour, blundered up the stream midway, like peasants on a holiday; and high and dark, with their lines of little prison-windows, these great dismasted wooden castles frowned upon the sunny water, dreary cages of punishment and convict crime. Then came the houses, straggling to the river's edge—then a passing glimpse of the great strong-ribbed bony skeletons which by-and-by should breast the sea-waves proudly, men-o'-war—then the grand placid breadth of the river palace, with the light lying quiet in its green quadrangle, and glimpses of blue sky relieving its cloistered fair arcade. Further on and further, and Jenny rubs her wide awake but very weary eyes, and shakes her clenched hand at the clumsy colliers and enterprising sloops which begin to shoot across "our boat's" encumbered way; and now we strike into the very heart of a maze of ships, built in rank and file against the river's side, and straying about here and there, even in the mid course of the stream: almost impossible, Menie, to catch anything but an uncertain glimpse of these quaint little wharfs, and strange small old-world gables, which grow like so many fungi at the water's edge; but yonder glows the golden ball and cross—yonder rises the world-famed dome, guardian of the world's chiefest city—and there it fumes and frets before us, stretching upward far away—far beyond the baffled horizon line, which fades into the distance, all chafed and broken with crowded spires and roofs—London—Babylon—great battle-ground of vexed humanity—the crisis scene of Menie Laurie's fate.

But without a thought or fear of anything like fate—only with some fluttering expectations, tremors, and hopes, Menie Laurie stood upon the steamer's deck as it came to anchor slowly and cumbrously before the vociferous pier. In presence of all this din and commotion, a silence of abstraction and reverie wrapt her, and Menie looked up unconsciously upon the flitting panorama which moved before her dreamy eyes. Mrs Laurie's brow had grown into curves of care again, and Jenny, jealous and alert, kept watch over the mountain of luggage which she had piled together by many a strenuous tug and lift—for Jenny already meditated kilting up her best gown round her waist, and throwing off her shawl to leave her sturdy arms unfettered, for the task of carrying some of these trunks and lighter boxes to the shore.

"Keep me, what's a' the folk wanting yonder?" said Jenny; "they canna be a' waiting for friends in the boat; and I reckon the captain durstna break the mail-bags open, so it canna be for letters. Eh, Miss Menie, just you look up there at that open in the houses—what an awfu' crowd's up in yon street! What'll be ado! I've heard say there's aye a great fire somegate in London, and folk aye troop to see a fire—but then they never happen but at night. My patience! what can it be?"

Whatever it is, Menie's eye has caught something less distant, which wakes up her dreaming face like a spell. While Jenny gazes and wonders at the thronging passengers of the distant street, Menie's face floods over with a flush of ruddy light like the morning sky. Her shy eyelids droop a moment over the warm glow which sparkles under them—her lips move, breaking into a host of wavering smiles—her very figure, slight and elastic, expands with this thrill of sudden pleasure. Your mother there looks gravely at the shore—a strange, alien, unkindly place to her—and already anticipates, with some care and annoyance, the trouble of landing, and the delay and further fatigue to be encountered before her little family can reach their new home; and Jenny is uttering a child's wonders and surmises by your side—what is this, Menie Laurie, that makes the vulgar pier a charmed spot to you?

Only another eager face looking down—another alert animated figure pressing to the very edge—impatient hands thrusting interposing porters and cabmen by—and eyes all a-glow with loving expectation, searching over all the deck for the little party which they have not yet descried. Involuntarily Menie raises her hand, her breath comes quick over her parted lips, and in her heart she calls to him with shy joy. He must have heard the call, surely, by some art magic, though the common air got no note of it, for see how he bends, with that sudden flush upon his face; and Menie meets the welcoming look, the keen gaze of delight and satisfaction, and lays her hand upon her mother's arm timidly, to point out where Randall Home waits for them; but he does something more than wait—and there is scarcely a possibility of communication with the crowded quay, as these unaccustomed eyes are inclined to fancy, when a quick step rings upon the deck beside them, and he is here.

But Menie does not need to blush for her betrothed—though those shy bright eyes of hers, wavering up and down with such quick unsteady glances, seem to light into richer colour every moment the glow upon her cheeks—for Randall is a true son of John Home of Crofthill, inheriting the stately figure, the high-crested head, with its mass of rich curls, the blue, clear, penetrating eyes. And Randall bears these natural honours with a grace of greater refinement, though a perfectly cool spectator might think, perchance, that even the more conscious dignity of the gentleman's son did not make up for the kindly gleam which takes from the farmer father's blue eyes all suspicion of coldness. But it is impossible to suspect coldness in Randall's glance now—his whole face sparkles with the glow of true feeling and genuine joy. The one of them did not think the other beautiful a few days—a few hours—ago, even with all the charm of memory and absence to make them fair—and neither are beautiful, nor near it, to everyday eyes; but with this warm light on them—happy, and true, and pure—they are beautiful to each other now.

"Weel, I wouldna say there was mony like him, 'specially amang thae English, after a'," said Jenny, under her breath.

"What do you say, Jenny?" Mrs Laurie, who has already had her share of Randall's greetings, and been satisfied therewith, thinks it is something about the luggage—which luggage, to her careful eyes, comes quite in the way of Randall Home.

"I was saying—weel, 'deed it's nae matter," said Jenny, hastily recollecting that her advice had not been asked before Menie's engagement, and that she had never deigned to acknowledge any satisfaction with the same, "but just it's my hope there's to be some safer gate ashore than yon. Eh, my patience! if it's no like a drove o' wild Irish, a' pouring down on us! But I would scarce like to cross the burn on that bit plank, and me a' the boxes to carry. I needna speak—the mistress pays nae mair heed to me; but, pity me! we're no out o' peril yet—they'll sink the boat!"

And Jenny watched with utter dismay the flood of invading porters and idle loungers from the quay, and with indignation looked up to, and apostrophised, the careless captain on the paddle-box, who could coolly look on and tolerate this last chance of "sinking the boat." From these terrors, however, Jenny was suddenly awakened into more active warfare. A parcel of these same thronging mercenaries assailed her own particular pile of trunks and boxes, and Jenny, furious and alarmed, flew to the defence.

But by-and-by—a tedious time to Mrs Laurie, though it flew like an arrow over the heads of Randall and Menie, and over Jenny's fierce contention—they were all safely established at last in a London hackney-coach, with so much of the lighter luggage as it could or would convey. Randall had permission to come to them that very night, so nothing farther was possible; he went away after he had lingered till he could linger no longer. Mrs Laurie leaned back in her corner with a long-drawn sigh—Jenny, on the front seat, muttered out the conclusion of her fuff—while Menie looked out with dazzled eyes, catching every now and then among the stranger passengers a distant figure, quick and graceful; nor till they were miles away did Menie recollect that now this vision of her fancy could not be Randall Home.

Miles away—it was hard to fancy that through these thronged and noisy streets one could travel miles. Always a long array of shops, and warehouses, and dingy houses—always a pavement full and crowded—always a stream of vehicles beside their own in the centre of the way—now and then a break into some wider space, a square, or cross, or junction of streets—here and there a great public building, or an old characteristic house, which Menie feels sure must be something notable, if anybody were by to point it out. Jenny, interested and curious at first, is by this time quite stunned and dizzy, and now and then cautiously glances from the window, with a strong suspicion that she has been singled out for a mysterious destiny, and that the cab-driver has some desperate intention of maddening his passengers, by driving them round and round in a circle of doom through these bewildering streets. Nothing but the hum of other locomotion, the jolting din of their own, the jar over the stones of the causeway, the stream of passengers left behind, and houses gliding past them, give evidence of progress, till, by-and-by, the stream slackens, the noises decrease—trees break in here and there among the houses—dusty suburban shrubberies—villakins standing apart, planted in bits of garden ground—and then, at last, the tired horse labours up a steep ascent; long palings, trees, and green slopes of land, reveal themselves to the eyes of the weary travellers, and, under the full forenoon sun, pretty Hampstead, eagerly looked for, appears through the shabby cab-windows, with London in a veil of mist lying far off at its feet.

Instinctively Mrs Laurie puts up her hands to draw her veil forward, and straighten the edge of her travelling-bonnet—instinctively Menie looses the ribbons of hers, to shed back the hair from her flushed cheek. Jenny, not much caring what the inhabitant of Heathbank Cottage may think of her, only gathers up upon her knee a full armful of bags and baskets, and draws her breath hard—a note of anticipatory disdain and defiance—as she nods her head backward, with a toss of impatience, upon the glass behind her. And now the driver looks back to point with his whip to a low house on the ascent before him, and demands if he is right in thinking this 'Eathbank.

Nobody can answer; but, after a brief dialogue with the proprietor of a passing donkey, the cabman stirs his horse with a chirrup, and a touch of the lash. It is 'Eathbank, and they are at their journey's end.

Home—well, one has seen places that look less like home. You can just see the low roof, the little bits of pointed gable, the small lattice-windows of the upper storey, above the thick green hawthorn hedge that closes round. A tall yew-tree looks out inquisitively over the hawthorns, pinched, and meagre, and of vigilant aspect, not quite satisfied, as it would seem, with the calm enjoyment of the cows upon this bank of grass without; but Jenny's heart warms to the familiar kye, which might be in Dumfriesshire—they look so home-like. Jenny's lips form into the involuntary "pruh." Jenny's senses are refreshed by the balmy breath of the milky mothers—and Menie's eyes rejoice over a glorious promise of roses and jasmine on yon sunny wall, and a whole world of clear unclouded sky and sunny air embracing yonder group of elm-trees. Even Mrs Laurie's curved brow smoothes and softens—there is good promise in the first glance of Heathbank.

At the little gate in the hedge, Miss Annie Laurie's favourite serving-maiden, in a little smart cap, collar, and embroidered apron, which completely overpower and bewilder Jenny, stands waiting to receive them. Everything looks so neat, so fresh, so unsullied, that the travellers grow flushed and heated with a sudden sense of contrast, and remember their own travel-soiled garments and fatigued faces painfully; but Menie has only cast one pleased look upon the smooth green lawn which shrines the yew-tree—made one step upon the well-kept gravel path, and still has her hand upon the carriage-door, half turning round to assist her mother, when a sudden voice comes round the projecting bow-window of Heathbank Cottage—a footstep rings on the walk, an appearance reveals itself in the bright air. Do you think it is some young companion whom your good aunt's kindness has provided for you, Menie—some one light of heart and young of life, like your own May-time? Look again, as it comes tripping along the path in its flowing muslin and streaming ringlets. Look and cast down your head, shy Menie, abashed you know not why—for what is this?

Something in a very pretty muslin gown, with very delicate lace about its throat and hands, and curls waving out from its cheeks. Look, too, what a thin slipper—what a dainty silken stocking reveals itself under the half-transparent drapery! Look at these ringing metallic toys suspended from its slender waist, at the laced kerchief in its hand, at its jubilant pace—anywhere—anywhere but at the smile that fain would make sunshine on you—the features which wear their most cordial look of welcome. Menie Laurie's eyes seek the gravel path once more, abashed and irresponsive. Menie Laurie's youthful cheek reddens with a brighter colour; her hand is slow to detach itself from the carriage door—though Menie Laurie's grand-aunt flutters before her with outstretched arms of gracious hospitality, inviting her embrace.

"My pretty little darling, welcome to Heathbank," says the voice; and the voice is not unpleasant, though it is pitched somewhat too high. "Kiss me, love—don't let us be strangers. I expect you to make yourself quite at home."

And Menie passively and with humility submits to be kissed—a process of which she has had little experience hitherto—and stands aside, suddenly very much subdued and silent, while the stranger flutters into the carriage window to tender the same sign of regard to Menie's mother. Menie's mother, better prepared, maintains a tolerable equanimity; but Menie herself has been struck dumb, and cannot find a word to say, as she follows with a subdued step into the sacred fastnesses of Heathbank. The muslin floats, the ringlets wave, before the fascinated eyes of Menie, and Menie listens to the voice as if it were all a dream.

CHAPTER XI

"My patience! but ye'll no tell me, Miss Menie, that yon auld antick is the doctor's aunt?"

"She was no older than my father, though she was his aunt, Jenny," said Menie Laurie, with humility. Menie was something ashamed and had not yet recovered herself of the first salute.

"Nae aulder than the doctor!—I wouldna say; your mamma hersel is no sae young as she has been; but the like o' yon!"

"Look, Jenny, what a pleasant place," said the evasive Menie; "though where the heath is—but I suppose as they call this Heathbank we must be near it. Look, Jenny, down yonder, at the steeple in the smoke, and how clear the air is here, and this room so pleasant and lightsome. Are you not pleased, Jenny?"

"Yon's my lady's maid," said Jenny, with a little snort of disdain. "They ca' her Maria, nae less—set her up! like a lady's sel in ane o' your grand novelles; and as muckle dress on an ilkaday as I've seen mony a young lady gang to the kirk wi', Miss Menie—no to say your ain very sel's been plainer mony a day. Am I no pleased? Is't like to please folk to come this far to an outlandish country, and win to a house at last wi' a head owre't like yon!"

"Whisht, Jenny!" Menie Laurie has opened her window softly, with a consciousness of being still a stranger, and in a stranger's house. The pretty white muslin curtains half hide her from Jenny, and Jenny stands before the glass and little toilet-table, taking up sundry pretty things that ornament it, with mingled admiration and disdain, surmising what this, and this, is for, and wondering indignantly whether the lady of the house can think that Menie stands in need of the perfumes and cosmetics to which she herself resorts. But the room is a very pretty room, with its lightly-draped bed, and bright carpet, and clear lattice-window. Looking round, Jenny may still fuff, but has no reason to complain.

And Menie, leaning out, feels the soft summer air cool down the flush upon her cheeks, and lets her thoughts stray away over the great city yonder, where the sunshine weaves itself among the smoke, and makes a strange yellow tissue, fine and light to veil the Titan withal. The heat is leaving her soft cheek, her hair plays on it lightly, the wind fingering its loosened curls like a child, and Menie's eyes have wandered far away with her thoughts and with her heart.

Conscious of the sunshine here, lying steadily on the quiet lawn, the meagre yew-tree, the distant garden-path—conscious of the soft bank of turf, where these calm cattle repose luxuriously—of the broad yellow sandy road which skirts it—of the little gleam of water yonder in a distant hollow—but, buoyed upon joyous wings, hovering like a bird over an indistinct vision of yonder pier, and deck, and crowded street—a little circle enclosing one lofty figure, out of which rises this head, with its natural state and grace, out of which shine those glowing ardent eyes—and Menie, charmed and silent, looks on and watches, seeing him come and go through all the ignoble crowd—the crowd which has ceased to be ignoble when it encloses him.

And voices of children ringing through the sunshine, and a sweet, soft, universal tinkle, as of some fairy music in the air, flow into Menie Laurie's meditation, but never fret its golden thread; for every joy of sight and sound finds some kindred in this musing; and the voices grow into a sweet all-hail, and the hum of distant life lingers on her ear like the silver tone of fame—Fame that is coming—coming nearer every day, throwing the glow of its purple royal, the sheen of its diamond crown upon his head and on his path,—and the girl's heart, overflooded with a light more glorious than the sunshine, forgets itself, its own identity and fate, in dreaming of the nobler fate to which its own is bound.

"A young friend of yours?—you may depend upon my warmest welcome for him, my dear Mrs Laurie," says a voice just emerging into the air below, which sends Menie back in great haste, and with violent unconscious blushes, from the window. "Mr Randall Home?—quite a remarkable name, I am sure. Something in an office? Indeed! But then, really, an office means so many very different things—may be of any class, in fact—and a literary man? I am delighted. He must be a very intimate friend to have seen you already."

Menie waits breathless for the answer, but in truth Mrs Laurie is very little more inclined to betray her secret than she is herself.

"We have known him for many years—a neighbour's son," said Mrs Laurie, with hesitation; "yet indeed it is foolish to put off what I must tell you when you see them together. Randall and my Menie are—I suppose I must say, though both so young—engaged, and of course it is natural he should be anxious. I have no doubt you will be pleased with him; but I was hurried and nervous a little this morning, or I should have postponed his first visit a day or two, till we ourselves were less perfect strangers to you, Miss Annie."

"I beg—" said Miss Annie Laurie, lifting with courteous deprecation her thin and half-bared arm. "I felt quite sure, when I got your letter, that we could not be strangers half an hour, and this is really quite a delightful addition;—true love—young love!—ah, my dear Mrs Laurie, where can there be a greater pleasure than to watch two unsophisticated hearts expanding themselves! I am quite charmed—a man of talent, too—and your pretty little daughter, so young and so fresh, and so beautifully simple. I am sure you could not have conferred a greater privilege upon me—I shall feel quite a delight in their young love. Dear little creature—she must be so happy; and I am sure a good mother like you must be as much devoted to him as your darling Menie."

Mrs Laurie, who was not used to speak of darling Menies, nor to think it at all essential that she should be devoted to Randall Home, was considerably confused by this appeal, and could only answer in a very quiet tone, which quite acted as a shadow to Miss Annie's glow of enthusiasm, that Randall was a very good young man, and that she had never objected to him.

"The course of true love never did run smooth," said the greatly interested Miss Annie. "My dear Mrs Laurie, I am afraid you must have had some other, perhaps more ambitious views, or you could not possibly— with your experience, too—speak with so little interest of your dear child's happiness."

Here Menie ventured to glance out. The lady of the house swayed lightly back and forward, with one foot on the ground and another on the close turf of the little lawn, switching the yew-tree playfully with a wand of hawthorn; and the wind blew Miss Annie's long ringlets against her withered cheek and fluttered the lace upon her arm, with a strange contempt for her airy graces, and for the levity so decayed and out of date, which Menie felt herself blush to see. Opposite, upon the grass, stood Mrs Laurie, the sun beating down upon her snowy matron-cap, her healthful cheek, her sober household dignity. But the sun revealed to Menie something more than the natural good looks of that familiar face. Mrs Laurie's cheek was flushed a little. Mrs Laurie's fine clear dark eye wandered uneasily over the garden, and Mrs Laurie's foot patted the grass with a considerable impatience. Half angry, disconcerted, abashed, annoyed, Menie's mother could but half conceal an involuntary smile of amusement, too.

"Yes, my child's happiness is very dear to me," said Mrs Laurie, with half a shade of offence in her tone. "But Menie is very young—I am in no haste to part with her."

"Ah, my dear, youth is the time," said Miss Annie pathetically—"the first freshness, you know, and that dear, sweet, early susceptibility, of which one might say so many charming things. For my part, I am quite delighted to think that she has given her heart so early, so many experiences are lost otherwise. I remember—ah, I remember!—but really, Mrs Laurie, you surprise me. I see I must give my confidence to Menie. Poor little darling—I am afraid you have not encouraged her to confide all her little romantic distresses to you."

"I have always respected Menie's good sense," said Mrs Laurie hastily. Then she made a somewhat abrupt pause, and then glanced up with her look of disconcertment and confusion, half covered with a smile. "I am Menie's mother, and an old wife now, Miss Annie. I am afraid I have lost a great deal of that early susceptibility you spoke of—and I scarcely think my daughter would care to find it in me—but we are very good friends for all that."

And Mrs Laurie's eye, glistening with mother pride, and quite a different order of sentiment from Miss Annie's, glanced up involuntarily to Menie's window. Menie had but time to answer with a shy child's look of love out of her downcast eyes—for Menie shrank back timidly from the more enthusiastic sympathy with which her grand-aunt waited to overpower her—and disappeared into the quiet of her room, to sit down in a shady corner a little, and wind her maze of thoughts into some good order. The sun was drawing towards the west—it was time to descend to the shady drawing-room of Heathbank, where Randall by-and-by should be received for the first time as Miss Annie Laurie's guest.

CHAPTER XII

It is very pleasant here, in the shady drawing-room of Heathbank. Out of doors, these grassy slopes, which Menie Laurie cannot believe to be the heath, are all glowing with sunshine; but within here, the light falls cool and green, the breeze plays through the open window, and golden streaks of sunbeams come in faintly at one end, through the bars of the Venetian blind, upon the pleasant shade, touching it into character and consciousness. It is a long room with a window at either end, a round table in the middle, an open piano in a recess, and pretty bits of feminine-looking furniture straying about in confusion not too studied. The walls are full of gilt frames too, and look bright, though one need not be unnecessarily critical about the scraps of canvass and broad-margined water-colour drawings, which repose quietly within these gilded squares. They are Miss Annie Laurie's pictures, and Miss Annie Laurie feels herself a connoisseur, and is something proud of them, while it cannot be denied that the frames do excellent service upon the shady drawing-room wall.

Mrs Laurie has found refuge in the corner of a sofa, and, with a very fine picture-book in her hand, escapes from the conversation of Miss Annie, which has been so very much in the style of the picture-book, that Menie's mother still keeps her flush of abashed annoyance upon her cheek, and Menie herself lingers shyly at the door, half afraid to enter. There is something very formidable to Menie in the enthusiasm and sympathy of her aunt.

"My pretty darling!" said Miss Annie—and Miss Annie lifted her dainty perfumed fingers to tap Menie's cheeks with playful grace. Menie shrunk back into a corner, blushing and disconcerted, and drooped her head after a shy girlish fashion, quite unable to make any response. "Don't be afraid, my love," said the mistress of the house, with a little laugh. "Don't fear any jesting from me—no, no—I hope I understand better these sensitive youthful feelings—and we shall say nothing on the subject, my dear Menie—not a word—only you must trust me as a friend, you know, and we must wait tea till he comes—ah, till *he* comes, Menie."

Poor Menie for the moment could have wished *him* a thousand miles away; but she only sat down, very suddenly and quietly, on a low seat by the wall, while Miss Annie tripped away to arrange some ornamental matters on the tea-table, where her little china cups already sparkled, and her silver tea-pot shone. Menie took courage to look at her kinswoman's face as this duty was being performed. Withered and fantastic in its decayed graces, there was yet a something of kindness in the smile. The face had been pretty once in its youthful days—a sad misfortune to it now, for if it were not for this long-departed, dearly remembered beauty, there might have been a natural sunshine in Miss Annie Laurie's face.

As it was, the wintry light in it played about gaily, and Miss Annie made very undeniable exertions to please her visitors. She told Menie of her own pursuits, as a girl might have done in expectation of a sharer in them; and to Mrs Laurie she gave a sketch of her "society," the few friends who, Menie thought, made up a very respectable list in point of numbers. Mrs Laurie from her sofa, and Menie on her seat by the wall, looking slightly prim and very quiet in her shy confusion, made brief answers as they could. Their entertainer did not much want their assistance; and by-and-by Menie woke with a great flush to hear the little gate swing open, to discern a lofty figure passing the window, and the sound of a quick step on the gravel path. Randall was at the door.

And Randall, looking very stately, very gracious and deferential, came through the shower of "delighteds" and "most happys" with which Miss Annie saluted him, with a bow of proud grace and much dignity of manner, to Mrs Laurie's extreme surprise, and Menie's shy exultation. Another hour passed over very well. The strangers grew familiar with Miss Annie; then by-and-by they strayed out, all of them, into the sweet evening air, so full of charmed distant voices, the hum and breath of far-off life; and Menie found herself, before she was aware, alone, under a sky slowly softening into twilight, in a pretty stretch of sloping turf, where some young birch-trees stood about gracefully, like so many children resting in a game, with Randall Home by her side.

And they had found time for various pieces of talk, quite individual and peculiar to themselves, before Menie lifted her face, with its flush of full unshadowed pleasure, and, glancing up to the other countenance above her, asked, "When is the next book coming, Randall?"

"What next book, May Marion?"

This was his caressing name for her, as May alone was his father's.

"*The* next book—our next book," said Menie. "I do not know much, nor maybe care much, about anybody else's. Randall—our own—when is it coming?"

"What if it should never come at all?"

Randall drew her fingers through his hand with playful tenderness, half as he might have done with a child.

"Yes—but I know it is to come at all, so that is not my question," said Menie. "I want to know *when*—not if. Tell me—for you need not be coy, or think of keeping such a secret from me." "Did you never hear that it is dangerous to hurry one work upon another?" was the answer somewhat evasively given. "I am to be prudent this time—there is peril in it."

"Peril to what?" Menie Laurie looked up with simple eyes into a face where there began to rise some faint mists. Looking into them, she did not comprehend at all these floating vapours, nor the curve of fastidious discontent which they brought to Randall's lip and brow.

"My simple Menie, you do not know how everything gets shaped into a trade," said Randall, with a certain condescension. "Peril to reputation, risk of losing what one has gained—that is what we all tremble for in London."

"Randall!" Menie looked up again with a flush of innocent scorn. He might speak it, indeed, but she knew he could mean nothing like this.

There was a slight pause—it might be of embarrassment—on Randall's part; certainly he made no effort to break the silence.

"But a great gift was not given for that," said Menie rapidly, in her unwitting enthusiasm. "People do not have unusual endowments given them to be curbed by such things as that; and you never meant it, Randall; it could not move *you*."

But Randall only drew his hand fondly over the fingers he held, and smiled—smiled with pleasure and pride, natural and becoming. He had not been sophisticated out of regard for the warm appreciation and praise of those most dear to him. He might distrust it—might think the colder world a better judge, and the verdict of strangers a safer rule, but in his heart he loved the other still.

But Menie's thoughts were disturbed, and moved into a sudden ferment. Her hand trembled a little on Randall's arm; her eyes forsook his face, and cast long glances instead over the bright air before them; and when she spoke her voice was as low as her words were quick and hurried.

"It does not become me to teach you, but, Randall, Randall, you used to think otherwise. Do you mind what you used to say about throwing away the scabbard, putting on the harness—Randall, do you mind?"

"I mind many a delightful hour up on the hillside yonder," said Randall affectionately, "when my May Marion began to enter into all my dreams and hopes; and I mind about the scabbard and the harness no less," he continued, laughing, "and how I meditated flashing my sword in the eyes of all the world, like a schoolboy with his first endowment of gunpowder. But one learns to know that the world cares so wonderfully little about one's sword, Menie; and moreover—you must find out for me the reason why—this same world seems to creep round one's-self strangely, and by-and-by one begins to feel it more decorous to hide the glitter of the trenchant steel. What a coxcomb you make me," said Randall, abruptly breaking off with a short laugh; "one would fancy this same weapon of mine was the sword of Wallace wight."

Menie made no answer, and the discontent on Randall's face wavered into various shades of scorn,—a strange scorn, such as Menie Laurie had never seen before on any face—scorn half of himself, wholly of the world.

"When I knew I had succeeded," said Randall at length, with still a tone of condescension in his confidence, "I was a little elated, I confess, Menie, foolish as it seems, and thought of nothing but setting to work again, and producing something worthy to live. Well, that is just the first impulse; by-and-by I came to see what a poor affair this applause was after all, and to think I had better keep what I had, without running the risk of losing my advantage by a less successful stroke. After all, this tide of popularity depends on nothing less than real 'merit,' as the critics call it; so I apprehend we will have no new book, Menie; we will be content with what we have gained."

"If applause is such a poor affair, why be afraid of the chance of losing it?" said Menie; but she added hastily, "I want to know about Johnnie Lithgow, Randall; is it possible that he has come to be a great writer too?"

"If I only knew what you meant by a great writer *too*," said Randall, with a smile. "Johnnie Lithgow is quite a popular man, Menie—one of the oracles of the press."

"Is it a derogation, then, to be a popular man?" said the puzzled Menie; "or is he afraid to risk his fame, like you?"

The lofty head elevated itself slightly. "No. Johnnie Lithgow is not a man for fame," said Randall, with some pride. "Johnnie does his literary work like any other day's work; and, indeed, why should he not?"

Menie looked up with a blank look, surprised, and not comprehending. Even the stronger emotions of life, the passions and the anguishes, had never yet taken hold of Menie; still less had the subtle refining, the artificial stoicism of mere mind and intellect, living and feeding on itself; and Menie's eye followed his slight unconscious gestures with wistful wonderment as Randall went on.

"After all, what does it signify—what does anything of this kind signify? One time or another appreciation comes; and if appreciation never should come, what then? So much as is good will remain. I do not care a straw for applause myself. I rate it at its own value; and that is nothing."

It began to grow somewhat dark, and Menie drew her shawl closer. "I think it is time to go home," she said softly; and as she spoke, a vision of the kindly home she had left—of the brave protecting hills, the broad fair country, the sky and atmosphere, all too humble for this self-abstraction, which answered in clouds and tears, in glorious laughter and sunshine, to every daily change—rose up before her; some tears, uncalled for and against her will, stole into Menie's eyes. With a little awe, in her innocence, she took Randall's arm again. He must be right, she supposed; and something very grand and superior was in Randall's indifference—yet somehow the night air crept into Menie's heart, as she had never felt it do before. Many an hour this soft night air had blown about her uncovered head, and tossed her hair in curls about her cheeks—to-night she felt it cold, she knew not why—to-night she was almost glad to hurry home.

CHAPTER XIII

"Randall Home is a very superior young man," said Mrs Laurie, with quiet approbation. "Do you know, Menie, I had begun to have serious thoughts about permitting your engagement so early?—if my only bairn should leave me—leave me, and get estranged into another house and home, with a man that was a stranger in his heart to me. Whisht, Menie—my darling, what makes you cry?"

But Menie could not tell; the night air was still cold at her heart, and she could not keep back these unseasonable tears.

"But I am better pleased to-night than I have been for many a day," said Mrs Laurie. "I never saw him so kindly, so like what I would desire. I was a little proud of him to-night, if it were for nothing but letting Miss Annie see that we are not all such common folk as she thinks down in the south country—though, I suppose, I should say the north country here. Menie! he will lose my good opinion again if I think he has vexed you. What ails you, bairn? Menie, my dear?"

"I don't know what it is, mother—no, no, he did not vex me. I suppose I am glad to hear you speak of him so," said the shy Menie, ashamed of her tears. The mother and daughter were in their own room preparing for rest, and Menie let down her hair over her face, and played with it in her fingers, that there might be no more remark or notice of this unwilling emotion. It was strange—never all her life before had Menie wept for anything indefinite: for childish provocations—for little vexations of early youth—for pity—she had shed bright transitory tears, but she had never "cried for nothing" until now.

"Yes, I am pleased," said Mrs Laurie, as she tied her muslin cap over her ears: "what did you say, Menie? I thought this coming to London would satisfy me on the one point which is likely to be more important than all others, and I was right. Yes, Menie, lie down, like a good girl; you must be wearied—and lie down with a good heart—you have a fair prospect, as fair as woman could wish. I am quite satisfied myself."

But how it came about that Menie only slept in broken snatches—that Menie dreamt uncomfortable dreams of harassment and annoyance—

dangers in which Randall forsook her—cares of which he had no part—Menie did not know. A day ago, and Mrs Laurie's unsolicited avowal of "satisfaction" had lifted Menie into the purest glow of joy, but to-night she cannot tell what makes her so restless and uneasy—what prompts her now and then to fall a-weeping, all unwillingly, and "for nothing." Alas for Menie Laurie's quiet heart!—something has come to trouble the waters, but in other guise than an angel's.

The grass is soft and mossy under the elm trees, and the morning air—a world of sweetness—beatifies their every branch and stem. Down yonder in the hollow, low at your feet, Menie Laurie, the great slave Titan has wakened to his daily toil. Is that the sweep of his mighty arm stirring the heavy mist which hangs above him? Is this the clang of his ponderous tools ringing up faintly into the quiet skies? The children are not astir yet, to seek their pleasure in these precincts. Nothing seems awake in this composed and sober place; but yonder, with many a conflict in his heart, with many a throbbing purpose in his brain, with life and strength tingling to his finger-points, with sighs and laughter swelling in his breath—yonder great vassal of the world is up and doing, holding the fate of a new day undeveloped in his busy hand.

And you, young wondering heart, look out upon him, innocent, ignorant, wistful, like an angel on the threshold of the world—nothing knowing the wiles and snares, the tortures and deliriums that live yonder under the battle-cloud, unacquainted with those prodigious penalties of social life, which yonder are paid and borne every hour; but looking out with your head bent forward, and your innocent eyes piercing far in the dreamy vision of reverie, making wistful investigation into the new marvels round you, pondering and bewildered in your own secret soul.

Randall—looking out thus through the morning light upon the city, one can see him in so many aspects;—the light shines upon his lofty head, reaching almost to the skies, like the hill of his quiet home—and Menie lifts her eyes to follow that noble daring look of his, piercing up through mortal clouds and vapours to do homage with the gifts God has given him, at his Master's throne and footstool. But anon there steals a cloud round the hero of Menie's vision—a dim background, which still reveals him, not less clearly, nor with less fascination, but with a sadder wonder of interest—for Randall's eyes are bent earthward, Randall's lofty head is bowed, and Menie, though she watches him with yearning curiosity, can never meet his downcast look to read what is there—can never fathom what lies within the veiled heart and self-abstracted soul. You would think now that her eyes are caught by the sunshine yonder, making each mischievous confusion among the city vapours: Not so; for Menie's eyes, under that troubled curve of her forehead, are studying Randall, and see only an incomprehensible something in him, overshadowing all the earth and all the skies.

With her little basket in her hand, with her dainty step, and fluttering muslin gown, Miss Annie brushes the dew from the grass, as she draws near the elm trees. But though Miss Annie has been very confidential with her grand-niece on the subject of her own juvenile occupations, one little piece of daily business Miss Annie has forborne to tell of, and that is a morning visit she pays to a poor pensioner or two in the village, where, if perhaps her charity may be sometimes intrusive, it is always real. For poor Miss Annie's heart, though it figures so much in her common talk, and is overlaid with so many false sentimentalities, has a true little fountain of human kindness in it, spite of the fantastic pretences that hide it from common view. Absorbed with her new thoughts, Menie neither heard nor saw her aunt's approach, till she woke with a start to hear a gay laugh behind her, and to feel the pressure of those long thin fingers upon her eyelids. "Dreaming, Menie? ah, my pretty love! but not 'in maiden meditation fancy free.'"

Startled and abashed, Menie drew back, but Miss Annie's ringlets had already touched her forehead, as Miss Annie bestowed the morning salutation upon Menie's cheek; and now they are seated side by side under shadow of the greatest elm.

"My dear, I am afraid your mamma does not encourage you to confide in her; you must tell me all your little trials, Menie," said Miss Annie, fluttering with her finger-points upon Menie's hand; "and now, my darling, speak to me freely—you were delighted to meet him last night."

But Menie had no voice to answer, and could only bend down her flushed face, and pluck up the grass with her disengaged hand.

"Don't be shy, love. I am so much interested; and tell me, Menie, you found him quite unchanged?—just as devoted as he used to be? I am sure one only needed to look at him—and how delightful to find him quite unchanged!"

"How far is it to London, aunt?" said Menie, with confusion.

"So near that your thoughts have travelled there this morning to find him out, I know," said Miss Annie,—"so near that he can come out every night, so we need not talk of London: but come now, darling; have you nothing to tell me?"

"You are very good," said Menie, with a slight falter in her voice. "I—I should like very well to take Jenny, if you please, to see some of the great sights."

Miss Annie shook her head—"Ah, Menie, how mischievous! Don't you think I deserve your confidence?"

"But, indeed, I have no confidence to give," said Menie, almost under her breath.

"My dear, I was just like you: the Scotch system is so restrictive—I was afraid to speak to any one," said Miss Annie; "and so you see I had a little misunderstanding; and he was angry, and I was angry; and first we quarrelled, and then we sulked at each other, and so at last it came about that we were parted. Yes, Menie, dear! just now you are happy; you do not care for a sympathising heart; but if you should chance to be disappointed—I trust not, my love, but such things will happen—you will then remember that I, too, have been blighted—oh, my dear child!"

And with a wave of her hand, expressing unutterable things, Miss Annie arranged her light silken mantle over this same blighted heart of hers, as if to hide the wound.

But Menie, whose mind already had recovered its tone—Menie, who now only remembered Randall unchanged, unchangeable, towering high above all vulgar quarrels and sullennesses, a very fortress for a generous heart to dwell in—Menie sprang lightly up from the elastic turf, and stood with her slight young figure relieved against the morning sky, and all her frame vibrating with pride and joy in her worthy choice. What chance that she should ever give this wished-for confidence—should ever turn to seek such sympathy—should ever find comfort or solace in hearing of Miss Annie Laurie's kindred woe?

CHAPTER XIV

"It is two years now since Randall came to London. From Dumfriesshire we send out a great many cadets into the world, Miss Annie; and some one who knew his father found a situation here for Randall Home. He brought his book with him, and it was published, and very successful; then he came home, and sought my consent to his engagement with Menie. That is all Randall's history in connection with us. The other young man you expect to-night, Miss Annie, is only a cottager's son—very clever, I hear, but not in any way, I fancy, to be put in comparison with Randall Home."

And Mrs Laurie took up her work with a little quiet pride, resolved to be very kind to Johnnie Lithgow, but by no means pleased to have him mentioned in the same breath with her future son-in-law.

"I adore talent," said Miss Annie, opening her work-table to take out a tiny bit of "fancy" work. "I could not describe the delight I have in the society of people of genius—self-taught genius too—so charming; and both of these delightful young men must be self-taught."

Mrs Laurie drew herself up with a little hauteur.

"Mr Home has had an excellent education; his father is a very superior man. Johnnie Lithgow, as I said before, is only a cottager's son."

But Miss Annie could not see the distinction, and ran on in such a flutter of delight in anticipation of her guests, that Mrs Laurie quietly retired into the intricacies of her work, and contented herself with a resolution to be very kind and condescending to the popular editor, the cottager's son.

The drawing-room is in special glory—the pinafores discarded from the chairs, the little tables crowded with gay books and toys and flowers, and everything in its company dress. Mrs Laurie—who never can be anything but Mrs Laurie, a matron of sober years, and Menie's mother—sits, in her grave-coloured gown and snowy cap, upon the sofa; while on a stool low down by her side, in a little tremor of expectation, Miss Annie perches like a bird, waiting the arrival of her visitors. Mrs Laurie, with her Dumfriesshire uses, quite believes what Miss Annie says, that only "a few friends" are coming to-night, and has not the slightest idea that the lady of the house will be greatly mortified if her rooms are not filled in an hour or two with a little crowd.

And up-stairs, resplendent in Jenny's gown, Menie Laurie stands before the glass, fastening on one or two simple ornaments, and admiring, with innocent enjoyment, her unusually elegant dress. You may guess by this glimpse of these well-known striped skirts, full and round, revealing themselves under cover of the curtains, that Jenny, too, has been admiring her own magnificent purchase. But Jenny by this time has grown impatient, and jealous that Menie's admiration prolongs itself only to please her, Jenny; so, giving premonition by sundry restless gestures of the advent of a "fuff," she has turned to look out from the window upon the sandy road which leads to 'Eathbank.

"Eh, Miss Menie! that brockit ane's a bonnie cow," said Jenny; "I never see onything else in this outlandish place that minds me o' hame, if it binna the mistress and yoursel. I'll just bide and look out for the young lads, Miss Menie. Ye needna clap your hands, as if Jenny was turning glaikit; if they werena lads frae our ain countryside, they might come and gang a twelvemonth for me."

"But the ladies and the gentlemen will see you from the window, Jenny," said Menie Laurie.

"Ise warrant they've seen waur sights," said Jenny briskly; "I'm no gaun to let down my ainsel, for a' I *have* a thraw; and I would just like to ken, if folk wanted to see a purpose-like lass, fit for her wark, wha they could come to in this house but me? There's my lady's maid—set her up!—in her grand gown, as braw as my lady; and there's the tither slaving creature put off a' this morning clavering to somebody, and no fit to be seen now; for a' they scoff at my short-gown and guid linsey coats. But they may scoff till they're tired, for Jenny; I'm no gaun to change, at my time o' life, for a' the giggling in London toun."

"But you'll put on your gown to-night, Jenny," said Menie, persuasively, patting her shoulder. "There's Randall did not see you last time he was here;

and Johnnie Lithgow, you would like to see him. Come, Jenny, and put on your gown."

"It's no muckle Randall Home heeds about me, and you ken that," said Jenny; "and for a' he didna see me, I saw him the last time he was here. I'll just tell you, Miss Menie, yon lad, to be a right lad, is owre heeding about himsel."

"You're not to say that, Jenny; it vexes me," said Menie, with simple gravity; "besides, it is not true. You mistake Randall—and then Johnnie Lithgow."

"I wouldna say but what I might be pleased to get a glint o' *him*," said Jenny. "Eh, my patience! to think o' Betty Armstrong's son sitting down with our mistress. But I'll be sure to ca' them by their right names afore the folk. I canna get my tongue about thae maisters. Maister Lithgow! and me minds him a wee white-headed laddie, hauding up his peeny for cakes on the Hogmanay, and pu'ing John Glendinning's kail-stocks at Hallowe'en. What would I put on my gown for, bairn? As sure as I gang into the room, I'll ca' him Johnnie."

But Jenny's scruples at last yielded, and Jenny came forth from her chamber glorious in a blue-and-yellow gown, printed in great stripes and figures, and made after an antediluvian fashion, which utterly shocked and horrified the pretty Maria, Miss Annie Laurie's favourite maid. Nor was Miss Annie Laurie herself less disconcerted, when honest Jenny, the high shoulder largely developed by her tight-fitting gown, and carrying a cake-basket in her brown hands, made her appearance in the partially-filled drawing-room, threading her way leisurely through the guests, and examining, with keen glances and much attention, the faces of the masculine portion of them. Miss Annie made a pause in her own lively and juvenile talk, to watch the strange figure and the keen inquiring face, over which a shade of bewilderment gradually crept. But Miss Annie no longer thought it amusing, when Jenny made an abrupt pause before her young mistress, then shily endeavouring to make acquaintance with some very fine young ladies, daughters of Miss Annie's loftiest and most aristocratic friends, and said in a startling whisper, which all the room could hear, "Miss Menie! ye might tell folk which is him, if he's here; but I canna see a creature that's like Johnnie Lithgow o' Kirklands, nor ony belanging to him, in the haill room."

Miss Annie Laurie, much horrified, rose from her seat somewhat hastily; but at the same moment up sprang by her side the guest to whom her most particular attentions had been devoted—"And Burnside Jenny has forgotten me!"

Burnside Jenny, quite forgetful of "all the folk," turned round upon him in an instant. Not quite Johnnie Lithgow, the merriest mischief-doer in Kirklands parish, but a face that prompted recollections of his without dispute—blue eyes, dancing and running over with the light of a happy spirit—and a wisp of close curls, not many shades darker in colour than those of the "white-headed laddie," whose merry tricks Jenny had not forgotten. "Eh, man! is this you?" said Jenny, with a sigh of satisfaction. "I aye likit the callant for a' his mischief, and it's just the same blithe face after a'."

Randall Home stood leaning his fine figure against the mantelpiece, and took no notice of Jenny. Randall was somewhat afraid of a similar recognition; but Johnnie Lithgow, who did not affect attitudes—Johnnie Lithgow, who was neither proud nor ashamed of being a cottager's son, and who had a habit of doing such kindly things as occurred to him without consideration of prudence—drew her aside by both her brown hands, out of which Jenny had laid the cake-basket, to talk to her of home. A slight smile curled on the lip of Randall Home. How well he looked, leaning upon his arm, his lofty head towering over every other head in Miss Annie's drawing-room, with his look of conscious dignity, his intellectual face! Menie Laurie and Menie Laurie's mother did not find it possible to be other than proud of him; yet the eyes of both turned somewhat wistfully to the corner, to dwell upon a face which for itself could have charmed no one, but which beamed and shone like sunshine upon Jenny, greeting her as an old friend.

"Your friend is a literary man?" said somebody inquiringly, taking up a respectful position by Randall's side.

"Yes, poor fellow; he spins himself out into daily portions for the press," said Randall.

"A high vocation, sir; leader of public opinions and movements," said the somebody, who professed to be an intellectual person, a man of progress.

"Say rather the follower," said Randall; "and well for those who have the happy knack of following wisely—chiming in, before itself is fully aware of it, with the humour of the time."

Menie Laurie, who was close at hand, and heard all this, ventured a whisper, while Randall's companion had for the moment turned away.

"Your words sound as if you slighted him, Randall, and you too call yourself a literary man."

"Good Johnnie Lithgow, I like him extremely," said Randall, with the half-scornful smile which puzzled Menie; "but he is only a literary workman after all. He does his literature as his day's labour—he will tell you so himself—a mere craft for daily bread."

And just then Lithgow turned round, with his radiant face—he who had no fame to lose, and did an honest day's work in every day, not thinking that the nature of his craft excused him from the natural amount of toil—and again Menie felt a little pang at her heart, as she thought of Randall's jealous guardianship of Randall's youthful fame.

CHAPTER XV

"I have been thinking of bringing up my mother to live with me," said the Mr Lithgow in whom Mrs Laurie and her daughter were beginning to forget the humble Johnnie: "I see no reason why she should live in poverty in Kirklands, while I am comfortable here."

His face flushed slightly as he concluded, and he began to drum with his fingers in mere shyness and embarrassment upon Miss Annie Laurie's work-table. Randall, a little distance from him, was turning over with infinite scorn Miss Annie's picture-books. The two young men had grown familiar in the house, though it was not yet a month since they entered it first.

"And I think you are very right," said Mrs Laurie cordially, "though whether Mrs Lithgow might be pleased with a town-life, or whether—"

She paused: it was not very easy to say "whether your mother would be a suitable housekeeper for you." Mrs Laurie could not do violence either to her own feelings or his by suggesting such a doubt.

"I think it would be a great risk," said Randall, "and, if you consulted me, would certainly warn you against it. Your mother knows nothing of London—she would not like it; besides, a young man seeking his fortune should be alone."

"Cold doctrine," said Lithgow, smiling, "and to come from *you*."

His eye fell unconsciously upon Menie; then as he met a quick upward glance from her, he stammered, blushed, and stopped short—for Johnnie Lithgow was as shy and sensitive as a girl, and had all the reverence of youthful genius for womanhood and love. With compunction, and an idea that he had been jesting profanely, Lithgow hurriedly began again.

"I am so vain as to think *I* myself would be London to my mother—old ground long known and well explored. If she would not like the change, of course—but I fancy she might."

"I advise you against it, Lithgow," said Randall "in your case I should never entertain such an idea. There is my father—no one can have a greater respect for him than I—but to bring him to live with me—to bring him to London—I should think it the merest folly, injurious to us both."

"Your wisdom is very safe at least," said Mrs Laurie, with a little asperity, "since there is no chance of your good father leaving his own respectable house for an unknown and strange place in any case; but I think your wish a very natural one, and very creditable to you, Mr Lithgow; and whether she comes or not, the knowledge that you wish for her will be joy to your mother's heart."

With his usual half-disdainful smile Randall had turned away, and there was a slight flush of anger upon Mrs Laurie's face. Indignation and scorn,—there was not much hope of friendliness where such unpromising elements had flashed into sudden existence. Menie looking on with terror, and perceiving a new obstacle thrown into her way, hastily endeavoured to make a diversion.

"Do you know, Mr Lithgow, that July Home is coming up to London to see me?"

There came a sudden brightening to all the kindly lines of the young man's face. "July Home! if I am too familiar, forgive me, Randall—but I have so many boyish recollections of her. She was such a sweet little timid simple womanly child too. I wonder if July minds me as I mind her."

Randall stood apart still, with his smile upon his lips. True, there had been a momentary curve on his brow at Lithgow's first mention of his sister's name, but his face cleared immediately. Poor little July! Randall might know her sufficiently timid and simple—but July was a baby, a toy, a good-hearted kindly little fool to her intellectual brother—and any higher qualities sweet or womanly about her remained to be found out by other eyes than his.

"And Miss Annie has promised us all the sightseeing in the world," said Menie with forced gaiety, anxious to talk, and to conciliate—to remove all trace of the little breaking of lances which had just passed. "July and Jenny and I, we are to see all manner of lions; and though they will be very dull at Crofthill when she is gone, Mr Home and Miss Janet have consented—so next week July is to come."

"Poor July! she will have enough to talk of all her life after," said her brother.

"Yes; our kindly country seems such a waste and desert place to you London gentlemen," said Mrs Laurie; "and it is wonderful, after all, how we manage to exist—ay, even to flourish and enjoy ourselves—in these regions out of the world."

But Randall made no response. A shivering chill came over Menie Laurie; this half-derisive silence on one side, this eager impulse of contradiction and opposition on the other, smote her to the heart. It had been rising gradually for some days past, and Menie, without being quite aware of it, had noticed the bias with which her mother and her betrothed listened and replied to each other; the unconscious inclination of each to give an unfavourable turn to the other's words, a harshness to the other's judgment, an air of personal offence to a differing opinion, of grave misdemeanour to a piece of blameless jesting. Lithgow, stranger as he was, discovered in a moment, so quick and sensitive was his nature, the incipient estrangement, and grew embarrassed and annoyed in spite of himself—annoyed, embarrassed, it looked so much like the last ebullition of some domestic quarrel; but Lithgow was a stranger, and had no interest farther than for the harmony of the moment in any strife of these conflicting minds.

But here sits one whose brow must own no curve of displeasure, whose voice must falter with no embarrassment. She is sitting by the little worktable in the window, her eyes, so wistful as they have grown, so large and full, and eloquent with many meanings, turning from one to the other with quick earnest glances, which are indeed whispers of deprecation and peacemaking. "He means something else than he says; he is not cold-hearted nor insincere; you mistake Randall," say Menie's eyes, as they labour to meet her mother's, and gaze with eager perturbation in her face, deciphering every line and wrinkle there. "Do not speak so—you vex my mother; but she does not mean to be angry," say the same strained and ever-changing eyes, as they turn their anxious regards to Randall's face. She sits between us and the light—you can see her girlish figure outlined against the window—her face falling from light to shadow, brightening up again from shadow to light, as she turns from one to the other; you can see how eagerly she listens, prompt to rush forward with her own softening gentle speech upon the very border of the harsher words, whose utterance she cannot prevent. The very stoop of her head—the changeful expression of her face, which already interprets the end of the sentence ere it is well begun—her sudden introduction of one subject after another, foreign to their former talk—her sudden interest in things indifferent, and all the wiles and artifices with which she hedges off all matters of personal or individual interest, and abstracts the conversation into the channel of mere curiosity, of careless and every-day talk—are all sufficiently visible exponents of Menie's new position and new trials. She is talking to Lithgow now so rapidly, and with so much demonstration of interest—you would almost fancy this poor loving Menie had caught a contagious enthusiasm from Miss Annie Laurie's juvenile delights—talking of these sights of the great unknown London, which have grown so indifferent and paltry to this suddenly enlightened and experienced mind of hers; but in the midst of all you can see how steadily her wakeful eyes keep watch upon Randall yonder by Miss Annie's miniature bookcases, and Mrs Laurie here, with that little angry flush upon her brow.

So slow the hours seem—so full of opportunities of discussion—so overbrimming with subjects on which they are sure to differ; till Menie, in her gradually increasing excitement, forgets to note the progress of time; but is so glad—oh, so glad and joyful—to see the evening fall dark around them, to hear Maria's step drawing near the door, while the lights she carries already throw their glimmer on the wall. It is late; and now the visitors take leave, somewhat reluctantly, for Lithgow begins to like his new friends greatly; and Randall, though something of irritation is in the face, where his smile of disdain still holds sway, is Menie's ardent wooer still, and feels a charm in her presence, simple though he has discovered her to be. But at last they are gone—safely gone; and Menie, when she has watched them from the door, and listened to their steps till they die away a distant echo upon the silent air, steals away in the dark to her own room—not for any purpose—simply to rest herself a little; and her manner of rest is, sitting down upon a low stool close by the window, where some pale moonlight comes in faintly, and bending down her face into her clasped hands, to weep a little silently and alone.

Is it but to refresh the wistful eyes which this night have been so busy? is it but to wash and flood away the pain that has been in their eager deprecating looks, their speeches of anxious tenderness? But Menie does not say even to herself what it is for, nor why. For some weeks now, Menie has been sadly given to "crying for nothing," as she herself calls it. She thinks she ought to be ashamed of her weakness, and would be afraid to acknowledge it to any living creature; but somehow, for these few days, Menie has come away about this same hour every night into the solitude here, to cry, with sometimes a little impatient sob bursting out among her tears—though she cannot tell you, will not tell you—would not whisper even to her own very secret heart, the reason why.

CHAPTER XVI

Mrs Laurie sits by the table with her work; but it is still an easy thing to perceive the irritation on Mrs Laurie's brow; her hand moves with an additional rapidity, her breath comes a little faster; and if you watch, you will see the colour gradually receding from her cheek, like an ebbing tide, and her foot ceasing to play so impatiently upon its supporting stool.

Very humbly, like a culprit, Menie draws forward her chair to the light. She is admonished, ere long, by a hasty answer, an abrupt speech, a slight pushing back from the table and erection of her figure, that Mrs Laurie is still angry. It is strange how this cows and subdues Menie—how eager she is to say something—how humble her tone is—and how difficult she feels it to find anything to say.

Poor heart! like many another bewildered moth, Menie flutters about the subject it behoves her most to avoid, and cannot help making timid allusions to their future life in London—that future life which begins to darken before her own vision under a cloudy horizon of doubt and dread. It has ceased to be a speculation now, this future; for even within these few days there has been talk of Menie's marriage.

"We will speak of some other thing; there is no very great charm in the future for me, Menie," said Mrs Laurie, with a sigh.

But Menie, with trembling temerity, begs to know the reason why. Why?—what concerns her concerns her mother also. Very timid, yet too bold, Menie insists, and will be satisfied—why?

"Because it is hard to lose my only child," said Mrs Laurie. "Let us not deceive ourselves; it is easy to say we will not be separated, that there shall be no change. I know better, Menie; well, well! do not cry—say it is only the natural lot."

"What is only the natural lot? O mother, mother! tell me." Menie is still pertinacious, even through her tears.

"I will tell you, Menie," said Mrs Laurie, quickly. "Randall Home and I cannot dwell under one roof in peace. I foresee a wretched life for you if we tried it; a constant struggle—a constant failure. Menie, I will try to be content; but your mother feels it hard to yield up you and your love to a stranger—very hard. I ought to be content and submissive. I ought to remember that it is the common necessity—an every-day trial; but we have been more to each other than mere mother and daughter. I cannot hide it from you, Menie; this trial is very grievous to me."

"Mother! mother!" It is not "for nothing" now that Menie Laurie weeps.

"You have been the light of my eyes for twenty years—my baby, my only bairn! I have nothing in the world when you are gone. Menie, have patience with your mother. I thought we might have been one household still. I never thought I could have hurt my bairn by clinging to her with all my heart. I see through another medium now. Menie, this that I say is better for us both. I would lose my proper place—I would lose even my own esteem—if I insisted, or if I permitted you to insist, upon our first plan. I do not mean to insist with Randall," said Mrs Laurie, with a sudden flush of colour, "but with ourselves. It is not for your credit, any more than mine, that your mother should be unnecessarily humiliated; and I choose to make this decision myself, Menie, not to have it forced upon me."

"If you think so—if I have nothing to hope but this—mother, mother!" cried Menie in her sobs, "there is yet time; we can change it all."

But Menie's voice was choked; her head bowed down upon her folded arms; her strength and her heart were overcome. The room was only partially lighted. So vacant—only these two figures, with their little table and their lamp at one end—it looked lonely, silent, desolate; and you could hear so plainly the great struggle which Menie had with these strong sobs and tears.

Mrs Laurie wiped a few hot hasty drops from her own eyes. She was not much used to contest; nor was it in her to be inflexible and stern; and the mother could not see her child's distress. "Menie!" Menie can make no answer; and Mrs Laurie rises to go to her side, to pass a tender caressing hand over the bowed head, to shed back the disordered hair. "Menie, my dear bairn, I did not mean to vex you. I will do anything—anything, Menie; only do not let me see you in such grief as this."

"He is not what you think, mother—he is not what you think," cried Menie; "it is not like this what he says of you. O mother! I do not ask you to do him justice—to think well of him. I ask a greater thing of you;—mother, hear me—I ask you to like him for Menie's sake."

And it will not do to evade this petition by caresses, by soothing words, by gentle motherly tenderness. "Yes, Menie, my darling, I'll try," said Mrs Laurie at last, with tearful eyes. "Do you think it is pleasant to me to be at strife with Randall? God forbid! and him my dear bairn's choice; but do not look at me with such a pitiful face. Menie, we'll begin again."

Was Menie content?—for the moment more than content, springing up into a wild exhilaration, a burst of confidence and hope. But by-and-by the conversation slackened—by-and-by the room became quite silent, with its dim corners, its little speck of light, and the two figures at its farther end. A heavy stillness brooded over them—they forgot that they had been talking—they forgot, each of them, that she was not alone. The leaves stirred faintly on the windows—the night-wind rustled past the yew-tree on the lawn. From the other end of the house came sometimes a stir of voices, the sound of a closed or opened door: but here everything was silent—as still as if these were weird sisters, weaving, with their monotonous moving fingers, some charm and spell; while, down to the depths—down, down, as far into the chill and dark of sad presentiment as a heart unlearned could go—fluttering, with its wings close upon its breast, its song changed into a mournful cry—down out of the serene heavens, where it had its natural dwelling, came Menie Laurie's quiet heart.

CHAPTER XVII

Through the depth and darkness of the summer-night, you can hear Mrs Laurie's quiet breathing as she lies asleep. With a pain at her heart she lay down, and when she wakes she will feel it, or ever she is aware that she has awaked; but still she sleeps: blessing on the kind oblivion which lays all these troubles for a time to rest.

But what is this white figure erecting itself from the pillow, sitting motionless and silent in the night? It is tears that keep these gentle eyelids apart—tears that banish from them the sleep of youth. Still, that she may not wake the sleeper by her side, scarcely daring to move her hand to wipe away this heavy dew which blinds her eyes. Menie Laurie, Menie Laurie, can this sad watcher be you?

And Menie's soul is vexing itself with plans and schemes, and Menie's heart is rising up to God in broken snatches of prayer, constantly interrupted and merging into the bewilderment of her thoughts. Startled once for all out of the early calm, the serene untroubled youthful life which lies behind her in the past, Menie feels the change very hard and sore as she realises it;—from doing nought for her own comfort—from the loving sweet dependence upon others, to which her child's heart has been accustomed—suddenly, without pause or preparation, to learn that all must depend upon herself,—to have the ghost of strife and discord, where such full harmony was wont to be,—to feel the two great loves of her nature—the loves which heretofore, in her own innocent and unsuspicious apprehension, have but strengthened and deepened each the other—set forth in antagonism, love against love, and her own heart the battle-ground. Shrinking and failing one moment, longing vainly to flee away—away anywhere into the utmost desolation, if only it were out of this conflict,—the next resolving, with such strong throbs and beatings of her heart, to take up her burden cordially, to be ever awake and alert, to subdue this giant difficulty with the force of her own strong love and ceaseless tenderness—praying now for escape, then for endurance, and anon breaking into silent tears over all. Alas for Menie Laurie in her unaccustomed solitude! and Menie thinks, like every other Menie, that she could have borne anything but this.

But by-and-by, in spite of tears and trouble, the natural rest steals upon Menie—steals upon her unawares, though she feels, in the sadness of her heart, as if she could never rest again; throws back her drooping head upon her pillow, folds her arms meekly on her breast, closes her eyelids over the unshed tear; and thus it is that the dawn finds her out, like a flower overcharged and drooping with its weight of evening dew, but wrapt in sleep as deep and dreamless and unbroken as if her youth had never known a tear.

The sun is full in the room when Menie wakes, and Mrs Laurie has but a moment since closed the door softly behind her, that the sleeper might not be disturbed. Even this tender precaution, when she finds it out, chills Menie to the heart; for heretofore her mother's voice has roused her, and even her mother's impatience of her lingering would be joy to her to-day; but Mrs Laurie is not impatient. Mrs Laurie thinks it better, for all the sun's unceasing proclamation that night and sleep are past, to let the young heart refresh itself a little longer, to leave the young form at rest.

Ay, Menie Laurie, kneel down by your bedside—kneel down and pray; it is not often that your supplications testify themselves in outward attitude. Now there is a murmur of an audible voice speaking words to which no mortal ear has any right to listen; and your downcast face is buried in your hands, and your tears plead with your prayers. For you never thought but to be happy, Menie, and the gentle youthful nature longs and yearns for happiness, and with the strength of a rebel fights against the pain foreseen— poor heart!

"Eh, Jenny! you're no keeping ill-will?" said a doleful voice upon the lawn below: very distinct, through the open window, it quickened Menie's morning toilette considerably, and drew her forward, with a wondering face, to make sure. "I'm sure it's no in me to be unfriends wi' onybody; and after ane coming a' this gate for naething but to ask a civil question, how you a' was. I'm saying, Jenny? you're no needing to haud ony correspondence wi' me except ye like; it's the mistress and Miss Menie I'm wanting to see."

"Am I to let in a' the gaun-about vagabones that want to see the mistress and Miss Menie?" said Jenny's gruff voice in reply. "I trow no; and how ye can have the face to look at Jenny after your last errand till her, I canna tell; ye'll be for undertaking my service ance mair? but ye may just as weel take my word ance for a'—the mistress canna bide ye ony mair than me."

"Eh, woman, Jenny, ye're a thrawn creature!" said Nelly Panton. "I'm sure I never did ye an ill turn a' my days. But ye needna even the like o' your service to me; I'm gaun to live wi' our Johnnie, and keep his house, and Johnnie's company are grander folk than the mistress; but I'm no forgetting auld friends, so I came to ask for Miss Menie because I aye likit her, and because she's a young lass like mysel; and I'll gang and speak to that ither servant-woman if ye'll no tell Miss Menie I'm here."

Jenny's fury—for very furious was Jenny's suppressed fuff at the presumptuous notion of equality or friendship between Menie Laurie and Nelly Panton—was checked by this threat; and fearful lest the dignity of her young mistress should be injured in the eyes of the household by the new-comer's pretensions, Jenny, who had held this colloquy out of doors, turned hastily round and pattered away by the back entrance to open the door for the visitor, muttering repeated adjurations. "My patience!" and Jenny's patience had indeed much reason to be called to her aid.

Menie's curiosity was a little roused—her mind, withdrawn from herself, lightened somewhat of its load—and she hastened down stairs less unwillingly than she would have done without this interruption. Jenny stood by the drawing-room door holding it open; and Jenny's sturdy little form vibrated, every inch of it, with anger and indignation. "Ane to speak to you, Miss Menie! ane used wi' grand society, and owre high for the like o' me. Ye'll hae to speak to her yoursel."

And Menie suddenly found herself thrust into the room, while Jenny, with an audible snort and fuff, remained in possession of the door.

Nelly Panton had too newly entered on her dignities to be able to restrain the ancient curtsy of her humility. Yes, undoubtedly, it was Nelly Panton—with the same faded gown, the same doleful shawl, the same wrapped-up and gloomy figure. Against the well-lighted, well-pictured wall of Miss Annie Laurie's drawing-room she stood in dingy individuality dropping her curtsy, while Menie, much surprised and silent, stood before her waiting to be addressed.

"Can nane o' ye speak?" said the impatient Jenny, from the door. "Miss Menie, are ye no gaun to ask what is her business here? A fule might hae kent this was nae place to come back to, after her last errand to Burnside; and when she kens I canna bide her, and the mistress canna bide her, to come and set up for a friendship wi' you."

"She's just as cankered as she aye was, Miss Menie," said Nelly Panton, compassionately, shaking her head. "It shows an ill disposition, indeed, when folk canna keep at peace wi' me, as mony a time I've telt my mother. But ye see, Miss Menie, I couldna just bide on in Kirklands when ye were a' away, so I just took my fit in my hand, and came on to London to see after Johnnie wi' my ain een. He needs somebody to keep him gaun, and set him right, puir callant; and he's in a grand way for himsel, and should be attended to—so I think I'll just stay on, Miss Menie; and the first thing I did was to come and ask for you."

"You are very kind, Nelly," said Menie Laurie; but Menie paused with a suppressed laugh when she saw Jenny's clenched hand shaken at her from the door.

"And ye'll maybe think I'm no just in condition to set up for friends wi' the like o' you," said Nelly, glancing down upon her dress; "but I only came in to London the day before yesterday, and I've naething yet but my travelling things. I'm hearing that little Juley Home of Braecroft's coming too; and between you and me, Miss Menie, no to let it gang ony farther, I think it was real right and prudent o' you to show us the first example, and draw us a' up to London to take care o' thae lads."

"What do you mean, Nelly?" exclaimed Menie, somewhat angrily.

"Ye may weel say what does she mean," said Jenny, making a sudden inroad from the door. "Do you hear, ye evil speaker!—the mistress is out, and there's naebody to take care o' this puir bairn but me; whatever malice and venom ye have to say, out wi't, and I'll tell the young lady what kind o' character ye are when a's done."

"I wouldna keep such a meddling body in my house—no, if she did the wark twice as weel," retorted Nelly, with calm superiority; "and I've nae call to speak my mind afore Jenny, and her aye misca'in' me; but it's nae secret o' mine. I was just gaun to say, that for a' our Johnnie's a very decent lad, and minds upon his friends, I never saw ane, gentle or simple, sae awfu' muckle tooken up about himsel as Randy Home. He's anither lad altogether to what he used to be; and it's no to be thocht but what he's wanting a grand wife like a' the rest. Now, ye'll just see."

Menie Laurie put down Jenny's passionate disclaimer by a motion of her hand. "If this was what you came to tell me, Nelly, I fear I shall scarcely be grateful for your visit. Do you know that it is an impertinence to say this to me? Whisht, Jenny, that is enough; and I came here to look after no one. Whatever you may have thought before, you will believe this now, since I say it. Jenny will see that you are comfortable while you stay out here; but I think, Nelly, you have said enough to me this morning, and I to you—Jenny, whisht."

"I'll no whisht," cried Jenny, at last, freed by Menie's pause. "Eh, ye evil spirit! will ye tell me what cause o' ill will ye ever could have against this innocent bairn? I'm no gaun to whisht, Miss Menie—to think of her coming up here anes errand to put out her malice on you! My patience! how ony mortal can thole the sight o' her, I dinna ken."

"I can forgie ye, Jenny," said the meek Nelly Panton, "for a' your passions and your glooms, and your ill words—I'm thankful to say I can forgie ye; but, eh, sirs, this is a weary world;—wherever I gang, at hame, or away frae hame, I'm aye miskent—naebody has the heart to take a guid turn frae me—though, I'm sure, I aye mean a'thing for the best, and it was right Miss Menie should ken. I thocht I would just come up this far to gie ye an advice, Miss Menie, when we were our lanes; and I'm no gaun to bleeze up into a fuff like Jenny because it's ill ta'en. I'm just as guid friends as ever. The next time I come I'll come wi' our Johnnie, so I bid you a very guid morning, Miss Menie Laurie, and mony thanks for your kind welcome. Jenny, fare-ye-weel."

Menie sat down in the window when the dark figure of her unwelcome visitor was gone. The sun came in upon her gaily—the genial August sun—and the leaves without fluttered in a happy wind and a maze of morning sounds, broken with shriller shouts of children, and rings of silvery laughter floated up and floated round her, of themselves an atmosphere fresh and sweet; but Menie bowed her face between her hands, and looked out with wistful eyes into the future, where so many fears and wonders had come to dwell; and vigilant and stern the meagre yew-tree looked in upon her, like an unkindly fate.

CHAPTER XVIII

"Eh, Menie, are you sure yon's London?"

So asked little July Home standing under the shadow of the elm trees, and looking out upon the sea of city smoke, with great St Paul's looming through its dimness. July did not quite understand how she could be said to be near London, so long as she stood upon the green sod, and saw above her the kindly sky. "There's no very mony houses hereaway," said the innocent July; "there's mair in Dumfries, Menie—and this is just a fine green park, and here's trees—are you sure yon's London?"

"Yes, it's London." Very differently they looked at it;—the one with the marvelling eyes of a child, ready to believe all wonders of that mysterious place, supreme among the nations, which was rather a superb individual personage from among the Arabian genii than a collection of human streets and houses, full of the usual weaknesses of humankind; the other with the dreamy gaze of a woman, pondering in her heart over the scene of her fate.

"And Randall's yonder, and Johnnie Lithgow?" said July—"I would just like to ken where. Menie, you've been down yonder in the town—where will Johnnie and our Randall be? Mrs Wellwood down in Kirklands bade me ask Randall if he knew a cousin of hers, Peter Scott, that lives in London; but nobody could ken a' the folk, Menie, in such a muckle town."

"My dear Miss July, muckle is an ugly word," said Miss Annie Laurie, "and you must observe how nicely your brother and his friend speak—quite marvellous for self-educated young men—and even Menie here is very well. You must not say muckle, my love."

"It was because I meant to say very big," said July with a great blush, holding down her head and speaking in a whisper. July had thrown many a wandering glance already at Miss Annie, speculating whether to call her the old lady or the young lady, and listening with reverential curiosity to all she said; for July thought "She—the lady," was very kind to call her my dear and my love so soon, and to kiss her when she went away wearied, on her first evening at Heathbank, to rest; though July could never be sure about Miss Annie, and marvelled much that Menie Laurie should dare to call any one in such ringlets and such gowns, aunt.

"You will soon learn better, my dear little girl," said the gracious Miss Annie, "and you must just be content to continue a little girl while you are here, and take a lesson now and then, you know; and above all, my darling, you must take care not to fall in love with this young man whom you speak of so familiarly. He must not be Johnnie any more, but only Mr Lithgow, your brother's friend and ours—for I cannot have both my young ladies falling in love."

"Me!" July's light little frame trembled all over, her soft hair fell down upon her neck. "It never will stay up," murmured July, with eager deprecation, as Miss Annie's eye fell upon the silky uncurled locks; but it was only shamefacedness and embarrassment which made July notice the descent of her hair—for July was trembling with a little thrill of fear and wonder and curiosity. Was it possible, then, that little July had come to sufficient years to be capable of falling in love?—and, in spite of herself, July thought again upon Johnnie Lithgow, and marvelled innocently, though with a blush, whether he "minded" her as she minded him.

But July could not understand the strange abstraction which had fallen upon her friend—the dreamy eye, the vacant look, the long intervals of silence. Menie Laurie of Burnside had known nothing of all this new-come gravity, and July's wistful look had already begun to follow those wandering eyes of hers—to follow them away through the daylight, and into the dark, wondering—wondering—what it was that Menie sought to see.

Jenny is busied in the remote regions of the kitchen at this present moment, delivering a lecture, very sharp, and marked with some excitement, to Miss Annie Laurie's kitchen-maid, who is by no means an ornamental person, and for that and many other reasons is a perpetual grief to Miss Annie's heart—so Jenny is happily spared the provocation of beholding the new visitor who has entered the portals of Heathbank. For a portentous shawl, heavy as a thundercloud, a gown lurid as the lightning escaping from under its shade, and a new bonnet grim with gentility, are making their way round the little lawn, concealing from expectant eyes the slight person and small well-formed head, with its short matted crop of curls, which distinguish Johnnie Lithgow. Johnnie, good fellow, does not think his sister the most suitable visitor in the world to the Laurie household; but Johnnie would not, for more wealth than he can reckon, put slight upon his sister even in idea—so Miss Annie Laurie's Maria announces Miss Panton at the door of Miss Annie Laurie's drawing-room, and Nelly, where she failed to come as a servant, is introduced as a guest.

"Thank'ye, mem," said Nelly. "I like London very weel so far as I've seen it—but it's a muckle place, I dinna doubt, no to be lookit through in a day—and I'm aye fleyed to lose mysel in thae weary streets; but you see I didna come here ance errand to see the town, but rather came with an object, mem—and now I'm to bide on to take care of Johnnie. My mother down by at hame has had mony thochts about him being left his lane, with naebody but himself to care about in a strange place—and it's sure to be a comfort to her me stopping with Johnnie, for she kens I'm a weel-meaning person, whatever folk do to me; and I would be real thankful if ye could recommend me to a shop for good linen, for I have a' his shirts to mend. To be sure, he has plenty of siller—but he's turning the maist extravagant lad I ever saw."

"Good soul! and you have come to do all those kind things for him," said Miss Annie Laurie: "it is so delightful to me to find these fine homely natural feelings in operation—so primitive and unsophisticated. I can't tell you what pleasure I have in watching the natural action of a kind heart."

"I am much obliged to ye, mem," said Nelly, wavering on her seat with a half intention of rising to acknowledge with a curtsy this complimentary declaration. "I was aye kent for a weel-meaning lass, though I have my fauts—but I'm sure Johnnie ought to ken how weel he can depend on me."

July Home was standing by the window—standing very timid and demure, pretending to look out, but in reality lost in conjectures concerning Johnnie Lithgow, whose image had never left her mind since Miss Annie took the pains to advise her not to think of him. July, innocent heart, would never have thought of him had this warning been withheld; but the fascination and thrill of conscious danger filled July's mind with one continual recollection of his presence, though she did not dare to turn round frankly and own herself his old acquaintance. With a slight tremble in her little figure, July stands by the window, and July's silky hair already begins to droop out of the braid in which she had confined it with so much care. A silk gown—the first and only one of its race belonging to July—has been put on in honour of this, her first day at Heathbank; and July, to tell the truth, is somewhat fluttered on account of it, and is a little afraid of herself and the unaccustomed splendour of her dress.

Menie Laurie, a good way apart, sits on a stool at her mother's feet, looking round upon all those faces—from July's innocent tremble of shy pleasure, to Johnnie Lithgow's well-pleased recognition of his childish friend. There is something touching in the contrast when you turn to Menie Laurie, looking up, with all these new-awakened thoughts in her eyes, into her mother's face. For dutiful and loving as Menie has always been, you can tell by a glance that she never clung before as she clings now—that never in her most trustful childish times was she so humble in her helplessness as her tender woman's love is to-day. Deprecating, anxious, full of so many wistful beseeching ways—do you think the mother does not know why it is that Menie's silent devotion thus pleads and kneels and clings to her very feet?

And there is a shadow on Mrs Laurie's brow—a certain something glittering under Mrs Laurie's eyelid. No, she needs no interpreter—and the mother hears Menie's prayer, "Will you like him—will you try to like him?" sounding in her heart, and resolves that she will indeed try to like him for Menie's sake.

"Mr Home, of course, will come to see us to-night," said the sprightly Miss Annie. "My dear Mrs Laurie, how can I sufficiently thank you for bringing such a delightful circle of young people to Heathbank? It quite renews my heart again. You can't think how soon one gets worn out and weary in this commonplace London world: but so fresh—so full of young spirits and life—I assure you, Mr Lithgow, yourself, and your friend, and my sweet girls here, are quite like a spring to me."

Johnnie, bowing a response, gradually drew near the window. You will begin to think there is something very simply pretty and graceful in this little figure standing here within shadow of the curtain, the evening sun just missing it as it steals timidly into the shade. And this brown hair, so silky soft, has slidden down at last upon July's shoulder, and the breath comes something fast on July's small full nether lip, and a little changeful flush of colour hovers about, coming and going upon July's face. Listen—for now a sweet little timid voice, fragrant with the low-spoken Border-speech, softened out of all its harshness, steals upon Johnnie Lithgow's ear. He knows what the words are, for he draws very near to listen—but we, a little farther off, hear nothing but the voice—a very unassured, shy, girlish voice; and July casts a furtive look around her, to see if it is not possible to get Menie Laurie to whisper her answer to; but when she does trust the air with these few words of hers, July feels less afraid.

Johnnie Lithgow!—no doubt it is the same Johnnie Lithgow who carried her through the wood, half a mile about, to see the sunset from the Resting Stane—but whether this can be the Mr Lythgoe who is very clever and a great writer, July is puzzled to know. For he begins to ask so kindly about the old homely Kirkland people—he "minds" every nook and corner so well, and has such a joyous recollection of all the Hogmanays and Hallowe'ens—the boyish pranks and frolics, the boyish friends. July, simple and perplexed, thinks within herself that Randall never did so, and doubts whether Johnnie Lithgow can be clever, after all.

CHAPTER XIX

"And July, little girl—you are glad to see Menie Laurie again?"

But July makes a long pause—July is always timid of speaking to her brother.

"Menie is not Menie now," said July thoughtfully. "She never looks like what she used to look at Burnside."

"What has changed her?" At last Randall began to look interested.

Another long pause, and then July startled him with a burst of tears. "She never looks like what she used to look at Burnside," repeated Menie's little friend, with timid sobs, "but aye thinks, thinks, and has trouble in her face night and day."

The brother and sister were in the room alone. Randall turned round with impatience. "What a foolish little creature you are, July. Menie does not cry like you for every little matter; Menie has nothing to trouble her."

"It's no me, Randall," said little July, meekly. "If I cry, I just canna help it, and it's nae matter; but, oh, I wish you would speak to Menie—for something's vexing *her*."

"I am sure you will excuse me for leaving you so long," said the sprightly voice of Miss Annie Laurie, entering the room. "What! crying, July darling? Have we not used her well, Mr Home?—but my poor friend Mrs Laurie has just got a very unpleasant letter, and I have been sitting with her to comfort her."

Randall made no reply, unless the smile of indifference which came to his lips, the careless turning away of his head, might be supposed to answer; for Randall did not think it necessary to pretend any interest in Mrs Laurie.

But just then he caught a momentary glimpse of some one stealing across the farthest corner of the lawn, behind a group of shrubs. Randall could not mistake the figure; and it seemed to pause there, where it was completely hidden, except to the keen eye which had watched it thither, and still saw a flutter of drapery through the leaves.

"Mem, if you please, Miss Menie's out," said Jenny, entering suddenly, "and the mistress sent me wi' word that she wasna very weel hersel, and would keep up the stair if you've nae objections. As I said, 'I trow no, you would have nae objections'—no to say there's company in the house to be a divert—and the mistress is far frae weel."

"But, Jenny, you must tell my darling Menie to come in," said Miss Annie. "I cannot want her, you know; and I am sure she cannot know who is here, or she would never bid you say she was out. Tell her I want her, Jenny."

"Mem, I have telt you," said Jenny, somewhat fiercely, "if she was ane given to leasing-making she would have to get another lass to gang her errands than Jenny, and I canna tell whatfor Miss Menie should heed, or do aught but her ain pleasure, for ony company that's here 'enow. I'm no fit mysel, an auld lass like me, to gang away after Miss Menie's light fit; but she's out-by, puir bairn—and it's little onybody kens Jenny that would blame me wi' a lee."

She had reached the door before Randall could prevail with himself to follow her; but at last he did hurry after Jenny, making a hasty apology as he went. Randall had by no means paid to Jenny the respect to which she held herself entitled: her quick sense had either heard his step behind, or surmised that he would follow her; and Jenny, in a violent fuff, strongly suppressing herself, but quivering all over with the effort it cost her, turned sharp round upon him, and came to a dead pause, facing him as he closed the door.

"Where is Miss Menie Laurie? I wish to see her," said Randall. Randall did not choose to be familiar, even now.

"Miss Menie Laurie takes her ain will commonly," said Jenny, making a satirical curtsey. "She's been used wi't this lang while; and she hasna done what Jenny bade her this mony a weary day. Atweel, if she had, some things wouldna have been to undo that are—and mony an hour's wark and hour's peace the haill house might have gotten, if she had aye had the sense to advise wi' the like o' me; but she's young, and she takes her ain gait. Puir thing! she'll have to do somebody else's will soon enough, if there's nae deliverance; whatfor should I grudge her her ain the now?"

"What do you mean? I want to see Menie," exclaimed Randall, with considerable haste and eagerness. "Do you mean to say she does not want to see me? I have never been avoided before. What does she mean?"

"Ay, my lad, that's right," said Jenny; "think of yoursel just, like a man, afore ye gie a kindly thocht to her, and her in trouble. It's like you a'; it's like the haill race and lineage o' ye, father and son. No that I'm meaning ony ill to auld Crofthill; but nae doubt he's a man like the lave."

Randall lifted his hand impatiently, waving her away.

"I wouldna wonder?" cried Jenny. "I wouldna wonder—no me. She's owre mony about that like her, has she?—it'll be my turn to gang my ways, and no trouble the maister. You would like to get her, now she's in her flower: you would like to take her up and carry her away, and put her in a cage, like a puir bit singing-burdie, to be a pleasure to you. What are you courting my bairn for? It's a' for your ain delight and pleasure, because ye canna help but be glad at the sight o' her, a darling as she is; because ye would like to get her to yoursel, like a piece o'land; because she would be something to you to be maister and lord of, to make ye the mair esteemed in ither folks' een, and happier for yoursel. Man, I've carried her miles o' gate in thae very arms o' mine. I've watched her grow year to year, till there's no ane like her in a' the countryside. Is't for mysel?—she canna be Jenny's wife—she canna be Jenny's ain born bairn? But Jenny would put down her neck under the darling's fit, if it was to gie her pleasure—and here's a strange lad comes that would set away *me*."

But Jenny's vehemence was touched with such depth of higher feeling as to exalt it entirely out of the region of the "fuff." With a hasty and trembling hand she dashed away some tears out of her eyes. "I'm no to make a fule o' mysel afore *him*," muttered Jenny, drawing a hard breath through her dilated nostrils.

Randall, with some passion, and much scorn in his face, had drawn back a little to listen. Now he took up his hat hurriedly.

"If you are done, you will let me pass, perhaps," he said angrily. "This is absurd, you know—let me pass. I warn you I will not quarrel with Menie for all the old women in the world."

"If it's me, you're welcome to ca' me names," said Jenny, fiercely. "I daur ye to say a word o' the mistress—on your peril. Miss Menie pleases to be her lane. I tell you Miss Menie's out-by; and I would like to ken what call ony mortal has to disturb the puir lassie in her distress, when she wants to keep it to hersel. He doesna hear me—he's gane the very way she gaed," said Jenny, softening, as he burst past her out of sight. "I'll no say I think ony waur o' him for that; but waes me, waes me—what's to come out o't a', but dismay and distress to my puir bairn?"

Distress and dismay—it is not hard to see them both in Menie Laurie's face, so pale and full of thought, as she leans upon the wall here among the wet leaves, looking out. Yes, she is looking out, fixedly and long, but not upon the misty far-away London, not upon the pleasant slope of green, the retired and quiet houses, the whispering neighbour trees. Something has brought the dreamy distant future, the unknown country, bright and far away—brought it close upon her, laid it at her feet. Her own living breath this moment stirs the atmosphere of this still unaccomplished world; her foot is stayed upon its threshold. No more vague fears—no more mere clouds upon the joyous firmament—but close before her, dark and tangible, the crisis and decision—the turning-point of heart and hope. Before her wistful eyes lie two clear paths, winding before her into the evening sky. Two; but the spectre of a third comes in upon her—a life distraught and barren of all comfort—a fate irrevocable, not to be changed or softened; and Menie's heart is deadly sick in her poor breast, and faints for fear. Alas for Menie Laurie's quiet heart!

She was sad yesterday. Yesterday she saw a cloudy sword, suspended in the skies, wavering and threatening above her unguarded head; to-day she looks no longer at this imaginative menace. From another unfeared quarter there has fallen a real blow.

CHAPTER XX

With the heat and flush of excitement upon his face, Randall Home made his way across the glistening lawn, and through the wet shrubs—for there had been rain—to that corner of the garden where he had seen Menie disappear. Impatiently his foot rung upon the gravel path, and crushed the fallen branches: something of an angry glow was in his eye, and heated and passionate was the colour on his cheek.

"You are here, Menie!" he exclaimed. "I think you might have had sufficient respect for me to do what you could to prevent this last passage of arms."

"Respect!" Menie looked at him with doubtful apprehension. She thought the distress of her mind must have dulled and blunted her nerves; and repeated the word vacantly, scarcely knowing what it meant.

"I said respect. Is it so presumptuous an idea?" said Randall, with his cold sarcastic smile.

But Menie made no answer. Drawing back with a timid frightened motion, which did not belong to her natural character, she stood so very pale, and chill, and tearful, that you could have found nowhere a more complete and emphatic contrast than she made to her betrothed. The one so full of strength and vigour, stout independence and glowing resentment— the other with all her life gone out of her, as it seemed, quenched and subdued in her tears.

"You have avoided me in the house—you will not speak to me now," said Randall. "Menie, Menie, what does this mean?"

For Menie had not been able to conceal from him that she was weeping.

"It is no matter, Randall," said Menie; "it is no matter."

Randall grew more and more excited. "What is the matter? Have you ceased to trust me, Menie? What do you mean?"

"I mean nothing to make you angry—I never did," said Menie, sadly. "I'm not very old yet, but I never grieved anybody, of my own will, all my days. Ill never came long ago; or, if it came, nobody ever blamed it on me. I wish you would not mind me," she said, looking up suddenly. "I came out here, because my mind was not fit to speak to anybody—because I wanted to complain to myself where nobody should hear of my unthankfulness. I would not have said a word to anybody—not a word. There was no harm in thinking within my own heart."

"There is harm in hiding your thoughts from me," said Randall. "Come, Menie, you are not to cheat me of my rights. I was angry—forgive me; but I am not angry now. Menie, my poor sorrowful girl, what ails you? Has something happened? Menie, you must tell *me*."

"It is just you I must not tell," said Menie, under her breath. Then she wavered a moment, as if the wind swayed her light figure, and held her in hesitating uncertainty; and then, with a sudden effort, she stood firm, apart from the wall she had been leaning on, and apart, too, from Randall's extended arm.

"Yes, I will tell you," said Menie, seriously. "You mind what happened a year ago, Randall: you mind what we did and what we said then—'For ever and for ever.'"

Randall took her hand tenderly into his own, "for ever and for ever." It was the words of their troth-plight.

"I will keep it in my heart," said poor Menie. "I will never change in that, but keep it night and day in my heart. Randall, we are far apart already. I have a little world you do not choose to share: you are entering a greater world, where I can never have any place. God speed you, and God go with you, Randall Home. You will be a great man: you will prosper and increase; and what would you do with poor Southland Menie, who cannot help yon in your race? Randall, we will be good friends: we will part now, and say farewell."

Abrupt as her speech was Menie's manner of speaking. She had to hurry over these disjointed words, lest her sobs should overtake and choke her utterance ere they were done.

Randall shook his head with displeased impatience. "This is mere folly, Menie. What does it mean? Cannot you tell me simply and frankly what is the matter, without such a preface as this? But indeed I know very well what it means. It means that I am to yield something—to undertake something—to reconcile myself to some necessity or other, distasteful to me. But why commence so tragically?—the threat should come at the end, not at the beginning."

"I make no threat," said Menie, growing colder and colder, more and more upright and rigid; "I mean to say nothing that can make you angry.

Already I have been very unhappy. I dare not venture, with our changed fortunes, to make a life-long trial—I dare not."

"Your changed fortunes!" interrupted Randall. "Are your fortunes to-day different from what they were yesterday?"

Menie paused. "It is only a very poor pride which would conceal it from you," she said at length. "Yes, they are different. Yesterday we had enough for all we needed—to-day we have not anything. You will see how entirely our circumstances are changed; and I hope you will see too, Randall, without giving either of us the pain of mentioning them, all the reasons which make it prudent for us, without prolonging the conflict longer, to say good-by. Good-by; I can ask nothing of you but to forget me, Randall."

And Menie held out her hand, but could not lift her eyes. Her voice had sunk very low, and a slight shiver of extreme self-constraint passed over her—her head drooped lower and lower on her breast—her fingers played vacantly with the glistening leaves; and when he did not take it, her hand gradually dropped and fell by her side.

There was a moment's silence—no answer—no response—no remonstrance. Perhaps, after all, the poor perverse heart had hoped to be overwhelmed with love which would take no denial: as it was, standing before him motionless, a great faintness came upon Menie. She could vaguely see the path at her feet, the trees on either hand. "I had better go, then," she said, very low and softly; and the light had faded suddenly upon Menie's sight into a strange ringing twilight, full of floating motes and darkness—and those few paces across the lawn filled all her mind like a life-journey, so full of difficulty they seemed, so weak was she.

Go quickly, Menie—quickly, ere those growing shadows darken into a blind unguided night—swiftly, ere these faltering feet grow powerless, and refuse to obey the imperative eager will. To reach home—to reach home—home, such a one as it is, lies only half-a-dozen steps away; press forward, Menie—are those years or hours that pass in the journey? But the hiding-place and shelter is almost gained.

When suddenly this hand which he would not take is grasped in his vigorous hold—suddenly this violent tremble makes Menie feel how he supports her, and how she leans on him. "I am going home," said Menie, faintly. Still he made no answer, but held her strongly, wilfully; not resisting, but unaware of her efforts to escape.

"I have wherewithal to work for you, Menie," said the man's voice in her ear. "What are your changed fortunes to me? If you were a princess, I would receive you less joyfully, for you would have less need of me. Menie, Menie, why have you tried yourself so sorely—and why should this be a cause of separating us? I wanted only you."

And Menie's pride had failed her. She hid her face in her hands, and cried, "My mother, my mother!" in a passion of tears.

"Your mother, your mother? But you have a duty to me," said Randall, more coldly. "Your mother must not bid you give me up: you have no right to obey. Ah! I see: I am dull and stupid; forgive me, Menie. You mean that your mother's fortunes are changed. She has the more need of a son then; and my May Marion knows well, that to be her mother is enough for me—you understand me, Menie. This does not change our attachment, does not change our plans, our prospects, in the slightest degree. It may make it more imperative that your mother should live with us, but *you* will think that no misfortune. Well, are we to have no more heroics now—nothing tragical—but only a little good sense and patience on all sides, and my Menie what she always is? Come, look up and tell me."

"I meant nothing heroic—nothing. What I said was not false, Randall," said Menie, looking up with some fire. "If you think it was unreal, that I did not mean it—"

"If you do not mean it now, is not that enough?" said Randall, smiling. "Let us talk of something less weighty. July says you do not look as you used to do; has this been weighing on your mind, Menie? But, indeed, you have not told me what the misfortune is."

"We knew it only to-day," said Menie. Menie spoke very low, and was very much saddened and humbled, quite unable to make any defence against Randall's lordly manner of setting her emotion aside. "My father's successors were young men, and the price they paid for entering on his practice was my mother's annuity. But now they are both gone; one died two years ago, the other only last week—and he has died very poor, and in debt, the lawyer writes; so that there is neither hope nor chance of having anything from those he leaves behind. So we have no longer an income; nothing now but my mother's liferent in Burnside."

Menie Laurie did not know what poverty was. It was not any apprehension of this which drew from her eyes those few large tears.

"Well, that will be enough for your mother," said Randall. It was impossible for Menie to say a word or make an objection, so completely had he put her aside, and taken it for granted that his will should decide all. "Or if it was not enough, what then? Provision for the future lies with me—and you need not fear for me, Menie. I am not quarrelsome. You need not look so deprecating and frightened: you will find no disappointment in me."

Was Menie reassured? It was not easy to tell; for very new to Menie Laurie was this trembling humility of tone and look—this faltering and wavering—as if she knew not to which side to turn. But Randall began to speak, as he knew how, of her own self, and of their betrothing, "for ever and for ever;" and the time these words were said came back upon her with new power. Her mind was not satisfied, her heart was not convinced, and very trembling and insecure now was her secret response to Randall's declaration that she should find no disappointment in him; but her heart was young, and all unwilling to give up its blithe existence. Instinctively she fled from her own pain, and accepted the returning hope and pleasantness. Bright pictures rose before Menie, of a future household harmonious and full of peace—of the new love growing greater, fuller, day by day—the old love sacred and strong, as when it stood alone. Why did she fear? why did a lurking terror in her heart cry No, no! with a sob and pang? After all, this was no vain impracticable hope; many a one had realised it—it was right and true for ever under the skies; and Menie put her hand upon the arm of her betrothed, and closed her eyes for a moment with a softening sense of relief and comfort, and gentle tears under the lids. Let him lead forward; who can tell the precious stores of love, and tenderness, and supreme regard that wait him as his guerdon? Let him lead forward—on to those bright visionary days—in to this peaceful home.

CHAPTER XXI

Perhaps next to the pleasure of doing all for those we love best, the joy of receiving all ranks highest. With her heart elate, Menie went in again to the house she had left so sadly—went in again, looking up to Randall, rejoicing in the thought that from him every daily gift—all that lay in the future—should henceforth come. And if it were well to be Menie's mother—chief over one child's heart which could but love—how much greater joy to be Randall's mother, high in the reverent thought of such a mind as his! Now there remained but one difficulty—to bring the mother and the son lovingly together—to let no misconception, no false understanding, blind the one's sight of the other—to clear away all evil judgment of the past—to show each how worthy of esteem and high appreciation the other was. She thought so in her own simple soul, poor heart! Through her own great affection she looked at both—to either of them *she* would have yielded without a murmur her own little prides and resentments; and the light of her eyes suffused them with a circle of mingling radiance; and sweet was the fellowship and kindness, pure the love and good offices, harmonious and noble the life of home and every day, which blossomed out of Menie Laurie's heart and fancy, in the reaction of her hopeless grief.

Mrs Laurie sits very thoughtful and still by the window. Menie's mother, in her undisturbed and quiet life, had never found out before how proud she was. Now she feels it in her nervous shrinking from speech of her misfortune—in the involuntary haughtiness with which she starts and recoils from sympathy. Without a word of comment or lamentation, the mere bare facts, and nothing more, she has communicated to Miss Annie; and Mrs Laurie had much difficulty in restraining outward evidence of the burst of indignant impatience with which, in her heart, she received Miss Annie's effusive pity and real kindness. Miss Annie, thinking it best not to trouble her kinswoman in the present mood of her mind, has very discreetly carried her pity to some one who will receive it better, and waits till "poor dear Mrs Laurie" shall recover her composure; while even July, repelled by the absorbed look, and indeed by an abrupt short answer, too, withdraws, and hangs about the other end of the room, like a little shadow, ever and anon gliding across the window with her noiseless step, and her stream of falling hair.

Mrs Laurie's face is full of thought—what is she to do? But, harder far than that, what is Menie to do?—Menie, who vows never to leave her—who will not permit her to meet the chill fellowship of poverty alone. A little earthen-floored Dumfriesshire cottage, with its kailyard and its one apartment, is not a very pleasant anticipation to Mrs Laurie herself, who has lived the most part of her life, and had her share of the gifts of fortune; but what will it be to Menie, whose life has to be made yet, and whose noontide and prime must all be influenced by such a cloud upon her dawning day? The mother's brow is knitted with heavy thought—the mother's heart is pondering with strong anxiety. Herself must suffer largely from this change of fortune, but she cannot see herself for Menie—Menie: what is Menie to do?

Will it be better to see her married to Randall Home, and then to go away solitary to the cot-house in Kirklands, to spend out this weary life—these lingering days? But Mrs Laurie's heart swells at the thought. Perhaps it will be best; perhaps it is what we must make up our mind to, and even urge upon her; but alas and alas! how heavily the words, the very thought, rings in to Mrs Laurie's heart.

And now here they are coming, their youth upon them like a mantle and a crown—coming, but not with downcast looks; not despondent, nor afraid, nor touched at all with the heaviness which bows down the mother's spirit to the very dust. Menie will go, then. Close your eyes, mother, from the light; try to think you are glad; try to rejoice that she will be content to part from you. It is "for her good"—is there anything you would not do "for her good," mother? It has come to the decision now; and look how she comes with her hand upon his arm, her eyes turning to his, her heart elate. She will be his wife, then—his Menie first, and not her mother's; but have we not schooled our mind to be content?

Yes, she is coming, poor heart!—coming with her new hope glorious in her eyes; coming to bring the son to his mother; coming herself with such a great embracing love as is indeed enough of its own might and strength to unite them for ever: and Menie thinks that now she cannot fail.

And now they are seated all of them about the window, July venturing forward to join the party; and as nothing better can be done, there commences an indifferent conversation, as far removed as possible from the real subject of their thoughts. There sits Mrs Laurie, sick with her heavy musings, believing that she now stands alone, that her dearest child has made up her mind to forsake her, and that in solitude and meagre poverty she will have to wait for slow-coming age and death. Here is Randall, looking for once out of himself, with a real *will* and anxiety to soften, by every means in his power, the misfortunes of Menie's mother, and rousing himself withal to the joy of carrying Menie home—to the sterner necessity of doing a man's work to provide for her, and for the new household; and all the wonder you can summon—no small portion in those days—flutters about the same subject, little July Home; and you think in your heart, if you but could, what marvellous things you *would* do for Menie Laurie, and Menie Laurie's mother; while Menie herself, with a wistful new-grown habit of observation, reads everybody's face, and knows not whether to be most afraid of the obstinate gloom upon her mother's brow, or exultant in the delicate attention, the sudden respectfulness and regard, of Randall's bearing. But this little company, all so earnestly engrossed—all surrounding a matter of the vitallest importance to each—turn aside to talk of Miss Annie Laurie's toys—Miss Annie Laurie's party—and only when they divide and separate, dare speak of what lies at their heart.

And Mrs Laurie is something hard to be conciliated. Mrs Laurie is much inclined to resent this softening of manner as half an insult to her change of fortune. Patience, Menie! though your mother rebuffs him, he bears it nobly. The cloud will not lighten upon her brow—cannot lighten—for you do not know how heavily this wistful look of yours, this very anxiety to please her—and all your transparent wiles and artifices—your suppressed and trembling hope, strikes upon your mother's heart. "She will go away—she will leave me." Your mother says so, Menie, within herself; and it is so hard, so very hard, to persuade the unwilling content with that sad argument, "It is for her good." Now, draw your breath softly lest she hear how your heart beats, for Randall has asked her to go to the garden with him, to speak of this; and Mrs Laurie rises with a sort of desolate stateliness—rises—accepts his offered arm, and turns away—poor Menie!—with an averted face, and without a glance at you.

And now there follows a heavy time—a little space of curious restless suspense. Wandering from window to window, from table to table; striking a few notes on the ever-open piano; opening a book now, taking up a piece of work then, Menie strays about, in an excitement of anxiety which she can neither suppress nor conceal. Will they be friends? such friends—such loving friends as they might be, being as they are in Menie's regard so noble and generous both? Will they join heartily and cordially? will they clasp hands upon a kindly bargain? But Menie shrinks, and closes her eyes—she dares not look upon the alternative.

"Menie, will you not sit down?" Little July Home follows Menie with her eyes almost as wistfully as Menie follows Randall and her mother. There is no answer, for Menie is so fully occupied that the little timid voice fails to break through the trance of intense abstraction in which her heart is separated from this present scene. "Menie!" Speak louder, little girl: Menie cannot hear you, for other voices speaking in her heart

So July steals across the room with her noiseless step, and has her arm twined through Menie's before she is aware. "Come and sit down—what are they speaking about, Menie? Do you no hear me? Oh, Menie, is it our Randall? Is it his blame?"

July is so near crying that she must be answered. "Nobody is to blame; there is no harm," said Menie, quickly, leading her back to her seat—quickly, with an imperative hush and haste, which throws July back into timid silence, and sets all her faculties astir to listen, too. But there comes no sound into this quiet room—not even the footsteps which have passed out of hearing upon the garden path, nor so much as an echo of the voices which Menie knows to be engaged in converse which must decide her fate. But this restless and visible solicitude will not do; it is best to take up her work resolutely, and sit down with her intent face turned towards the window, from which at least the first glance of them may be seen as they return.

No,—no need to start and blush and tremble; this step, ringing light upon the path, is not the stately step of Randall—not our mother's sober tread. "It's no them, Menie—it's just Miss Laurie," whispers little startled July from the corner of the window. So long away—so long away—and Menie cannot tell whether it is a good or evil omen—but still they do not come.

"My sweet children, are you here alone?" said Miss Annie, setting down her little basket "Menie, love, I have just surprised your mamma and Mr Randall, looking very wise, I assure you; you ought to be quite thankful that you are too young to share such deliberations. July, dear, you must come and have your lesson; but I cannot teach you to play that favourite tune,—oh no, it would be quite improper,—though he has very good taste, has he not, darling? But somebody will say I have designs upon Mr Lithgow, if I always play his favourite tune."

So saying, Miss Annie sat down before the piano, and began to sing, "For bonnie Annie Laurie I'll lay down my head and dee." Poor Johnnie Lithgow had no idea, when he praised the pretty little graceful melody and delicate verses, that he was paying a compliment to the lady of Heathbank.

And July, with a blush, and a little timid eagerness, stole away to Miss Annie's side. July had never before touched any instrument except Menie Laurie's old piano at Burnside, and with a good deal of awe had submitted to Miss Annie's lessons. It did seem a very delightful prospect to be able to play this favourite tune, though July would have thought very little of it, but for Miss Annie's constant warnings. Thanks to these, however, and thanks to his own kindly half-shy regards, Johnnie Lithgow's favourite tunes, favourite books, favourite things and places, began to grow of great interest to little July Home. She thought it was very foolish to remember them all, and blushed in secret when Johnnie Lithgow's name came into her mind as an authority; but nevertheless, in spite of shame and blushing, a great authority Johnnie Lithgow had grown, and July stood by the piano, eager and afraid, longing very much to be as accomplished as Miss Annie, to be able to play his favourite tune.

While Menie Laurie still sits by the window, intent and silent, hearing nothing of song or music, but only aware of a hum of inarticulate voices, which her heart longs and strains to understand, but cannot hear.

CHAPTER XXII

The music is over, the lesson concluded, and July sits timidly before the piano, striking faint notes with one finger, and marvelling greatly how it is possible to extract anything like an intelligible strain from this waste of unknown chords. Miss Annie is about in the room once more, giving dainty touches to its somewhat defective arrangement—throwing down a book here, and there altering an ornament. Patience, Menie Laurie! many another one before you has sat in resolute outward calm, with a heart all a-throb and trembling, even as yours is. Patience; though it is hard to bear the rustling of Miss Annie's dress—the faint discords of July's music. It must have been one time or another, this most momentous interview—all will be over when it is over. Patience, we must wait.

But it is a strange piece of provocation on Miss Annie's part that she should choose this time, and no other, for looking over that little heap of Menie's drawings upon the table. Menie is not ambitious as an artist— few ideas or romances are in these little works of hers; they are only some faces—not very well executed—the faces of those two or three people whom Menie calls her own.

"Come and show them to me, my love." Menie must not disobey, though her first impulse is to spring out of the low opened window, and rush away somewhere out of reach of all interruption till this long suspense is done. But Menie does not rush away; she only rises slowly—comes to Miss Annie's side—feels the pressure of Miss Annie's embracing arm round her—and turns over the drawings; strangely aware of every line in them, yet all the while in a maze of abstraction, listening for their return.

Here is Menie's mother—and here again another, and yet another, sketch of her; and this is Randall Home.

"Do you know, I think they are very like," said Miss Annie: "you must do my portrait, Menie, darling—you must indeed. I shall take no denial; you shall do me in my white muslin, among my flowers; and we will put Mr. Home's sweet book on the table, and open it at that scene—that scene, you know, I pointed out to you the other day. I know what inspired him when he wrote that. Come, my love, it will divert you from thinking of this trouble—your mamma should not have told you—shall we begin now! But,

Menie, dear, don't you think you have put a strange look in this face of Mr. Randall? It is like him—but I would not choose you to do me with such an expression as that."

Half wild with her suspense, Menie by this time scarcely heard the words that rang into her ears, scarcely saw the face she looked upon; but suddenly, as Miss Annie spoke, a new light seemed to burst upon this picture, and there before her, looking into her eyes, with the smile of cold supervision which she always feared to see, with the incipient curl of contempt upon his lip—the pride of self-estimation in his eye—was Randall's face, glowing with contradiction to all her sudden hopes. Her own work, and she has never had any will to look at him in this aspect; but the little picture blazes out upon her like a sudden enlightenment. Here is another one, done by the loving hand of memory a year ago; but, alas! there is no enchantment to bring back this ideal glory, this glow of genial love and life that makes it bright—a face of the imagination, taking all its wealth of expression from the heart which suffused these well-remembered features with a radiance of its own; but the reality looks out on Menie darkly; the face of a man not to be moved by womanish influences—not to be changed by a burst of strong emotion—not to be softened, mellowed, won, by any tenderness—a heart that can love, indeed, but never can forget itself; a mind sufficient for its own rule, a soul which knows no generous *abandon*, which holds its own will and manner firm and strong above all other earthly things. This is the face which looks on Menie Laurie out of her own picture, startling her heart, half distraught with fond hopes and dreams into the chill daylight again— full awake.

"I will make portraits," said Menie, hastily, in a flood of sudden bitterness, "when we go away, when we go home—I can do it—this shall be my trade."

And Menie closed the little portfolio abruptly, and went back to her seat without another word; went back with the blood tingling through her veins, with all her pride and all her strength astir; with a vague impetuous excitement about her—an impulse of defiance. So long—so long: what keeps them abroad lingering among these glistening trees? perhaps because they are afraid to tell her that her fate is sealed; and starting to her feet, the thought is strong on Menie to go forth and meet them, to bid them have no fear for her, to tell them her delusion is gone for ever, and that there is no more light remaining under the skies.

Hush! there are footsteps on the path. Who are these that come together, leaning, the elder on the younger, the mother on the son! With such a grace this lofty head stoops to our mother; with such a kindly glance she lifts her eyes to him; and they are busy still with the consultation which has occupied so long a time. While she stands arrested, looking at them as they draw near—growing aware of their full amity and union—a shiver of great emotion comes upon Menie—then, or ever she is conscious, a burst of tears. In another moment all her sudden enlightenment is gone, quenched out of her eyes, out of her heart—and Menie puts the tears away with a faltering hand, and stands still to meet them in a quiet tremor of joy, the same loving Menie as of old.

"*My* bairn!" Mrs Laurie says nothing more as she draws her daughter close to her, and puts her lips softly to Menie's brow. It is the seal of the new bond. The mother and the son have been brought together; the past is gone for ever like a dream of the night; and into the blessed daylight, full of the peaceful rays God sends us out of heaven, we open our eyes as to another life. Peace and sweet harmony to Menie Laurie's heart!

Put away the picture; lay it by where no one again shall believe its slander true; put away this false-reporting face; put away the strange clearsightedness which came upon us like a curse. No need to inquire how much was false—it is past, and we begin anew.

CHAPTER XXIII

"Yes, Menie, I am quite satisfied." It is Mrs Laurie herself who volunteers this declaration, while Menie, on the little stool at her feet, looks up wistfully, eager to hear, but not venturing to ask what her conversation with Randall was. "We said a great many things, my dear—a great deal about you, Menie, and something about our circumstances too. The rent of Burnside will be a sufficient income for me. I took it kind of Randall to say so, for it shows that he knew I would not be dependent; and as for you, Menie, I fancy you will be very well and comfortable, according to what he says. So you will have to prepare, my dear—to prepare for your new life."

Menie hid her face in her mother's lap. Prepare—not the bridal garments, the household supplies—something more momentous, and of greater delicacy—the mind and the heart; and if this must always be something solemn and important, whatever the circumstances, how much more so to Menie, whose path had been crossed already by such a spectre? She sat there, her eyes covered with her hands, her head bowing down upon her mother's knee; but the heavy doubt had flown from her, leaving nothing but lighter cloudy shadows—maidenly fears and tremblings—in her way. Few hearts were more honest than Menie's, few more wistfully desirous of doing well; and now it is with no serious anticipations of evil, but only with the natural thrill and tremor, the natural excitement of so great an epoch drawing close at hand, that Menie's fingers close with a startled pressure on her mother's hand, as she is bidden prepare.

What is this that has befallen little July Home? There never were such throngs of unaccountable blushes, such a suffusion of simple surprise. Something is on her lips perpetually, which she does not venture to speak—some rare piece of intelligence, which July cannot but marvel at herself in silent wonder, and which she trembles to think Menie and "a'body else" will marvel at still more. Withdrawing silently into dark corners, sitting there doing nothing, in long fits of reverie, quite unusual with July; coming forward so conscious and guilty, when called upon; and now, at this earliest opportunity, throwing her arms round Menie Laurie's neck, and hiding her little flushed and agitated face upon Menie's shoulder. What has befallen July Home?

"Do you think it's a' true, Menie? He wouldna say what he didna mean: but I think it's for our Randall's sake—it canna be for me!"

For July has not the faintest idea, as she lets this soft silken hair of hers fall down on her cheek without an effort to restrain it, that Johnnie Lithgow would not barter one smile upon that trembling child's lip of hers for all the Randalls in the world.

"He says he'll go to the Hill, and tell them a' at hame," said July. "Eh, Menie, what will they say? And he's to tell Randall first of all. I wish I was away, no to see Randall, Menie; he'll just laugh, and think it's no true—for I see mysel it canna be for me!"

"It is for you, July; you must not think anything else; there is nobody in the world like you to Johnnie Lithgow." And slowly July's head is raised—a bright shy look of wonder gradually growing into conviction, a sudden waking of higher thought and deeper feeling in the open simple face; a sudden flush of crimson—the woman's blush—and July withdrew herself from her friend's embrace, and stole a little apart into the shadow, and wept a few tears. Was it true? For her, and not for another! But it is a long time before this grand discovery can look a truth, and real, to July's humble eyes.

But, nevertheless, it is very true. Randall's little sister, Menie's child-friend, the little July of Crofthill, has suddenly been startled into womanhood by this unexpected voice. After a severer fashion than has ever confined it before, July hastily fastens up her silky hair, hastily wipes off all traces of the tears upon her cheek, and is composed and calm, after a sweet shy manner of composure, lifting up her little gentle head with a newborn pride, eager to bring no discredit on her wooer's choice. And already July objects to be laughed at, and feels a slight offence when she is treated as a child—not for herself, but for him, whom now she does not quite care to have called *Johnnie* Lithgow, but is covetous of respect and honour for, as she never was for Randall, though secretly in her own heart July still doubts of his genius and cannot choose but think Randall must be cleverer than his less assuming friend.

And in this singular little company, where all these feelings are astir, it is hardly possible to preserve equanimity of manners. Miss Annie herself, the lady of the house, sits at her little work-table, in great delight, running over now and then in little outbursts of enthusiasm, discoursing of Mr Home's sweet book, of Mr Lithgow's charming articles, and occasionally making a demonstration of joy and sympathy in the happiness of her darling girls, which throws Menie—Menie always conscious of Randall's eye upon her, the eye of a lover, it is true, but something critical withal—into grave and painful embarrassment, and covers July's stooping face with blushes. Mrs. Laurie, busy with her work, does what she can to keep the conversation "sensible," but with no great success. The younger portion of the company are too completely occupied, all of them, to think of ordinary intercourse. Miss Annie's room was never so bright, never so rich with youthful hopes and interests before. Look at them, so full of individual character, unconscious as they are of any observation—though Nelly Panton, very grim in the stiff coat armour of her new assumed gentility, sits at the table sternly upright, watching them all askance, with vigilant unloving eye.

Lithgow, good fellow, sits by Miss Annie. Though he laughs now and then, he still does not scorn the natural goodness, the natural tenderness of heart, which make their appearance under these habitual affectations—the juvenile tricks and levities of her unreverent age. Poor Miss Annie Laurie has been content to resign the reverence, in a vain attempt at equality; but Lithgow, who is no critic by nature, remembers gratefully her true kindness, and smiles only as little as possible at the fictitious youthfulness which Miss Annie herself has come to believe in. So he sits and bears with her, her little follies and weaknesses, and, in his unconscious humility, is magnanimous, and does honour to his manhood. Within reach of his kindly eye, July bends her head over her work, glancing up now and then furtively to see who is looking at him—to see, in the second place, who is noticing or laughing at her; and July, with all her innocent heart, is grateful to Miss Annie. So many kind things she says—and in July's guileless apprehension they are all so true.

Graver, but not less happy, Menie Laurie pursues her occupation by July's side, rarely looking up at all, pondering in her own heart the many weighty things that are to come, with her tremor of fear, her joy of deliverance scarcely yet quieted, and all her heart and all her mind engaged—in dreams no longer, but in sober thought; sober thought—thoughts of great devotion, of life-long love and service, of something nobler than the common life. Very serious are these ponderings, coming down to common labours, the course of every day; and Menie does not know the nature of her dreamings—they look to her so real, so sober, and so true—and would scorn your warning, if you told her that not the wildest story of Arabian genii was more romance than those, her sober plans and thoughts.

Apart, and watching all, stands Randall Home. There is love in his eye—you cannot doubt it—love and the impulse of protection, the strong, appropriating grasp. There is something more. Look how his head rises in the dimmer background above the table and the lights, above the little company assembled there. With something like laughter, his eye turns upon July—upon July's wooer, his own friend—kindly, yet with a sense of superiority, an involuntary elevation of himself above them both. And this glance upon Miss Annie is mere scorn, nothing higher; and his eye has scarcely had time to recover itself, when its look falls, bright and softened, upon his betrothed; a look of love—question it not, simple Menie—but is calm, superior above you still.

CHAPTER XXIV

"They tell me it's a haill month since it was a' settled, but I hear naething o' the house or the plenishing, and no a word o' what Jenny's to do. If they're no wanting me, I'm no wanting them—ne'er a bit. It's aye the way guid service is rewarded; and whatfor should there be ony odds wi' Jenny? I might hae kent that muckle, if I had regarded counsel, or thocht o' my ainsel; but aye Jenny's foremost thocht was o' them, for a' sic an ill body as she is now."

And a tear was in Jenny's eye as she smoothed down the folds of Menie's dress—Menie's finest dress, her own present, which Menie was to wear to-night. And Menie's ornaments are all laid out carefully upon the table, everything she is likely to need, before Jenny's lingering step leaves the room. "I canna weel tell, for my pairt, what like life'll be without her," muttered Jenny, as she went away—"I reckon no very muckle worth the minding about; but I'm no gaun to burden onybody that doesna want me—no, if I should never hae anither hour's comfort a' my days."

And slowly, with many a backward glance and pause, Jenny withdrew. Neglect is always hard to bear. Jenny believed herself to be left out of their calculations—forgotten of those to whom she had devoted so many years of her life; and Jenny, though she tried to be angry, could not manage it, but felt her indignant eyes startled with strange tears. It made a singular cloud upon her face this unusual emotion; the native impatience only struggled through it fitfully in angry glimpses, though Jenny was furious at herself for feeling so desolate, and very fain would have thrown off her discomfort in a fuff—but far past the region of the fuff was this her new-come solitude of heart. Her friends were dead or scattered, her life was all bound up in her mistress and her mistress's child, and it was no small trial for Jenny to find herself thus cast off and thrown aside.

The next who enters this room has a little heat about her, a certain atmosphere of annoyance and displeasure. "I will be a burden"—unawares the same words steal over Mrs Laurie's lip, but the sound of her voice checks her. Two or three steps back and forward through the room, a long pause before the window, and then her brow is cleared. You can see the shadows gradually melting away, as clouds melt from the sky, and in another moment she has left the room, to resume her place down stairs.

This vacant room—nothing can you learn from its calm good order, its windows open to the sun, its undisturbed and home-like quiet, of what passes within its walls. There is Menie's little Bible on the table; it is here where Menie brings her doubts and troubles, to resolve them, if they may be resolved. But there is no whisper here to tell you what happens to Menie, when, as has already chanced, some trouble comes upon her which it is not easy to put away. Hush! this time the door opens slowly, gravely—this time it is a footstep very sober, something languid, which comes in; and Menie Laurie puts up her hand to her forehead, as if a pain was there; but not a word says Menie Laurie's reverie—not a word. If she is sad, or if she is merry, there is no way to know. She goes about her toilette like a piece of business, and gives no sign.

But this month has passed almost like age upon Menie Laurie's face. You can see that grave thoughts are common now, everyday guests and friends in her sobered life, and that she has begun to part with her romances of joy and noble life—has begun to realise more truly what manner of future it is which lies before her. Nothing evil, perhaps—little hardship in it; no great share of labour, of poverty, or care—but no longer the grand ideal life, the dream of youthful souls.

And now she stands before the window, wearing Jenny's gown. It is only to look out if any one is visible upon the road—but there is no passenger yet approaching Heathbank, and Menie goes calmly down stairs. As it happens, the drawing-room is quite vacant of all but Nelly Panton, who sits prim by the wall in one corner. Nelly is not an invited guest, but has come as a volunteer, in right of her brother's invitation, and Miss Annie shows her sense of the intrusion by leaving her alone.

"Na, I'm no gaun to bide very lang in London," said Nelly. "Ye see, Miss Menie, you're an auld friend. I'm no sae blate, but I may tell you. I didna come up here anes errand for my ain pleasure, but mostly to see Johnnie, and to try if I couldna get ony word o' a very decent lad, ane Peter Drumlie, that belangs about our countryside. We were great friends, him and me, and then we had an outcast—you'll ken by yoursel—but we've made it up again since I came to London, and I'm gaun hame to get my providing, and comfort my mother a wee while, afore I leave her athegither. It's a real duty comforting folk's mother, Miss Menie. I'm sure I wouldna forget that for a' the lads in the world."

"And where are you to live, Nelly?" Nelly's moralising scarcely called for an answer.

"We havena just made up our minds; they say ae marriage aye makes mair," said Nelly, with a grim smile. "Miss Menie, you've set us a' agaun."

Perhaps Menie did not care to be classed with Nelly Panton. "July Home will be a very young wife," she said; "I think your brother should be very happy with her, Nelly."

"I wouldna wonder," said Nelly, shortly; "but you see, Miss Menie, our Johnnie's a weel-doing lad, and might hae lookit higher, meaning nae offence to you; though nae doubt it's true what Randall Home said when he was speaking about this. 'Lithgow,' says he (for he ca's Johnnie by his last name—it's a kind o' fashion hereaway), 'if you get naething wi' your wife, I will take care to see you're no cumbered wi' onybody but hersel;' which nae doubt is a great comfort, seeing there might hae been a haill troop o' friends, now that Johnnie's getting up in the world."

"What was that Randall Home said?" Menie asked the question in a very clear distinct tone, cold and steady and unfaltering—"What do you say he said?—tell me again."

"He said, Johnnie wouldna be troubled wi' nane o' her friends," said Nelly; "though he has her to keep, a bit wee silly thing, that can do naething in a house—and nae doubt a maid to keep to her forby—that he wouldna hae ony o' her friends a burden on him; and a very wise thing to say, and a great comfort. I aye said he was a sensible lad, Randall Home. Eh, preserve me!"

For Randall Home stands before her, his eyes glowing on her with haughty rage. He has heard it, every single deliberate word, and Randall is no coward—he comes in person to answer for what he has said.

Rise, Menie Laurie! Slowly they gather over us, these kind shadows of the coming night; no one can see the momentary faltering which inclines you to throw yourself down there upon the very ground, and weep your heart out. Rise; it is you who are stately now.

"This is true?"

She is so sure of it, that there needs no other form of question, and Menie lays her hand upon the table to support herself, and stands firmly before him waiting for his answer. Why is it that now, at this moment, when she should be most strong, the passing wind brings to her, as in mockery, an echo of whispering mingled voices—the timid happiness of July Home? But Menie draws up her light figure, draws herself apart from the touch of her companions, and stands, as she fancies she most do henceforth, all her life, alone.

"This is true?"

"I would disdain myself, if I tried to escape by any subterfuge," said Randall, proudly. "I might answer that I never said the words this woman attributes to me; but that I do not need to tell you. I would not deceive you, Menie. I never can deny what I have given expression to; and you are right—it is true."

And Randall thinks he hears a voice, wavering somewhere, far off, and distant like an echo—not coming from these pale lips which move and form the words, but falling out upon the air—faint, yet distinct, not to be mistaken. "I am glad you have told me. I thank you for making no difficulty about it: this is very well."

"Menie! you are not moved by this gossip's story? This that I said has no effect on you? Menie! is a woman like this to make a breach between you and me?"

In stolid malice Nelly Panton sits still, and listens with a certain melancholy enjoyment of the mischief she has made, protesting, under her breath, that "she meant nae ill; she aye did a'thing for the best;" while Randall, forgetful of his own acknowledgment, repeats again and again his indignant remonstrance, "a woman like this!"

"No, she has no such power," said Menie firmly—"no such power. Pardon me—I am wanted to-night. My strength is not my own to be wasted now; we can conclude this matter another time."

Before he could say a word the door had closed upon her. There was a hustle without, a glimmer of coming lights upon the wall. In a few minutes the room was lighted up, the lady of the house in her presiding place—and Randall started with angry pride from the place where he stood, by the side of Nelly Panton, whose gloomy unrelieved figure suddenly stood out in bold relief upon the brightened wall.

Another time! Menie Laurie has not gone to ponder upon what this other conference shall be—she is not by her window—she is not out of doors—she has gone to no such refuge. Where she never went before, into the heart of Miss Annie's preparations—into the bustle of Miss Annie's hospitality—shunning even Jenny, far more shunning her mother, and waiting only till the room is full enough, to give her a chance of escaping every familiar eye. This is the first device of Menie's mazed, bewildered mind. These many days she has lived in hourly expectation of some such blow; but it stuns her when it comes.

Forlorn! forlorn! wondering if it is possible to hide this misery from every eye—pondering plans and schemes of concealment, trying to invent—do not wonder, it is a natural impulse—some generous lie. But Menie's nature, more truthful than her will, fails in the effort. The time goes on, the lingering moments swell into an hour. Music is in her ears, and smiling faces glide before her and about her, till she feels this dreadful pressure at her heart no longer tolerable, and bursts away in a sudden passion, craving to be alone.

Another heart, restless by reason of a gnawing unhappiness, wanders out and in of these unlighted chambers—oftenest coming back to this one, where the treasures of its life rest night by night. This wandering shadow is not a graceful one—these pattering hasty footsteps have nothing in them of the softened lingering tread of meditation. No, poor Jenny, little of sentiment or grace embellishes your melancholy—yet it is hard to find any poem so full of pathos as a desolate heart, even such a one as beats in your homely breast to-night.

Softly—the room is not vacant now, as it was when you last entered here. Some one stands by the window, stooping forward to look at the stars; and while you linger by the door, a low cry, half a sigh, half a moan, breaks the silence faintly—not the same voice which just now bore its part so well below;—not the same, for that voice came from the lips only—this is out of the heart.

"Bairn, you're no weel—they've a' wearied you," said Jenny, stealing upon her in the darkness: "lie down and sleep; its nae matter for the like o' me, but when you sigh, it breaks folk's hearts."

The familiar voice surprised the watcher into a sudden burst of childish tears. All the woman failed in this great trial. "Oh, Jenny, dinna tell my mother!" Menie Laurie was capable of no other thought.

CHAPTER XXV

But this Menie Laurie, rising up from her bed of unrest, when the morning light breaks, cold and real, upon a changed world, has wept out all her child's tears, and is a woman once again. No one knows yet a whisper of what has befallen her, not even poor Jenny, who sobbed over her last night, and implored her not to weep.

Now, how to tell this—how to signify, in the fewest and calmest words, the change that has come upon her. Sitting, with her cheek leant on her hand, by the window where she heard it, before any other eyes are awake, Menie ponders this in her heart. Always before in little difficulties counsel and help have been within her reach; few troublous things have been to do in Menie's experience; and no one ever dreamt that *she* should do them, when they chanced to come to her mother's door.

But now her mother's honour is involved—she must not be consulted—she must not know. With a proud flush Menie draws up herself—herself who must work in this alone. Ah, sweet dependence, dear humility of the old times! we must lay them by out of our heart to wait for a happier dawn. This day it is independence—self-support—a strength that stands alone; and no one who has not felt such an abrupt transition can know how hard it is to take these unused weapons up.

"Will you let me speak to you, aunt?" Menie's heart falters within her, as she remembers poor Miss Annie's unaccepted sympathy. Has she indeed been driven to seek refuge here at last?

"My love! how can you ask such a question, darling, when I am always ready to speak to you?" exclaimed Miss Annie, with enthusiasm.

"But not here—out of doors, if you will permit me," said Menie in a half whisper. "I—I want to be out of my mother's sight—she must not know."

"You delightful creature," said Miss Annie, "are you going to give me your confidence at last?"

Poor Menie, sadly dismayed, was very ill able to support this strain of sympathy. She hastened out, not quite observing how it tasked her companion to follow her—out to the same green overgrown corner, where once before she had spoken of this same subject to Randall himself. With a slight shudder she paused there before the little rustic seat, from which she had risen at his approach; but Menie knew that she must harden herself against the power of associations; enough of real ill was before her.

"I want to tell you, aunt, if you will please to listen to me, that the engagement of which you were told when we came here is dissolved—broken. I do not know if there is any stronger word," said Menie, a bewildered look growing on her face. "I mean to say that it is all over, as if it had never been."

And Menie folded her hands upon her breast, and stood patiently to listen, expecting a burst of lamentation and condolence; but Menie was not prepared for the laugh which rung shrilly on her ears—the words that followed it.

"My sweet simple child, I have no doubt you quite believe it—forgive me for laughing, darling; but I know what lovers' quarrels are. There, now, don't look so grave and angry; my love, you will make it all up to-morrow."

And Miss Annie Laurie patted Menie's shrinking shoulder encouragingly. It was a harder task this than Menie had anticipated; but she went on without flinching.

"This is no lovers' quarrel, aunt; do not think so. My mother is in some degree involved in this. I cannot consult her, or ask her to help me; it is the first time I have ever been in such a strait;" and Menie's lip quivered as she spoke. "You are my only friend. I am serious—as serious as mind can be, which feels that here it decides its life. Aunt, I apply to you."

Miss Annie Laurie looked up very much confused and shaken: very seldom had any one spoken to her with such a sober seriousness of tone; she could not think it unreal, for neither extravagance nor despair were in these grave sad words of Menie. The poor frivolous heart felt this voice ring into its depths, past all superficial affectations and sentiments. No exuberance of sympathy, no shower of condoling words or endearments, could answer this appeal; and poor Miss Annie faltered before this claim of real service—faltered and shrank into a very weak old woman, her self-delusions standing her in no stead in such a strait; and the only answer she could make was to cry, in a trembling and strangely altered voice, "Oh, child, do not speak so. What can I do for you?"

Most true, what can you do, indeed, poor soul! whose greatest object for all these years has been to shut out and darken the daylight truth, which mocked your vain pretences? You could give charity and gentle words—be thankful; your heart is alive in you because of these: but what can you do in such a difficulty as this? where is your wisdom to counsel, your strength to uphold? This grave girl stands before you, sadly bearing her burden, without an effort to conceal from you that she feels it hard to bear; but you, whose age is not grave, whose heart has rejected experience, whose mind has refused to learn the kindly insight of advancing years—shrink into yourself, poor aged butterfly; feel that it is presumption to call yourself her counsellor, and say again—again, with a tremble in your weakened voice, "What can I do for you?"

"Aunt, I apply to you," said Menie Laurie; "I ask your help, when I resolve to decide my future life according to my own will and conviction of what is best. I have no one else to assist me. I apply to you."

Miss Annie melted into a fit of feeble crying; her hands shook, her ringlets drooped down lank about her cheeks. "I will do anything—anything you like; tell me what to do, Menie—Menie, my dear child."

It was pitiful to see her distress. Menie, whom no one comforted, felt her heart moved to comfort her.

"I will not grieve you much," said Menie gently; "only I beg you to give me your countenance when I see Randall—Mr Home. I want you to be as my mother might have been in other circumstances; but I will not trouble you much, aunt—I will not trouble you."

Miss Annie could not stop her tears; she was very timid and afraid, sobbing helplessly. "What will I do? what can I do? Oh, Menie, love, you will make it up to-morrow;" for poor Miss Annie knew no way of conquering grief except by flying out of its sight.

Menie led her back to the house tenderly. Menie had never known before this necessity of becoming comforter, when she had so much need to be comforted. It was best for her—it gave her all the greater command over her own heart.

And to hear poor innocent July, in her own young unclouded joy—to hear her unsuspicious mother at their breakfast-table—to have Randall's name cross her now and then like a sudden blow—Randall, Randall;— Menie knew nothing of all these depths, nor how such sorrows come in battalions; so, one by one, her inexperienced heart gained acquaintance with them now,—gained acquaintance with that sorest of human truths, that it is possible to love and to condemn—possible to part, and know that parting is the best—yet withal to cling and cling, and hold, with the saddest gripe of tenderness, the heart from which you part. Poor Menie! they said she looked very dark and heavy; that last night's exertions had wearied her—it was very true.

Miss Annie sent a message that she was not well, and would breakfast in her own room. In the forenoon, when she came down stairs again, even Menie was startled at the change. Miss Annie's ringlets were smoothed out and braided on her poor thin cheek—braided elaborately with a care and study worthy of something more important; her step tottered a little: when any one spoke to her, a little gush of tears came to her eyes; but, notwithstanding, there was a solemnity and importance in the hush of Miss Annie's manner, which no one had ever seen in her before. Half-a dozen times that day she asked in a startling whisper, "Menie, when is he to come?" Poor Menie, sick at heart, could scarcely bear this slow prolonging of her pain.

CHAPTER XXVI

"Aunt, he has come."

No one knows; July is out on a ramble in this pleasant heath, where she cannot lose herself; Mrs Laurie has gone out for some private errands of her own. In her first day, Menie has managed well. True, they all know that Menie has been wearied last night; that her eye looks dull and heavy; that her cheek has lost its slight bloom of colour; that she says something of a headache; but nobody knows that headache has come to be with Menie Laurie, as with many another, only a softer word for heartache—no one suspects that the quiet heart, which feared no evil when this spring began, is now a battle-ground and field of contest, and that sometimes, when she sits quiet in outward seeming, she could leap up with a start and scream, and feels as if madness would come to her underneath their unsuspicious eyes.

"Aunt, he has come."

Miss Annie Laurie is very nervous; she has to be supported on Menie's arm as they go down stairs. "You will make it all up, Menie; yes, my darling;" but Miss Annie's head nods spasmodically, and there is a terrified troubled expression about her face, which looks so meagre in its outline under that braided hair.

Slightly disturbed, something haughty, rather wondering what Menie has got to say for herself, Randall sits waiting in the drawing-room. It is no small surprise to him to see Miss Annie—especially to see her so moved and nervous; and Randall restrains, with visible displeasure, the words which rose to his lip, on Menie's entrance, and coldly makes his bow to the lady of the house.

"My dear Mr Home, I am very much grieved; I hope you are ready to make it all up," murmurs Miss Annie; but she trembles so much that it is not easy to hear what she says, except the last words, which flush Randall's cheek with a sudden disdainful anger. A lovers' quarrel!—that he should be fancied capable of this.

"My aunt has come with me," said Menie steadily, "to give the weight of her presence to what I say. Randall, I do not pretend that my own feelings are changed, or that I have ceased to care for you. I do not need to seem to quarrel, or to call you by a less familiar name. We know the reason, both of us; there is no use for discussing it—and I have come to have it mutually understood that our engagement is broken. We will go away very soon. I came to say good-by."

Before she concluded, Menie had bent her head, and cast down her wavering eyes upon Miss Annie's hand, which she held firmly in her own. Her voice was very low, her words quick and hurried; she stood beside Miss Annie's chair, holding fast, and twining in her own Miss Annie's nervous fingers; but she did not venture to look up to meet Randall's eyes.

"What does this mean? it is mere trifling, Menie," said Randall impatiently. "You hear a gossip's story of something I said; true or false, it did not affect you—it had no bearing on you; you know very well that nothing has happened to make you less precious to me—that nothing can happen which will ever change my heart. Menie, this is the second time; is this the conduct I have a right to expect from you? Deal with me frankly; I have a title to it. What do you mean?"

"My darling, he will make it up," said Miss Annie, with a little overflow of tears.

But Menie was very steady—so strange, so strange—she grew into a startling acquaintance with herself in these few hours. Who could have thought there were so many passionate impulses in Menie Laurie's quiet heart?

"We will not discuss it, Randall," she said again; "let us simply conclude that it is best for both of us to withdraw. Perhaps you will be better content if I speak more strongly," she continued, with a little trembling vehemence, born of her weakness, "if I say it is impossible—impossible—you understand the word—to restore the state of mind, the hope, the trust, and confidence that are past. No—let us have no explanation—I cannot bear it, Randall. Do we not understand each other already? Nothing but parting is possible for us—for me. I think I am saying what I mean to say—good-by."

"Look at me, Menie."

It is hard to do it—hard to lift up those eyes, so full of tears—hard to see his lips quiver—hard to see the love in his face; but Menie's eyes fall when they have endured this momentary ordeal; and again she holds out her hand and says, "Good-by."

"Good-by—I answer you," said Randall, wringing her hand, and throwing it out of his grasp. "Good-by—you are disloyal, Menie, disloyal to Nature and to me; some time you will remember this; now I bid you farewell."

Something crossed her like an angry breath—something rang in her ears, confused and echoing like the first drops of a thunder-shower; and Menie can see nothing in all the world but Miss Annie weeping upon her hand, and, like a culprit, steals away—steals away, not knowing where she goes—desolate, guilty, forsaken, feeling as if she had done some grievous wrong, and was for ever shut out from peace or comfort in this weary world.

Yes—there is no one to see you. Lie down upon the ground, Menie Laurie—down, down, where you can be no lower, and cover your eyes from the cheerful light. How they pour upon you, these dreadful doubts and suspicions of yourself!—wisely—wisely—what should make it wise, this thing you have done? You yourself have little wisdom, and you took no counsel. If it was not wise, what then?—it is done, and there is nothing for it now but to be content.

CHAPTER XXVII

"It must not be—I cannot permit it," said Mrs Laurie. "Menie, is this all that your mother deserves at your hands? to take such a step as this without even telling me—without giving me an opportunity of remonstrance? Menie! Menie!"

And with hasty steps Mrs Laurie paces backward and forward the narrow room. Beside the window, very pale, Menie stands with a half-averted face, saying nothing—very pale—and there is a sullen suffering in Menie Laurie's darkened face.

"I cannot have it—I will not permit it"—Mrs Laurie is much excited. "My own honour is compromised; it will be said it is I who have separated you. Menie! it is strange that you should show so little regard either to Randall or to me. I must do something—I must make an effort—I cannot have this."

"Mother, hear me," exclaimed Menie. "No one shall do anything; I will not bear it either. In everything else you shall make of me what you will—here I am not to be swayed; I must decide this for myself—and I have decided it, mother."

With astonished eyes Mrs Laurie looked upon her daughter's face. Flushed with passion, full of a fierce unrespecting will—was this Menie Laurie? but her mother turned aside from her. "I am sorry, Menie—I am very sorry—to see you show such a spirit; another time I will speak of it again."

Another time!—Menie Laurie laughed a low laugh when her mother left the room. Something like a scowl had come to Menie's brow; a dark abiding cloud was on her face: and in her heart such bitterness and universal disappointment as killed every gentle feeling in her soul: disloyal to the one love, disrespectful and disobedient to the other—bitterly Menie's heart turned upon itself—she had pleased no one; her life was nothing but a great blot before her. She was conscious of a host of evil feelings—evil spirits waging war with one another in her vexed and troubled mind. Sullenly she sat down once more upon the ground, not to seek if there was any comfort in the heavens above or the earth beneath, but to brood upon her grief, and make it darker, till the clouds closed over her, and swallowed her up, and not a star remained.

There is a certain obstinate gloom; satisfaction in despair. To decide that everything is hopeless—that nothing can be done for you—that you have reached to the pre-eminence of woe—no wonder Menie's race was dark and sullen—she had come to this point now.

Like a thunder-storm this intelligence came upon little July Home—she could not comprehend it, and no one took the trouble to explain to her. Lithgow, knowing but the fact, was surprised and grieved, and prophesied their reunion; but no hope was in Menie's sullen gravity—none in the naughty resentment of Randall Home.

And Mrs Laurie once more with a troubled brow considers of her future—will Menie be best in the Dumfriesshire cottage, where no one will see their poverty, or pursuing some feminine occupation among the other seamstresses, teachers, poor craftswomen of a less solitary place? For now that all is done that can be done, there is no hope of recovering anything of the lost income,—and Mrs Laurie will not live on Miss Annie's bounty. She is anxious with all her heart to be away.

Miss Annie herself has not recovered her trial: autumn winds grow cold at night—autumn rains come down sadly upon the little world which has had its cheerfulness quenched out of it—and when Randall takes away his little sister to carry her home, Miss Annie looks a mournful old woman, sitting there wrapped up by the early lighted fire. These two or three mornings she has even been seen at the breakfast-table with a cap protecting the head which is so sadly apt to take cold—and Miss Annie cries a little to herself, and tells bits of her own love-story to Menie, absorbed and silent, who sits unanswering beside her—and moans to herself sadly sometimes, over this other vessel of youthful life, cast away.

But Miss Annie Laurie never wears ringlets more. Strangely upon her conscience, like a reproach for her unnatural attenuated youth, came

Menie's appeal to her for help and comfort. Feeling herself so frivolous and feeble, so unable to sustain or strengthen, Miss Annie made a holocaust of her curls, and was satisfied. So much vanity was relinquished not without a struggle; but great comfort came from the sacrifice to the heroic penitent.

And Jenny, discontented and angry with them all, furiously now takes the part of Randall Home, and wonders, in a fuff and outburst, what Miss Menie can expect that she "lightlies" a bonnie lad like yon. A great change has taken place on Menie; no one can say it is for the better—and sullenly and sadly this bright year darkens over the house of Heathbank.

CHAPTER XXVIII

"You're to bide away—you're no to come near this place. Na, you may just fecht; but you've nae pith compared to Jenny, for a' sae auld and thrawn as Jenny has been a' her days. It's no me just—it's your mamma and the doctor. Bairn! will you daur struggle wi' me?"

But Menie would dare straggle with any one—neither command nor resistance satisfies her.

"Let me in—I want to see my mother."

"You can want your mother for a day—there's mair than you wanting her. That puir old haverel there—guid forgie me—she's a dying woman—has sairer lack o' her than you. Keep to your ain place, Menie Laurie—muckle made o'—muckle thocht o'—but you're only a bairn for a' that—you're no a woman o' judgment like your mamma or me. I tell yon to gang away—I will not let you in."

And Jenny stood firm—a jealous incorruptible sentinel in the passage which led to Miss Annie Laurie's room. "Miss Menie, ye'll no take it ill what I say," said Jenny; "there's death in the house, or fast coming. I ken what the doctor means. Gang you ben the house, like a guid bairn; look in your ain glass, and see if there should be a face like that in a house where He comes."

Menie looks silently into the countenance before her—the keen, impatient, irascible face; but it was easy to see a hasty tear dashed away from Jenny's cheek.

And without another word, Menie Laurie turned away. Some withered leaves are lying on the window-sill—the trees are yielding up their treasures, dropping them down mournfully to the disconsolate soil—but the meagre yew-tree rustles before her, darkly green in its perennial gloom. Rather shed the leaves, the hopes—rather yield to winter meekly for the sake of spring—rather be cut down, and rooted up altogether, than grow to such a sullen misanthrope as this.

And Menie Laurie looks into her own face; this gloomy brow—these heavy eyes—are these the daylight features of Menie Laurie?—the interpretation of her heart? Earnestly and long she reads—no lesson of vanity, but a stern sermon from that truthful mirror. Hush!—listen!—what was that?—a cry!

The doctor is leaving Miss Annie Laurie's room—the cry is over—there is only now a feeble sound of weeping; but a shadow strangely still and sombre has fallen upon the house, and the descending step rings like a knell upon the stairs. What is it?—what is coming?—and what did it mean, that melancholy cry?

Alas! a voice out of a startled soul—a cry of wild and terrified recognition—acknowledgment. Years ago, age came gently to this dwelling—gently, with light upon his face, and honour on his grey hairs. There was no entrance for him through the jealous door; but now has come another who will not be gainsaid.

Gather the children, Reaper—gather the lilies—take the corn full in the ear—go to the true souls where thought of you dwells among thoughts of other wonders, glories, solemn things to come—leave this chamber here with all its poor devices. No such presence has ever stood within its poverty-stricken walls before. Go where great love, great hope, great faith, great sorrow, sublimer angels, have made *you* no phantom—leave this soul to its toys and delusions—it is a poor triumph—come not here.

Hush, be still. They who have sent him have charged him with a message; hear it how it rings slow and solemn into the ear of this hushed house. "There is a way, and it shall be called the way of holiness; the wayfaring man, though a fool, shall not err therein." Stay your weeping, poor fool—poor soul; prayers have gone up for you from the succoured hearts of some of God's poor. Unawares, in your simplicity, you have lent to the Lord. Your gracious debtor gives you back with the grand usury of heaven—gives you back opportunity—hope—a day to be saved—lays aside those poor little vanities of yours under the cover of this, His great magnanimous divine grace—and holds open to your feeble steps the way, where wayfaring men, though fools, shall not err any more for ever.

"I'll let you pass, Miss Menie, if you'll bide a moment," said Jenny, wiping her eyes; "he says it's no the fever he thocht it was, but just a natural decay. Did you hear yon? she wasna looking for Him that's at the door, and he'll no wait lang where ance He's gien His summons—pity me! I would like to see him coming the road mysel, afore I just found him at my doorstane."

The room is very still; through the quiet you can only hear the panting of a frightened breath, and now and then a timid feeble sob. She has to go away—knows and feels to the depth of her heart that she must go upon this solemn road alone; but, with a sad panic of terror and curiosity, she watches her own feelings, wondering if this and this be death.

And now they sit and read to her while the daylight flushes in noon—while it fades and wanes into the night—the night and dark of which she has a childish terror—read to her this gracious blessed Gospel, which does not address itself alone to the wise and noble, but is for the simple and for fools. Safe ground, poor soul, safe ground—for this is no scheme of electicism, no portal to the pagan heavens—and you cannot know yourself so low, so mean, as to escape the range of this great wide embracing arm.

"I have not done all that I ought to have done," murmurs poor Miss Annie. "Don't leave me:" for she cannot rest except some one holds her hand, and has a faint superstitious trust in it, as if it held her sure.

A little pause—again the fingers close tightly upon the hand they hold. "I never did any harm." The words are so sad—so sad—falling out slow and feeble upon the hushed air of this darkening room.

"But I never did any good—never, never." The voice grows stronger. "Does anybody think I did? I—I—I never was very wise. I used to try to be kind sometimes;" and in a strain of inarticulate muttering, the sound died away once more.

And then again the voice of the reader broke the silence. They scarcely thought the sufferer listened; for ever and anon she broke forth in such wavering self-justifications, self-condemnings, as these. But now there is a long silence; strange emotions come and go upon this old, old, withered face. The tears have been dried from her eyes for hours, now they come again, bedewing all her poor thin cheeks; but a strange excitement struggles with her weakness. Looking about to her right hand and to her left, the dying woman struggles with an eager defiance—struggles till, at a sudden climax, her broken voice breaks forth again.

"Who said it was me—me—it's not me! I never could win anything in this world—nothing in this world—not a heart to care for me. Do you think I could win Heaven? I say it is not me; it's for His sake."

"For His sake—for His sake." If it is a prayer that ends thus—if it is a sudden assurance of which she will not loose her hold for ever—no one can know; for by-and-by her panic returns upon Miss Annie. Close in her own cold fingers she grasps the hand of Menie Laurie, and whispers, "Is it dark—is it so dark to you?" with again a thrill of terror and trembling, and awful curiosity, wondering if this, perchance, is the gloom of death.

"It is very dark—it is almost night." The lamp is lighted on the table; let some one go to her side, and hold this other poor wandering hand. "Oh!

not in the night—not in the night—I am afraid to go out in the night," sobs poor Miss Annie; and with a dreadful suspicion in her eyes, as if of some one drawing near to murder her, she watches the falling of this fated night.

A solemn vigil—with ever that tight and rigid pressure upon their clasped hands. Mother and daughter, silent, pale, keep the watch together; and below, the servants sit awe-stricken, afraid to go to sleep. Jenny, who is not afraid, goes about the stairs, up and down, from room to room, sometimes serving the watchers, sometimes only straying near them, muttering, after her fashion, words which may be prayers, and dashing off now and then an intrusive tear.

Still, with many a frightened pause—many a waking up, and little pang of terror, this forlorn heart wanders back into the life which is ending now—wanders back to think herself once more engaged in the busier scenes of her youth, in the little occupations, the frivolities and gaiety of her later years; but howsoever her mind wanders, she never ceases to fix her eyes upon the span of sky glittering with a single star, which shines pale on her through the window, from which, to please her, they have drawn the curtain. "I am afraid to go out in the dark;" again and again she says it with a shudder, and a tightened hold upon their hands—and stedfastly watches the night.

At last her eyes grow heavy—she has fallen asleep. Little reverence has Miss Annie won at any time of all her life—but the eyes that look on her are awed and reverent now. Slowly the hours pass by—slowly the gradual dawn brightens upon her face—the star has faded out of the heavens—on her brow, which is the brow of death, the daylight glows in one reviving flush. The night is over for evermore.

And now her heavy eyes are opened full—her feeble form is raised; and, with a cry of joy, she throws out her arms to meet the light. Lay her down tenderly; her chains are broken in her sleep; now she no more needs the pressure of your kindly hands. Lay her down, she is afraid no longer; for not in the night, or through the darkness, but with the morning and the sun, the traveller fares upon her way—where fools do not err. By this time they have taken her in yonder at the gate. Lay down all that remains of her to its rest.

CHAPTER XXIX

The curtains are drawn again in Miss Annie Laurie's house of Heathbank—drawn back from the opened windows to let the fresh air and the sunshine in once more to all the rooms. With a long breath and sigh of relief, the household throws off its compelled gloom. With all observances of honour, they have laid her in her grave, and a few natural tears have been wept—a few kindly words spoken—a reverent memento raised to name the place where she lies. Now she is passed away and forgotten, her seat empty—her house knowing her no more.

In Miss Annie's desk, a half-written paper, intimating vaguely that, in case of "anything happening" to her at any future time, she wished all that she had to be given to Menie Laurie—was found immediately after the funeral. But some superstitious terror had prevented her from finishing it, far more from making a will. Menie was her next of kin; it pleased them to have this sanction of her willingness to the inheritance of the natural heir.

Miss Annie had been rather given to speak of her savings; but no vestige of these savings was to be found. She had practised this on herself like many another delusion; and saving the furniture of Heathbank, and a profusion of ornaments not valuable, there remained little for Menie to inherit. Miss Annie's maid was her well-known favourite, and had been really attentive, and a good servant to her indulgent mistress. Her name was mentioned in the half-written paper, and Maria's own report of many conversations, modestly hinted at a legacy. Miss Annie's furniture, pretty and suitable for her house as it was, was not valuable in a sale; and Mrs Laurie, acting for her daughter, bestowed almost the whole amount received for it upon Maria, as carrying out the will of her mistress. Having done this, they had done all, Mrs Laurie thought, and would now go home to live as they could upon what remained to them. Burnside, with all its plenishing, brought in no greater revenue than fifty pounds a-year, and Mrs Laurie had two or three hundred pounds "in the bank." This was all. She began to calculate painfully what the home-journey would cost them, and called Jenny to consult about their packing. They were now in a little lodging in the town of Hampstead. They had no inducement to stay here; and Menie's face looked very pale—very much in want of the fresh gale on the Dumfriesshire braes. True, they knew not where they were going, but the kindly soil was home.

When her mother and Jenny began to take enumeration of the bags and boxes which must go with them, Menie entered the room. Menie looked very slight, very pale, and exhausted, almost shadowy in her mourning dress; but Menie's now was a face which had looked on Death. The conflict and sullen warfare were gone out of it. Dead and silent within her lay her chilled heart, like a stricken field when the fight is over, with nothing but moans and sighs, and voices of misery, where the music and pomp of war has so lately been. The contest was over; there was nothing to struggle for or struggle with, in this dull unhappiness—and a heavy peace lay upon Menie like a cloud.

"There is a wee kistie wi' a lock. I set it by mysel for Miss Menie; and there's the muckle ane that held the napery at hame; but I'm no gaun owre them a'. I'll just lay in the things as I laid them when we came. Miss Menie! gang away your ways, like a guid bairn, and read a book; your mamma's speaking about the flitting, and I can only do ae thing at a time."

"Are we going home, mother?"

"There is nothing else we can do, Menie," said Mrs Laurie. "I suppose none of us have any inducement now to stay in London."

A flush of violent colour came to Menie's cheeks. She paused and hesitated. "*I* have, mother."

"Bless me, I aye said it," muttered Jenny quickly, under her breath, as she turned round with an eager face, and thrust herself forward towards the mother and daughter. "The bairn's come to hersel."

Mrs Laurie coloured scarcely less than Menie. "I cannot guess what you mean," she said hurriedly. "You did not consult me before—I am, perhaps, an unsuitable adviser now; but I cannot stay in London without having a reason for it. This place has nothing but painful associations for me. You are not well, Menie," continued the mother, softening; "we shall all be better away—let us go home."

The colour wavered painfully on Menie Laurie's cheek, and it was hard to keep down a groan out of her heart. "I am not come to myself—my mind is unchanged," she said with sudden meekness. "I want you to stay for a month or two—as short a time as possible—and to let me have some lessons. Mother, look at these."

Menie had brought her little portfolio. With some astonishment Mrs Laurie turned over its contents, and delicately—almost timidly too—lest

Randall's face should look out upon her as of old. But all the sketches of Randall were removed. Jenny pressed forward to see; but Jenny, as bewildered as Menie's mother, could only look up with a puzzled face. What did she mean?

"They are not very well done," said Menie; "but, for all that, they are portraits, and like. I want to have lessons, mother. Once before, long ago,"—poor Menie, it seemed to be years ago,—"I said this should be my trade. I will like the trade; let me only have the means of doing it better, and it will be good for me to do it. This is why I ask you to stay in London."

Jenny, very fierce and red, grasping the back of a chair, thrust it suddenly between them at this point, with a snort of emphatic defiance.

"Ye'll no let on ye hear her!" exclaimed Jenny; "you'll let her get her whimsey out like ony ither wean!—ye'll pay nae attention to her maggots and her vanities! Trade! My patience! to think I should live to hear a bairn o' ours speak o' a trade, and Jenny's twa hands to the fore!"

And a petulant reluctant sob burst out of Jenny's breast—an angry tear glittered in her eye. She drew a long breath to recover herself—

"Jenny's twa hands to the fore, I say, and the bere a' to shear yet, and the 'taties to gather—no to say the mistress is to buy me twa kye, to take butter to the market! I would just like to ken where's the pleasure in working, if it's no to gie ease to folk's ain? I've a' my ain plans putten down, if folk would just let me be; and we'll can keep a young lass to wait upon Miss Menie," cried Jenny, with a shrill tone in her voice, "and the first o' the cream and the sweetest o' the milk, and nae occasion to wet her finger. You're no gaun to pay ony heed to her—you're no gaun to let on you hear what she says!"

Reaching this point, Jenny broke down, and permitted, much against her will, a little shower of violent hot tears to rain down upon the arms which she folded resolutely into her apron. But Jenny shook off, with indignation, the caressing hand which Menie laid upon her shoulder. Jenny knew by experience that it was better to be angry than to be sad.

"I would think with you too, Jenny," said Mrs Laurie, slowly. "I could do anything myself; but a bairn of mine doing work for money—Menie, we will not need it—we will try first—"

"Mother," said Menie, interrupting her hastily, "*I* will need it—I will never be wilful again—let me have my pleasure now."

It was a thing unknown in the household that Menie should not have her pleasure. Even Jenny yielded to this imperative claim. The boxes were piled up again in Jenny's little bedchamber. Jenny herself, able to do nothing else, set to knitting stockings with great devotion. "I'll hae plenty to do when we get hame, without ever taking wires in my hand," said Jenny. "Nae doubt it's just a providence to let me lay up as mony as will serve."

Their parlour was in the first floor, over one of the trim little ladies' shops, which have their particular abode in little towns of competence and gentility. Toys and Berlin wool—a prim, neat, gentle Miss Middleton sitting at work on some pretty bit of many-coloured industry behind the orderly counter—gay patterns and specimens about—little carts and carriages, and locomotive animals upon the floor—bats, balls, drums, shining tin breastplates, and glorious swords hanging by the door, and a linen awning without, throwing the little shop into pleasant shade. This was the ground floor; above it was a very orderly parlour, and the sun came glistening in upon the little stand of flowers through the bright small panes of the old-fashioned window, and fell upon Mrs Laurie, always at work upon some making or mending—upon Jenny's abrupt exits and entrances—her keen grey eyes and shining "wires," the latter of which were so nobly independent of any guidance from the former—and upon Menie's heavy meditations, and Menie's daily toil.

For toil it came to be, exalted from the young lady's accomplishment to the artist's labour. She worked at this which she harshly called her trade with great zeal and perseverance. Even herself did not know how deficient she was till now; but Menie worked bravely in her apprenticeship, and with good hope.

CHAPTER XXX

"I wouldna hae come hame as I gaed away, if I had been you, Jenny." The speaker stands at the door of Jenny's little byre, looking on, while Jenny milks her favourite cow. "Ye see what Nelly Panton's done for hersel; there's naething like making up folk's mind to gang through wi' a'thing; and you see Nelly's gotten a man away in yon weary London."

"I wouldna gang to seek a misfortune—no me," said Jenny; "ill enough when it comes; and I wonder how a woman like you, wi' twelve bairns for a handsel, could gie sic an advice to ony decent lass; and weel I wat Nelly Panton's gotten a man. Puir laddie! it's the greatest mercy ever was laid to his hands to make him a packman—he'll no be sae muckle at hame; but you'll make nae divert o' Jenny. If naebody ever speered my price, I'm no to hang my head for that. I've aye keepit my fancy free, and nae man can say that Jenny ever lookit owre her shouther after him. A' the house is fu' 'enow, Marget; we've scarcely done wi' our flitting; I canna ask you to come in."

So saying, Jenny rose with her pail, and closed the byre door upon Brockie and her black companion. The wind came down keen from the hills; the frosty wintry heavens had not quite lost the glow of sunset, though the pale East began to glitter with stars. Sullen Criffel has a purple glory upon his cap of cloud, and securely, shoulder to shoulder, this band of mountain marshals keep the border; but the shadows are dark about their feet, and night falls, clear and cold, upon the darkened grass, and trees that stir their branches faintly in the wind.

The scene is strangely changed. Heaths of other nature than the peaceful heath of Hampstead lie dark under the paling skies, not very far away; and the heather is brown on the low-lying pasture hills, standing out in patches from the close-cropped grass. Yonder glow upon the road is the glow of fire-light from an open cottage door, and on the window ledge within stand basins of comfortable Dumfriesshire "parritch," cooling for the use of those eager urchins, with their fair exuberant locks and merry faces, and waiting the milk which their loitering girl sister brings slowly in from the byre. It is cold, and she breathes upon her fingers as she shifts her pail from one hand to the other; yet bareheaded Jeanie lingers, wondering vaguely at the "bonnie" sky and deep evening calm.

Another cottage here is close at hand, faintly throwing out from this back-window a little light into the gathering gloom. Brockie and Blackie are comfortable for the night; good homely sages, they make no account of the key turned upon them in the byre door; and Jenny, in her original dress, her beloved shortgown and warm striped skirts, stands a moment, drawing in, with keen relish, the sweep of cold air which comes full upon us over the free countryside.

"I'm waiting for Nelly's mother," says Jenny's companion, who is Marget Panton from Kirklands, Nelly's aunt; "she's gane in to speak to your mistress. You'll no be for ca'ing her mistress now, Jenny, and her sae muckle come down in the world. I'm sure you're real kind to them; they'll no be able now to pay you your fee."

"Me kind to them! My patience! But it's because ye dinna ken ony better," said Jenny, with a little snort. "I just wish, for my part, folk would haud by what concerns themselves, and let me abee. I would like to ken what's a' the world's business if Jenny has a guid mistress, and nae need to seek anither service frae ae year's end to the ither—and it canna advantage the like o' you grudging at Jenny's fee. It's gey dark, and the road's lanesome; if I was you, I would think o' gaun hame."

"I wouldna be sae crabbed if I got a pension for't," returned Marget, sharply; "and ye needna think to gar folk believe lees; it's weel kent your house is awfu' come down. 'Pride gangs before a fa',' the Scripture says. Ye'll no ca' that a lee; and I hear that Miss Menie's joe just heard it, and broke off in time."

"I'm like to be driven daft wi' ane and anither," exclaimed Jenny furiously. "If Miss Menie hadna been a thrawart creature hersel, I wouldna have had to listen to the like o' this. Na, that might have been a reason—but it was nane o' the siller; she kens best hersel what it was. I'm sure I wouldna hae cast away a bonnie lad like yon if it had been me; but the like o' her, a young leddy, behoves to hae her ain way."

"Weel, it's aye best to put a guid face on't," said Jenny's tormentor. "I'm no saying onything at my ain hand; it's a' Nelly's story, and Johnnie being to marry July Home—it's a grand marriage for auld Crofthill's daughter, sic a bit wee useless thing—we're the likest to ken. Ye needna take it ill, Jenny. I'm meaning nae reproach to you."

"I'm no canny when I'm angered," said Jenny, setting down her pail in the road; "ye'll gang your ways hame, if you take my counsel; there's naething for you here. Pity me for Kirklands parish, grit and sma'l wi' Nelly at the Brokenrig, and you at the Brigend; but I canna thole a lee—it makes my heart sick; and I tell ye I'm no canny when I'm angered. Guid night to you, Marget Panton; when I want to see you I'll send you word. You can wait here, if you maun get yon puir decent woman hame wi' you. I reckon I would get mony thanks if I set her free; but I dinna meddle wi' ither folk's business; you can wait for her here."

And, taking up her pail again rapidly, Jenny pattered away, leaving Marget somewhat astonished, standing in the middle of the road, where this energetic speech had been addressed to her. With many mutterings Jenny pursued her wrathful way.

"Ye've your ainsel to thank, no anither creature, Menie Laurie; and now this painting business is begun, they'll be waur and waur. Whatfor could she no have keepit in wi' him? A bonnie ane, to hae a' her ain way, and slaving and working a' day on her feet, as if Jenny was na worth the bread she eats; and the next thing I'll hear is sure to be that she's painting for siller. Pity me!"

Full of her afflictions, very petulant and resentful, Jenny entered the cottage door. It was a but and a ben—that is to say, it had two apartments, one on each side of the entrance. The larger of the two was boarded—Mrs Laurie had ventured to do this at her own expense—and had been furnished in an extremely moderate and simple fashion. It was a very humble room; but still it was a kind of parlour, and, with the ruddy fire-light reddening its further corners, and blinking on the uncovered window, it looked comfortable, and even cheerful, both from without and within. Mrs Laurie, with her never-failing work, sat by a little table; Menie, whose day's labour was done, bent over the fire, with her flushed cheeks supported in her hands; the conflict and the sullen glow had gone out of Menie's face, but a heavy cloud oppressed it still.

Conscious that she is an intruder, divided between her old habitual deference and her new sense of equality, as Johnnie Lithgow's mother, with any Mrs Laurie under the sun, Mrs Lithgow sits upon the edge of a chair, talking of Nelly, and Nelly's marriage.

"Nelly says you were real kind. I'm sure naething could be kinder than the like o' you taking notice o' her, when she was in a strange place her lane, though nae doubt, being Johnnie's sister made a great difference. I can scarcely believe my ainsel whiles, the awfu' odds it's made on me. I have naething ado but look out the best house in Kirklands, and I can get it bought for me, and an income regular, and nae need to do a thing, but be thankful to Providence and Johnnie. It's a great blessing a guid son."

As there was only a murmur of assent in answer to this, Mrs Lithgow proceeded:—

"I'm sure it's naething but neighbourlike—you'll no take it amiss, being in a kindly spirit—to say if there's onything ane can do.—There's Nelly gotten her ain house now, and wonderful weel off in the world; and for me, I'm just a miracle. If there was ought you wanted, no being used to a sma' house, or ony help in ae way or anither, from a day's darg wi' Jenny, to— —"

But Mrs Lithgow did not dare to go any further. The slight elevation of Mrs Laurie's head, the sudden erectness of that stooping figure by the fireside, warned the good woman in time; so, after a hurried breathless pause, she resumed:—

"I would be real glad—it would be naething but a pleasure; and I'll ne'er forget how guid you were to me when I was in trouble about Johnnie, and aye gied me hope. Puir laddie! next month he's coming down to be married—and I'm sure I hope he'll be weel off in a guid wife, for he canna but be a guid man, considering what a son he's been to me."

"He will be very well off," said Mrs Laurie; "and poor little July goes away next month, does she? Has Jenny come in yet, Menie? We have scarcely had time to settle in our new house, Mrs Lithgow; but I will remember your kind offer, and thank you. How dark the night grows—and it looks like snow."

"I'll have to be gaun my ways," said the visitor, rising; "it's a lanesome road, and I'm no heeding about leaving my house, and a' the grand new things Johnnie's sent me, their lane in the dark. I'll bid you good night, ladies, kindly, and I'm real blithe to see you in the countryside again."

She was gone, and the room fell into a sudden hush of silence, broken by nothing but the faint rustling of a moved hand, or the fall, now and then, of ashes on the hearth. The bustle and excitement of the "flitting" were over—the first pleasure of being home in their own country was past. Grey and calm their changed fate came down upon them, with no ideal softening of its everyday realities. This sliding panel here opens upon their bed; this little table serves all purposes of living; these four dim walls, and heavy raftered roof, shut in their existence. Now, through the clear frosty air without, a merry din breaks into the stillness. It is little Davie from the cot-house over the way, who has just escaped from the hands which were preparing him for rest, and dares brothers and sisters in a most willing race after him, their heavy shoes ringing upon the beaten way. Now, you hear them coming back again, leading the truant home, and by-and-by all the urchins are asleep, and the mother closes the ever-open door. So good night to life and human fellowship. Now—none within sight or hearing of us, save Jenny humming a broken song, on the other side of the wooden partition, which, sooth to say, is Jenny's bed—we are left alone.

Menie, bending, in her despondent attitude, over the fire, which throws down, now and then, these ashy flakes upon the hearth—our mother, pausing from her work, to bend her weary brow upon her hand. So very still, so chill and forsaken. Not one heart in all the world, except the three which beat under this thatched roof, to give anything but a passing thought to us or our fate; and nothing to look to but this even path, winding away over the desolate lands of poverty into the skies.

Into the skies!—woe for us, and our dreary human ways, if it were not for that blessed continual horizon line; so we do what we have not been used to do before—we read a sad devout chapter together, and have a faltering prayer; and then for silence and darkness and rest.

Say nothing to your child, good mother, of the bitter thoughts that crowd upon you, as you close your eyes upon the wavering fire-light, and listen, in this stillness, to all the stealthy steps and touches of the wakeful night. Say nothing to your mother, Menie, of the tears which steal down between your cheek and your pillow, as you turn your face to the wall. What might have been—what might have been; is it not possible to keep from thinking of that? for even Jenny mutters to herself, as she lies wakefully contemplating the glow of her gathered fire—mutters to herself, with an indignant fuff, and hard-drawn breath, "I wish her muckle pleasure of her will: she's gotten her will: and I wouldna say but she minds him now—a bonnie lad like yon!"

CHAPTER XXXI

Courage, Menie Laurie! Heaven does not send this breeze upon your cheek for nought—does not raise about you these glorious limits of hill and cloud in vain. Look through the distance—look steadily. Yes, it is the white gable of Crofthill looking down upon the countryside. Well, never veil your eyes—are you not at peace with them as with all the world?

Little Jessie here wearies where you have left her waiting, and trembles to move a finger lest she spoil the mysterious picture at which she glances furtively with awe and wonder. "The lady just looks at me," says little Jessie; "no a thing mair. Just looks, and puts it a' down like writing on a sclate." And Jessie cannot understand the magic which by-and-by brings out her own little bright sun-burnt face from that dull canvass which had not a line upon it when Jessie saw it first.

Come to your work, Menie Laurie; they make your heart faint these wistful looks and sighs. No one doubts it is very heavy—very heavy—this poor heart; no one doubts it is full of yearnings—full of anxious thought, and fears, and solitude. What then!—must we leave it to brood upon its trouble? Come to little Jessie here, and her picture—find out the very soul in these surprised sweet eyes—paint the loveliest little heart upon your canvass, fresh and fair out of the hands of God—such a face as will warm cold hearts, and teach them histories of joyous sacrifice—of love that knows no evil—of life that remembers self last and least of all. You said it first in bitterness and sore distress; but, nevertheless, it is true. You can do it, Menie. It is "the trade" to which you were born.

And with a long sigh of weariness Menie comes back. No, it is not a very fine picture; the execution is a woman's execution, very likely no great thing in the way your critics judge; but one can see how very like it is, looking at these little simple features—one could see it was still more like, looking in to the child's sweet generous heart.

"What were you crying for this morning, Jessie?"

A cloud came over the little face—a mighty inclination to cry again; but Jessie glanced at the picture once more, and swallowed down her grief, feeling herself a very guilty Jessie, as one great blob of a tear fell upon her arm.

"It wasna little Davie's blame—it was a' me." Poor little culprit, she dares not hang her head for terror of that picture. "He was paidling in the burn—and his new peeny gae a great screed, catching on the auld saugh-tree; but it wasna his blame—he's owre wee—it was a' mine for no looking after him. Just, I was awfu' busy; but that's nae excuse—and my mother gae Davie his licks, for a' I could say."

Another great tear; no one knows so well what an imp this said little Davie is—but Jessie sighs again. "It was a' me."

But it is not this little cloud of childish trouble that throws a something of pensive sadness into Jessie's pictured face. The face is the face before you; but the atmosphere, Menie Laurie, is in your own heart. Something sad—touched with that sweet pathos which lies on the surface of all great depths—and this true picture grows under Menie's hand to a heroic child.

It is a strange place for an artist to be. From this dark raftered threatening roof which catches your first glance, you look down to the mother by the fire with her unpretending look of gentlewoman—to the daughter's graceful head bending over her work—to pretty little Jessie here, with her flutter of extreme stillness, looking at the grey walls and sober thatch without. You would never think to surprise such a group within; and yet, when you look at them again, there is something of nobleness in the primitive cottage where these women have come to live independent and unpitied—come down in the world—very true; but it would be hard to presume upon the tenants of this wayside house.

You need not fear to enter, little July. Half-weeping, blushing, trembling, and with all these beseeching deprecations of yours, you may come in boldly at this narrow entrance. "It is no blame of hers, poor bairn," Mrs Laurie says, with a little sigh. No blame of hers nor of Randall's either, for Menie has kept her secret religiously, and will never tell to mortal ear what broke her engagement. Nelly Panton knows it, it is true; but Nelly, with the obtuse comprehension of a mercenary mind, thinks Randall broke off the match in consequence of Mrs Laurie's poverty, and knows of no more delicate difficulties behind. Come in, boldly, July Home—for no manner of interpretation could disclose to you the sudden pang which seizes Menie as she bends her head down for an instant, when she discovers you at the door. Now she says nothing, as she holds out her hand; but Menie is busy; it is only her left hand she extends to her friend; that in why she does not speak.

"I'm not to come out again," whispers July, sitting back into Mrs Laurie's shadow, and speaking under her breath. "I came here the very last place—and oh, Menie, will you come?"

The colour mounts high to Menie's temples; this means, will she come to July's marriage, which is to happen a week hence. Will she be there? Some one else will be there, the thought of whose coming makes Menie's heart beat strong and loud against her breast. But Menie only shakes her head in reply—shakes her head and says steadily, "No."

"You might come, for me. I never had a friend but you, and you've aye been good to me. Mrs Laurie, she might come?"

But Mrs Laurie too, after quite a different fashion, shakes her head with a look of regret—of only partial comprehension, but unmistakeable solicitude. "No," she says doubtfully; "I do not see how Menie could go;" but, as she speaks, she looks at Menie with an eager wish that she would.

Courage, Menie Laurie! If your hand falters, they will see it; if a single tear of all this unshed agony bursts forth, your mother's heart will be overwhelmed with pain and wonder—your little friend's with dismay. This is best—to look at the child and go on—though little Jessie has much ado to keep from weeping when she meets, with her startled face, the great gloom and darkness of Menie's eye.

"This is from Menie and me," said Mrs Laurie, taking out a pretty ring. "You are to wear it for our sake, July. Menie, can you put it on?"

Yes—Menie takes the little trembling hand within her own, and fits her mother's present to a slender finger—and no one knows how Menie presses her own delicate ankle under her chair, to keep herself steady by the pain. "You must try to be very happy, July," says Menie, with a faint smile, holding the hand a moment in her own; then she lets it drop, and turns to her work once more.

What can July do but cry? She does cry, poor little trembling heart, very abundantly, and would fain whisper a hundred hesitations and terrors into Menie's ear. But there is nothing of encouragement in Menie's face—so steady and grave, and calm as it looks. The little bride does not dare to pour forth her innocent confidences—but only whispers again, "I never had another friend but you, and you were aye so good to me;" and weeps a flood of half-joyful, half-despairing tears, out of her very heart.

CHAPTER XXXII

"No one can doubt that Randall is unhappy; but Randall is not a humble man, Mrs Laurie; he will not woo and plead and supplicate, I am afraid; he will honour only those who honour him, and never obtrude his love where he thinks there is no response. You know them both—could anything be done?"

Alas! good Johnnie Lithgow, we are all proud. This is not the wisest line of attack, in the circumstances. Mrs Laurie sits gravely by the fireside to listen. Mrs Laurie was Mrs Laurie before Randall Home was born. It is wonderful how she recollects this; and, recollecting, it is not difficult to see which of the two, in the opinion of Menie's mother, has the best right to stand on their dignity.

"I cannot advise," said Mrs Laurie somewhat coldly. "Menie has made no explanation to me. Mr Home has not addressed me at all on the subject. I am sorry I cannot suggest anything—especially when I have to take into consideration the lofty ideas of your friend."

It was a little bitter this. Lithgow felt himself chilled by it, and she saw it herself immediately; but Mrs Laurie said no word of atonement, till a sudden recollection of Menie's strangely altered and sobered fate broke upon her. Her countenance changed—her voice softened.

"I would be glad to do anything," she said, with a slight faltering. "To make Menie happy, I could accept any sacrifice. I will see—I will try. No," she continued, after a considerable pause, "I was right after all—your friend is what you call him. My Menie has a very high spirit, and in this matter is not to be controlled by me. They must be left to themselves—it is the wisest way."

Lithgow made no answer. Mrs Laurie sank into silence and thought. As they sat opposite to each other by the little fireplace, the young man's eye wandered over the room. His own birthplace and home was such another cottage as this; and Lithgow's mother, with her homely gown and check apron—her constant occupation about the house—her peasant tastes and looks and habits—was suitable and homogeneous to the earthen floor and rude hearth of the cottars' only room. But very strangely out of place was

Menie's easel—Menie's desk—Mrs Laurie's delicate basket of work—her easy-chair and covered table; strangely out of place, but not ungracefully—bearing, wherever they might be, a natural seemliness and fitness of their own. And if a rapid cloud of offence—a vapour of pride and resentment, might glide over Mrs Laurie's brow, it was never shaded by so much as a momentary shame. As undisturbed in her household dignity as at her most prosperous time, she received her visitor in the cot-house, nor ever dreamt she had cause to be ashamed of such an evidence of her diminished fortunes.

But Lithgow's thoughts were full of Randall; he was not willing to give up his attempt to reconcile them. "Randall is working very hard," said his generous fellow-craftsman. "I think his second success will lift him above all thought of hazard. He does his genius wrong by such unnecessary caution; he could not produce a commonplace thing if he would."

"And you, Mr Lithgow"—Mrs Laurie's heart warmed to him, plebeian though he was.

"I do my day's work," said the young man, happily, "thanking God that it is very sufficient for the needs of the day; but between Randall and myself there is no comparison. I deal with common topics, common manners, common events, like any other labouring man. But Randall is an artist of the loftiest class. What he does is for generations to come, no less than for to-day."

This enthusiasm threw a flush upon his face. As it receded, gradually fading from his forehead, a quick footstep went away from the cottage threshold. Menie Laurie had paused to listen whose the voice was before she entered, and, pausing, had heard all he had to say.

The happy golden purple of the sunset has melted from Criffel and his brother hills; but there is a pale light about all the east, whither Menie Laurie's face is turned as she leaves the cottage door. From her rapid step, you would fancy she was going somewhere. Where will she go? Nowhither, poor heart—only into the night a little—into the silence. It would not be possible to sit still in that noiseless house, by that lonely fireside, with such a tumult and commotion in this loud throbbing heart—forcing up its rapid cadence into the ears that thrill with sympathetic pulses—leaping to the very lips that grow so parched and faint. Oh! for the din of streets, of storms, the violence of crowds and noise of life—anything to drown this greater violence, these strong perpetual throbs that beat upon the brain like hailstones—anything to deaden this.

But all the air remains so still—so still; not a sound upon the silent road, but the heart and the footsteps, so rapid and irregular, which keep each other time. But by-and-by, as Menie goes upon her aimless way, another sound does break the silence—voices in the air—the sound of wheels and of a horse's feet. Listen, Menie—voices in the air!

But Menie will not listen—does not believe there are voices in the world which could wake her interest now—and so, unconsciously, looks up as this vehicle dashes past—looks up, to receive—what? The haughty salutation— uncovered brow and bending head, of Randall Home.

She would fain have caught at the hedge for a support; but he might look back and see her, and Menie hurried on. She had seen him; they had looked again into each other's eyes. "I never said I was indifferent," sobbed Menie to herself, and, in spite of herself, her voice took a shriller tone of passion—her tears came upon her in an agony. "I never said I was indifferent; it would have been a lie."

Hush!—be calm. It is safe to sit down by the roadside on this turf, which is unsullied by the dust of these passing wheels; safe to sit down and let the flood have vent, once and never more. And the soft whispering air comes stealing about Menie, with all its balmy gentle touches, like a troop of fairy comforters; and the darkness comes down with gracious speed to hide her as she crouches, with her head upon her hands, overcome and mastered;— once, and never more.

Now it is night. Yonder the lights are glimmering faintly in the cottage windows of the Brigend. Far away above the rest shines a little speck of light from the high window of Burnside, where once was Menie Laurie's chamber—her land of meditation, her sanctuary of dreams. The wind rustles among the firs—the ash-trees hold up their bare white arms towards the heavens, waiting till this sweet star, lingering at the entrance of their arch, shall lead her followers through, like children in their dance. And—hush!— suddenly, like a bird new awaked, the burn throws out its voice upon the air, something sad. The passion is overpast. Look up, Menie Laurie; you are not among strangers. The hills and the heavens stretch out arms to embrace you; the calm of this great night, God's minister, comes to your heart. Other thoughts—and noble ones—stretch out helping hands to you like angels. Rise up; many a hope remains in the world, though this one be gone for ever.

And Menie, rising, returns upon her way—away from Burnside, her old beloved home, and, going, questions with herself if aught is changed since she made the bitter and painful decision which in her heart she thought it right to make. Nothing is changed—the severance has been made—the shock is over. At first we knew it would be very hard; at first we thought of nothing but despair. We never took into our calculation the oft-returning memories—the stubborn love, that will not be slain at a blow; and this it is that has mastered mind, and heart, and resolution now.

There is no one else upon the road. The night, and the hills, and Menie Laurie, look up through the silence to heaven—and no one knows the conflict that is waging—none is here with human voice or hand to help the struggle. Fought and won—lie still in her religious breast, oh heart! Fittest way to win your quiet back again, Menie Laurie has laid you down—come good or evil, come peace or contest—laid you down once for all at the feet of God.

CHAPTER XXXIII

A brilliant company—the very newspapers would say so if they had note of it; distinguished people—except here and there a few who are only wives or sisters of somebody; the ladies and gentlemen present, individual by individual, are somebodies themselves. For a very pretty collection of Lions, as one could wish to see, is drawn together into Mr Editor Lithgow's drawing-room, to do honour to his wedding-day.

And you may wonder at first to hear such a moderate amount of roaring; Lions of the present day are not given to grandiloquence. If the truth must be told, the talk sounds somewhat professional, not unlike the regimental talk of soldier officers, and the ladies pertaining to the same. True, that a picturesque American, bolder than her compeers on this side the Atlantic, *poses* in one corner, and by-and-by makes a tableau, lying down in wild devotion at the feet of two respectable and somewhat scared good people—literary ladies of a modest standing, who have done just work enough to make their names known, but are by no means prepared for such homage as this. And for the rest of the company, it must be said that they sit or stand, lean back or lean forward, as propriety or common custom enjoin;—that there is a great talk of babies in that other corner, where the mistress of the house is surrounded by a band of matron friends;—and that there is in reality very little out of the common in this company, if it were not for the said professional talk.

The young mistress of the house! she talks pretty nearly as much now as other people talk—quite as much, indeed, when her heart is opened with that all-interesting subject, babies—or when her tongue has leisure to talk of the marvellous feats of certain babies of her own. July Home has been a married wife five years.

There is nothing very costly or rare in this drawing-room; but it is well-sized and well-furnished, notwithstanding, and a pretty apartment. Lithgow himself, not a very stately host, attends to his guests with an unassuming kindliness which charms these somewhat sophisticated people in spite of themselves; and Lithgow is full of the talk of the profession, and speaks great names with the confidence of friendship. In these five years, mother though she be, and mistress of a London household, all you can say of July is that she has grown a pretty girl—a little taller, a little more mature in action—but a girl, just as she was when we saw her last.

Being addressed, but of his own will scarcely speaking to any one, there is a remarkable-looking person among Mr Lithgow's guests. Looking up to his great height, you can just see some threads of white among his hair, though his age does not justify this, for he is a young man still; and a settled cloud upon his brow gives darkness to his face. It is not grief—it is not care; a gloomy self-absorbed pride is much more like what it is.

"That is Mrs Lithgow's brother," says another guest, in answer to the "who's that?" of an unaccustomed visitor. Mrs Lithgow's brother! Is this all the distinction that remains to the lofty Randall Home?

"And a literary man like all the rest of us," continues, condescendingly, this gentleman, who is a critic, and contemptuous in right of his craft. "He made a great success with his first publication six or seven years ago. I saw it on that table in the corner, covered with a pile of prints and drawings. They say Home cannot bear to see it now. Well; he lingered a long time polishing and elaborating, and retouching his second book, expecting, no doubt, a universal acclamation. Poor fellow! the public never so much as looked at it—it was a dead failure."

"Was it not equal to the first?" inquired breathlessly the original speaker, who in his heart was a warm adherent of Randall, though personally unknown to him, and who was a great deal better acquainted with the work in question than his informant.

"There was merit in the book," said the critic, poising a pretty paper-knife carelessly on his forefinger—"merit, such as it was; and Lithgow, here, gave him an article, and tried hard to get up a feeling; but he's a supercilious fellow, sir—proud as Lucifer; he is constantly running against somebody, and we put him down."

The critic turned to speak to another critic on his other hand; the interrogator stood aside. Solitary in the midst of this animated company—dark, where all was glowing with a modest brilliancy—it was not wonderful that this good man should inquire of himself whether there was nought of the evil thing called affectation in the gloom and pride of Randall Home. One thing at least it was not difficult to see—that Randall knew people were looking at him—wondering about him—and that more than one lady of sentiment and enthusiasm had marvelled already, with wistful melancholy, whether any one knew what the grief was which had blighted the young author's life.

The young author's life was not blighted. On him, like a nightmare, sat a subtle spirit, self-questioning, self-criticising. He was disappointed;—a bitter stream had come into his way, and by its side he walked, his eyes bent downward on it, pondering the evils of his fate, trying with a cold philosophy to believe them no evils, assuming to despise them, yet resenting them with bitterness in his own secret heart.

"Randall, look at this; it minds me of home," said his sister in his ear. He took mechanically what she put into his hand—carelessly: not the slightest interest in *his* face for poor July's enthusiasm—as like as not he would smile and put it down with a careless glance. Things that other people look on with interest were matters of chilled and disappointed indifference to Randall Home.

Yet he looks at this child's face that has been brought before him; insensibly a smile breaks upon his lips in answer to this sweet child's smile. He, who is a critic, knows it is no *chef-d'œuvre*, and has little claim to be looked upon as high art; but for once Randall thinks nothing of the execution—as on a real countenance he gazes upon this. These sweet little features seem to move before him with the throng of gracious childlike thoughts that hover over the unclouded brow—childlike thoughts—thoughts of the great eternal simplicities which come nearest to angels and to children. This man, through his intricacies and glooms, catches for an instant a real glimpse of what that atmosphere must be through which simple hearts look up into the undoubted heavens; for scarcely so much as a summer cloud can float between this child and the sky.

Come this way, Randall. Here is a little room, vacant, half-lighted, where lie other things akin to this. Take them up after your careless fashion. What message can they have to you? Be ready, if you can, to put them aside with a word of bitter criticism—only leave out this child's portrait. Say with your lips it is good and you like it; feel in your heart as if it spoke to you long, loving, simple speeches; and when you turn from it—hush! it is irreverent—do not try with either sarcasm or jest to cheat this sudden desolateness which you feel at your heart.

A cloudy face—is this no portrait? The wind is tossing back wildly the curls from its white high brow, and out of a heavy thunder-cloud it looks down darkly, doubtfully, with a look which you cannot fathom. Uneasily the spectator lays it aside to lift another—another and another; they are very varied, but his keen eye perceives in a moment that every face among them which is a man's bears the same features. Other heads of children unknown to Randall—pictures of peasant women, real and individual, diversify the little collection; but where the artist has made a man's face, everywhere a subtle visionary resemblance runs through each and all. Through altered features the same expression—through changed moods and tempers the same sole face. The room swims about him as he looks—is it a dream or a vision—what does it mean?

The long white curtains faintly stir in the autumn night-wind which steals in through the open window; the shaded lamp upon the table throws down a little circle of light—a larger circle of shadow—upon these pictures, and faintly shines in the mirror above the vacant hearth. He has sunk on one knee to look at them again. What memory is it that has kept this face, what sad recollection has preserved its looks and changes so faithfully and so long? No ideal, noble, and glorious, such as a heart might make for itself—no human idol either, arrayed in the purple and gold of loving homage—and the heart of Randall, startled and dismayed, hides its face and beholds itself for the first time truly. He knows that none of these is meant for him—feels with certain confidence that reproach upon him is the last thing intended by this often portraiture; yet stands aside, and marvels, with a pang—a great throb of anguish and hope—to see himself, changed in habit and in aspect, with years added, and with years taken away; but he feels in every one that the face is his own.

Love that thinks you loftiest, noblest—love that worships in you its type of grace and high perfection, its embodiment of dreams and longings—rejoice in it, oh youth! But if you ever come to know a love that is disenchanted—a love that with its clear and anxious sight has found you out and read your heart—knowing not the highest part alone, but, in so far as human creature can, *all* that is written there—yet still is love; if you rejoice no longer, pause at least, and tremble. Light is the blind love of the old poets—frail, and in constant peril. Heaven help those to whom is given the love that sees as nothing else can see—It struck to the heart of Randall Home.

Through secrets of his being, which himself had never guessed, this lightened eye had pierced like a sunbeam. Unwitting of its insight, nought could it say in words of its discovery, but unconsciously they came to light under the artist-hand. Menie Laurie—Menie Laurie!—little you wist when your pencil touched so dreamily these faces, which were but so many shadows of one face in your heart—little you wist how strange a revelation they would carry to another soul.

"Something has happened to Randall—he will not hear me," said July to her husband when the guests went away. "He makes me no answer—he never hears me speak, but stands yonder steadfast at the mirror, looking in his own face."

CHAPTER XXXIV

The sun has struck on Criffel's sullen shoulder. Look you how it besets him, with a glorious burst of laughter and triumph over his gloom. And now a clown no longer, but some grand shepherd baron, he draws his purple cloak about him, and lifts his cloudy head into the sky. Marshal your men-at-arms, Warder of the Border! Keep your profound unbroken watch upon the liege valleys and homes at your feet—for the sun is setting in a stormy glory, and the winds are gathering wild in their battalions in the hollows of the hills.

Travelling with his face towards the east, is one wayfarer on this lonely road. He knows the way, but it is long to his unaccustomed feet; and he is like to be benighted, whatever speed he makes. The sky before him is cold and clear, the sky of an autumn night, gleaming itself with an intense pale lustre, while great mountain-heaps of clouds, flung upon it, stand out round and full against its glittering chilly light; and with a wild rush the wind comes down upon the trees, seizing them in a sudden convulsion. The road ascends a little, and looks from this point as if it went abruptly into the skies; and on either side lies the low breadth of a peat-moss, on which it is too dark now to distinguish the purple patches of heather, or anything but the moorland burn and deep drain full of black clear water, from which is thrown back again, in long flying glimmers of reflection, the pale light of the sky.

There is not a house in sight. Here and there a doddered oak or thorn, or stunted willows trailing their branches into the pools, give a kind of edge, interrupted and broken, to the moorland road; and now and then on a little homely bridge—one arch of stone, or it may be only two or three planks—it crosses a burn. With every gust of wind a shower of leaves comes rustling down from the occasional trees we pass, and the same cold breath persuades this traveller very soon to regret that his breast is not guarded by the natural defence—the grey plaid of the Border hills.

He does not lift his foot high and cumbrously from the ground, as the men of this quarter, used to wading through the moss and heather, are wont to do; nor does he oppose to this wild wind the broad expanded chest and weather-beaten face of rural strength; but he knows the way along which he walks so smartly—pauses now and then to recognise some ancient landmark—and pushes forward without hesitation, very well aware where he is going to, nor fearing to choose that shorter way across the moss, like one to the manner born.

A narrower path, broken in upon here and there by young sapling trees, self-sown willows, and bushes, which are scattered over all the moss. Suddenly—it may be but a parcel of stones, a little heap of peats—but there is something on the edge of the way.

Going forward, the traveller finds seated on the fallen trunk of a tree two children—a little girl drawing in to her side the uncovered flaxen head of a still younger boy, and holding him firmly with her arm. The little fellow, with open mouth and close shut eyes, is fast asleep, and his young guardian's head droops on her breast. You can see she watched long before she yielded to it; but she too has dropped asleep.

The traveller, touched with sudden interest, pauses and looks down upon them. Indistinctly, in her sleep, hearing his step, or conscious of the human eye upon her which breaks repose, the little girl moves uneasily, tightens the firm pressure of her arm, murmurs something—of which the spectator, stooping down, can hear only "little Davie"—and then, throwing back her head and changing her attitude, settles again into her profound child's sleep.

What arrests him that he does not wake her? What makes him pause so long after his previous haste? Yes, look closer—stoop down upon the damp and springy soil—bend your knee. The pale faint light has not deceived you, neither has the memory which holds with unwonted tenacity the likeness of this face—for this is indeed the original. Sweet in its depth of slumber, its lips half-closed, its eye-lash warm upon its cheek, the same sweet heart you saw in London in the picture—the very child.

Eleven years old is Jessie now; and to keep little Davie out of mischief is a harder task than ever. So helpless, yet in such an attitude of guardianship and protection, the traveller's eyes, in spite of himself, fill with tears. He is almost loth to wake her, but the wind rushes with growing violence among the cowering trees.

He touches her shoulder—she does not know how gently—as suddenly she starts up broad awake. One terrified look Jessie gives him—another at the wild sky and dreary moor. "You're no to meddle wi' Davie; it's a' my blame," said Jessie with one frightened sob; "and oh, it's dark night, and we'll never win hame!"

"How did you come here?" said the stranger, gently. Jessie was reassured; she dried her eyes, and began to look up at him with a little returning confidence.

"I dinna ken; it was Davie would rin—no, it was me that never cam the road before—and we got on to the moss. Oh, will you tell me the airt I'm to gang hame?"

He put his hand upon the child's head kindly. This was not much like Randall Home. The Randall of old days, if he never failed to help, scarcely ever knew himself awakened to interest. There was a great delight of novelty in this new spring opened in his heart.

"Were you not afraid to fall asleep?"

Poor little Jessie began to cry; she thought she had done wrong. "I couldna keep wakin. I tried as lang as I could, and then I thocht I would just ask God to take care o' Davie, and then there would be nae fear. That was the way I fell asleep."

A philosopher! But how have these tears found their way to his face? Somehow he cannot look on this little speaker—cannot perceive her small brother laying his cheek upon her breast, without a new emotion which ought to have no place in the mind of an observing moralist whose thought is of cause and effect. Again he lays his hand upon her head—so kindly that Jessie looks up with a shy smile—and says, "You are used to say your prayers?"

"I aye do't every night." Jessie looks up again wistfully, wondering with a sudden pity. Can it be possible that he does not say his prayers, gentleman though he be!

"Say them here, little girl—I would like to hear your prayers"—and his own voice sounds reverent, low, as one who feels a great presence near.

But Jessie falters and cries—does not know what to answer, though it is very hard to contend against the impulse of instant obedience. "Oh! I dinna like—I canna say them out-by to a man," she says in great trouble, clasping and unclasping her hands. "I just mind a'body, and little Davie—and give my soul to Christ to keep," added the little girl solemnly, "for fear I shouldna wake the morn."

There is a little silence. She thinks this kindly stranger is angry with her, and cries; but it is only a something of strong unusual emotion, which he must swallow down.

"Now, you must wake up little Davie, and I will take you home. Is it far? You do not know, poor little guardian. Come away—it is near Brigend?

Well, we will manage to get there. Come, little fellow, rouse up and give me your hand."

But Davie, very wroth at such a sudden interruption of his repose, shook his little brown clenched hand in the stranger's face instead, and would hold by no other but his sister. So in this order they went on, Jessie, with much awe, permitting her hand to be held in Randall's, and sleepy Davie dragging her back at the other side. They went on at a very different pace from Randall's former rate of walking—threading their encumbered way with great difficulty through the moorland path—but by-and-by, to the general comfort, emerged once more upon the high-road, and near the cheerful light from a cottage door.

And here he would pause to ask for some refreshment for the lost children, but does not fail to glance in first at the cottage window. This woman sitting before the fire has a face he knows, and she is rolling up a heavy white-faced baby, and moving with a kind of monotonous rock back and forward upon her seat. But there is not a murmur of the mother-song—instead, she is slowly winding up to extremest aggravation a little girl in a short-gown and apron, who stands behind her in a flood of tears, and whose present state of mind suggests no comfort to her, but to break all the "pigs" (*Anglicè* crockery) in the house and run away.

"Will I take in twa bairns?—what would I do wi' twa bairns? I've enow o' my ain; but folk just think they can use ony freedom wi' me," said the woman, in answer to Randall's appeal made from the door. "I'm sure Peter's pack might be a laird's lands for what folk expect; and because there's nae ither cause o' quarrelling wi' a peaceable woman like me, I maun aye be askit to do things I canna do. It's nane o' my blame they didna get their denner. Lad, you had best take them hame."

"I will pay for anything you give them cheerfully; but the little creatures are exhausted," said Randall again from the door. He thought he had altered a good deal his natural voice.

The woman suddenly raised her head. "I'm saying, that's a tongue I ken," she said in an undertone. "This is nae public to gie meat for siller, lad," she continued; "but they may get a bit barley scone and a drink o' milk—I've nae objections. Ye'll no belang to this country yoursel?" For with a rapidity very unusual to her, she had suddenly deposited her gaping baby in the cradle, and now stood at the door. Randall kept without in the darkness. The lost children were admitted to the fire.

"No."

"I wouldna say but you're out o' London, by your tongue. I've been there mysel before I was married, biding wi' a brother o' mine that's real weel-off and comfortable there. I've never been up again, for he's married, and her and me disna gree that weel. It's an awfu' world—a peaceable person has nae chance—and I was aye kent for that, married and single. Ye'll ha heard o' my man, Peter Drumlie, if you come out o' Cumberland; but I reckon you're frae London, by your tongue."

With a bow, and a sarcastic compliment to her discrimination, Randall answered her question; but the bow and the sarcasm were lost upon the person he addressed: she went on in her dull tone without a pause.

"Ay, I aye was kent for discrimination," she said with modest self-approval, "though it's no everybody has the sense to allow't. But you'll hae come to see your friends, I reckon—they'll be biding about this pairt?"

"Just so," said Randall.

"Ye'll ken mony a change in the countryside," continued the woman. "There's the auld minister dead in Kirklands parish, and a' the family scattered, and a delicate lad, a stranger, in the Manse his lane; and maister and mistress gane out o' Kirklands House, away some gate in foreign pairts; and Walter Wellwood, the young laird, he's married upon a grand lady and joined to the Papishes; and—but ye'll maybe ken better about the common folk o' the parish. There's auld Crofthill and Miss Janet their lee lane up the brae yonder, and ne'er a word frae Randy—maybe you would ken Randy?—the awfullest lad for thinking o' himsel; and then there's the family at Burnside—they're come down in the world, wi' a' their pride and their vanity—living in naething but a cot-house on the siller Jenny makes wi' her kye; and Miss Menie, she makes pictures and takes folk's likenesses, and does what she can to keep hersel. Eh, man, there's awfu' changes!—And wee July Home, Crofthill's daughter, she's married upon our Johnnie, keepit like a leddy, and never has a hand's turn laid to her, wet day or dry—it's a grand marriage for the like o' her;—and there's mysel—I was ance Nelly Panton, till I got my man—but I've nae occasion to do a thing now but keep the house gaun, and mind the siller—for Peter, he's a man o' sense, and kens the value o' a guid wife—and I live real comfortable among my ain folk in a peaceable way, as I was aye disposed—though they're an ill set the folk hereaway—they're aye bickering amang themsels. Will you no come in-by and rest?"

Randall, who felt his philosophy abandon him in this respect as well as others, and who could not persuade himself by any arguments of her insignificance to quench the passion which this slow stream of malicious disparagement raised within him, answered very hotly, and with great abruptness, that he could not wait longer. A moment after he found himself again upon the road, with the reluctant children dragging him back, and Nelly looking out after him from her door. He had time to be annoyed at himself for betraying his anger; but Randall began to have changed thoughts—began to lose respect for the self-constraint which once had been his highest form of dignity—began to think that no natural emotion was unworthy of him—of *him*. For the first time he laughed at the words with bitterness as he looked up to the pale gleaming sky, with its clouds and stars. Unworthy of him—who then was he?

CHAPTER XXXV

"The man's right—they'll hae strayed in on the moss. Oh, my bairns! my bairns!" cried the distressed mother into the night. "And Patie was telling, nae farther gane than yestreen, what a bogilly bit it was, till a' the weans were fleyed; and if they're no sunk in the moss itsel, they'll be dead wi' fright by this time. Oh, my bonnie Jessy! that was aye doing somebody a guid turn; and wee Davie—puir wee Davie! he was aye the youngest, and got his ain way. My bairns! my bairns!"

A snort came through the misty gloom. By this time it was very dark, and Randall could hear the voices as they approached.

"What's the woman greeting for? Her bairns?—her bairns? I would just like to ken what suld ail her bairns—little mischiefs! They're warm at somebody's ingle-neuk, Ise warrant. That wee Davie's an imp o' Satan; neither fright nor bogles will harm him. Come this road, woman. What gart ye leave the lantern? If there werena better wits than yours"—

Jenny's voice was interrupted by a sudden footstep crushing the bramble branches on the side of the way, and by a sudden glow of light thrown full upon the dazzled eyes of little Jessie, who left Randall's hand with a cry of joy—"Oh, it's the leddy—we're safe at hame."

The lantern flashed about through the darkness. Randall's heart beat loudly. With a great start he recognised the voice which gave kindly welcome to the strayed child, and he could distinguish the outline of her figure, as she shaded the lantern with her hand; then she raised it—he felt the light suddenly burst upon his face—another moment, and it was gone. Little Jessie flew back to him dismayed; voice and figure and light had disappeared as they came; one other step upon the brambles, and they were alone once more.

He had no time to marvel or to follow, for now the mother and Jenny, suddenly drawing close to them, fell upon the lost children, with cried of mingled blame and joy. "It was the gentleman brought us hame."

"Thanks to the gentleman—would he no come in and rest?—he would be far out o' his way—the guidman would take a lantern, and convoy him"—and a hundred other anxious volunteerings of gratitude poured upon Randall's ears. "I must go on—I must go on!" He burst past them impatiently; he did not know where the house was, or if she had gone home; but Menie had seen him, and Menie he must see.

Step softly, Randall! In her high excitement, she hears every stir of the falling leaves without, and could not miss your footstep, if you trod as softly as a child. She has reached to her shelter already—she has put out her mother's lights, and stands in the darkness, pressing her white face against the window, looking out, wondering if she will see you again—wondering why you come here—praying in a whisper that you may not cross her path any more, but contradicting the prayer in her heart. Mrs Laurie stands by the door without, watching for the children's return; and now they come, Davie lifted into his mother's arms (for he has been almost asleep on his feet), Jessie eager that everybody should understand "it was my blame," and Jenny smartly lecturing each and all. The rest of the family—all but the goodman, who has gone to the moss to seek the children—are gathered in a group before the cottage; and the red light of the fire glows out upon them, and some one has picked up the lantern which Menie Laurie dropped. A little crowd—the inner circle of faces brightened by the lamp, the outer ones receding into partial gloom, hearing little Jessie tell her story, speculating what part of the moss it could be, and "where was the gentleman?"—a question which none could answer.

"Though I've heard his tongue afore, mysel," said Jenny, "I'm just as sure—woman, will ye no take that little Satan to his bed?—and puir wee Jessie's een's gaun thegither. It wasna your blame, you deceitful monkey! Ye may cheat the wife there, but ye'll no cheat Jenny. It was a' that little bother—it wasna you. Gang out o' my gate, callant! If nane o' the rest o' ye will stir, I maun pit the bairn to her bed mysel."

From her window Menie Laurie looks out upon this scene—upon the darkness around—the one spot of light, and the half-illuminated faces; looks out wistfully, straining her eyes into the night, wondering where he has gone, and getting time now, as her agitation calms, to be ashamed and annoyed at her own weakness. Very calm for many a day has been Menie Laurie's quiet heart—soberly, happily contented, and at rest. Little comforts and elegancies, which neither Mrs. Laurie's income nor Jenny's kye could attain, Menie has managed to collect into this little room. Her "trade," as she still calls it—for Menie is the person of all others least satisfied with her own performances, and will not assume to be an artist—has brought her in contact with many pleasant people; her mother is pleased that they have even better "society" here, in the cot-house, than they had in prosperous Burnside; and it even seems a thing probable, and to be hoped for, that by-and-by they may go back to Burnside, and be able to live without its fifty yearly pounds. This success could not come without bringing some content and satisfaction with it; and constant occupation has restored health and ease to Menie's mind; while almost as calm as of old, but with a deeper, loftier quiet, a womanly repose—light, within her eased breast, has lain Menie Laurie's heart.

And why this face of strange excitement now, Menie cannot tell. She found him out so suddenly—flashing her light upon the face which least of all she thought to see. But Menie wonders to feel this strong thrill of agitation returning on her as she touches the window with her pale cheek, and wonders if she will see him again.

The night falls deeper—darker; the wind over-head comes shouting down upon the trees, throwing their leaves from them in wild handfuls, and tearing off their feebler branches in a frenzy. Here where we stand, you can hear it going forth with its cry of defiance against the hills, flinging a magic circle round the startled homesteads, attacking bridges upon rivers, stacks in farmyards. The goodman, who has returned with a glad heart to find his children safe, says, when he closes the cottage door, that it is a wild night; but here, amid all its violence, waiting a moment when he may see her—strangely excited, strangely emancipated, owning the sway of one most passionate and simple emotion, and for the first time forgetting, not only himself, but everything else—here, with his bare forehead to the wind, stands Randall Home.

Now come hither: Jenny's candle in the kitchen thriftily extinguished, leaving her window only lightened by the firelight, proves that Jenny has come "ben" to the family service—the daily meeting-ground of mistress and servant, child and mother. There is no need to close the shutters on this window, which no one ever passes by to see. Calm in her fireside corner sits Mrs Laurie, with her open Bible in her lap; Jenny is close by the table, drawing near the light, and poring very closely upon the "sma' prent," which runs into a confused medley before her, not to be deciphered—for Jenny will not be persuaded to try spectacles, lest they should "spoil her een;" while Menie, who reads the chapter aloud, reverently turns over the leaves of the family Bible, and, with all her quiet restored, speaks the words which say peace to other storms than that storm never to be forgotten, in the Galilean Sea.

You remember how she was when you saw her last—you remember her through the flash of your own anger, the mortification of your own pride—but pride and mortification have little to do with this atmosphere which surrounds our Menie now. Her delicate hand is on the open Book— her reverent eyes cast down upon it—her figure rising out of its old girlish freedom and carelessness, into a womanly calm and dignity. He follows the motion of her head and lips with an unconscious eager gesture—follows them with devotion, longing to feel himself engaged with her; and hears, his frame quivering the while—rising upon his heart with a command, that hushes all these violent strong voices round—the low sound of *her* voice.

Now they are at prayer. Her face is folded in her hands, Randall; and there may be a prayer in Menie's heart, which Mrs Laurie's voice, always timid at this time, does not say. Whatever there is in Menie's heart, you know what is in your own—know at once this flood of sudden yearning, this sudden passion of hope and purpose, this sudden burst of womanish tears. Now then, over-mastered, subdued, and won, turn away, Randall Home—but not till Jenny, starting from her knees, has burst into a violent sob and scream. "I dreamt he was come back this very night; I dreamt o' him yestreen—Randall—Randall Home!" But with an awed face, Jenny returned from the door to which she had flown. Randall was not there!

CHAPTER XXXVI

Something of languor is in this chill morning, as its quiet footstep steals upon the path of the exhausted storm—something worn out and heavy are Menie's eyes, as she closes them, wearily upon the daylight when Jenny has cleared the little breakfast-table, and it is time for the day's work to begin. They speak to her softly, you will perceive, and are very tender of Menie, as if she were ill, and Jenny cannot forgive herself for the shock that her exclamation caused last night.

A heavy stupor is on Menie's mind, lightened only with gleams of wild anxiety, with fruitless self-questionings, which she fain would restrain, but cannot. Jenny, firm in the belief that she has seen a spirit, is melancholy and mysterious, and asks suggestive questions—whether they have heard if there is "ony great trouble in London 'enow," or who it was that was prayed for in the kirk last Sabbath—a young man in great distress. Mrs Laurie, uneasy and solicitous, cannot stay these pitiful looks which unawares she turns upon her daughter, and hangs perpetually about her with tender touches, consoling words, and smiles, till poor Menie's heart is like to break.

The day's work is over in Jenny's "redd-up kitchen;"—the uneven earthen floor is carefully swept—the hearth as white and the fireside as brilliant as Jenny's elaborate care can make them; and Jenny has drawn aside a little the sliding panel which closes in her bed, to show the light patch-work quilt, and snowy linen of the "owrelay." Bright brass and pewter carefully polished above the high mantelshelf—bright plates and crockery against the walls—with a glance of satisfaction Jenny surveyed the whole as she passed into the private corner where she made her toilette—a "wiselike" kitchen; it was worthy of Jenny.

And now, in her blue and yellow gown, in her black and red checked plaiden shawl, in her great Leghorn bonnet, fashioned in antique times, Jenny sets out from the cottage door. No one knows where Jenny is going, and there has been some surprise "ben the house" at her intimation of her proposed absence. But Jenny keeps her own counsel, and walks away soberly, seeing Mrs Laurie at the window, in the direction of Burnside. "Nae occasion to let the haill town see the gate Jenny was gaun," she says to herself, with a slight fuff; and, altering her course before she reaches the Brigend, Jenny turns rapidly towards the hills.

And something of growing gravity, almost awe, is on Jenny's face. "Eh, puir callant, he's young to take fareweel o' this life. Weel, laddie, mony's the time Jenny's grutten for ye; and maybe it's best, after a', if ane could but think sae." These lamentations fall like so many tears on Jenny's way—and she is rapidly climbing the brae, as she utters them, towards the house of Crofthill.

It is a wintery autumn afternoon—so dull, that the potato-gatherers in the fields are chilled into silence, and the ploughmen scarcely can whistle into the heavy atmosphere, which droops upon them laden with unfallen rain. The paths of the little triangular garden of Crofthill are choked with masses of brown leaves, fallen from the trees, which sway their thin remaining foliage drearily, hanging lank from the crest of the hill. The goodman is thrashing to-day; you can hear the heavy tramp of the horses, the swing of the primitive machine; it is almost the only sound that breaks the silence of the place.

Nay, listen—there is another sound; a slow monotonous voice, wont to excite in Jenny certain sentiments the reverse of peaceable. The kitchen door is open, a great umbrella rests against the lintel, and Miss Janet's tall figure is just visible in a gown not much unlike Jenny's own, standing before the fire listening, as Jenny, arrested at the threshold, must be content to listen too.

"Na; I can do nae mair than tell what's true; I canna gie folk the judgment to put trust in me. I'm no ane that meddles wi' ither folk's concerns—but I thocht it right ye should ken—I'm no saying whether it's in the flesh or the spirit—that Randall Home was seen upon the Kirklands road last night."

"But I tell ye, woman, it couldna be our Randy—it couldna be my bairn," exclaimed Miss Janet in great distress. "Do you think Crofthill's son would ca' upon the like o' you, and no come hame? It's been some English lad, that's spoken grand, like Randall; and how was you to ken to look at his presence, that never ane had like him? Na, it wasna our son."

"Presence or no presence, I mind him weel," said Nelly, emphatically. "I wouldna think, mysel, an appearance or a wraith could hae grippit thae weans, and kent the road sae weel to carry them hame—no to say that spirits would hae little patience, as I think, wi' barley scones, when they canna partake themsels; and I tried him about the Burnside family, and Crofthill as weel; and I saw his een louping wi' passion and he scarce gae me thanks for my charity. It's an awfu' thing to see as I do ilka day—and I canna think but what it's just because I'm sae peaceable mysel that a'body flees into raptures wi' me. But I just ken this—I saw Randall Home."

Miss Janet turned round to wring her hands unseen. She was very much troubled and shaken, and turning, met, to her dismay, the keen inquisitive face of Jenny. With a little start and cry, Miss Janet turned again to dash some tears off her cheek. Then she addressed the new-comer in a trembling voice. "Ye'll have heard her story—your house is on the same road—have ye seen anything like this?"

"I wouldna put a moment's faith in her—no me!" said Jenny, promptly. "It's a dull day to her when she disna put somebody in trouble; and its just because there's no a single mischief to the fore in Kirklands that she's come to put her malice on you. Put strife amang neibors, woman—naebody can do't sae weel; but what would ye come here for to frighten honest folk in their ain houses?"

"For every friendly word I say, I aye get twa ill words back," said Nelly meekly, with a sigh of injury. "But it's weel kent the spirit that's in Burnside Jenny, and I wouldna take notice, for my pairt, o' what the like o' her might say; but I canna help aye being concerned for what happens to Crofthill, minding the connection; and if I didna see Randall Home's face, and hear Randall Home's tongue, in the dark at my ain door yestreen I never saw mortal man. If he's in the flesh, I wouldna say but he was hiding for some ill-doing—for you may be sure he didna want me to see his face, kenning me for far sight langsyne; and if it was an appearance, I'll no gie you muckle hope o' his state, for the awsome passion he got in, though he never said a word to me; and, as I said before, I can tell you what's true, but I canna gie ye faith to believe—sae I'll bid ye guid-day, Miss Janet; and ye'll just see if ye dinna think mair o' what I've said, afore you're a day aulder—you and the auld man too."

Slowly Nelly took her departure, Miss Janet looking on like one stupefied. As the unwelcome visitor disappeared, Miss Janet sank into a chair, and again wrung her hands; but looking up with sudden fright to perceive Jenny's elaborate dress, and look of mystery, hastily exclaimed, "Jenny, woman—it's no but what you're aye welcome,—but what's brought you here the day?"

"I cam o' my ain will; naebody kens," said Jenny abruptly.

"But ye maun have come wi' an errand—I'm no feared to greet before you, Jenny," said Miss Janet, with humility. "Oh, woman, tell me—do you ken anything o' my bairn?"

"Me! what should I ken?" said Jenny, turning her face away. "You'll have gotten word? Nae doubt, being grand at the writing, he aye sends letters. What gars ye ask the like o' me?"

Miss Janet caught her visitor's hand, and turned her face towards the light with a terrified cry, "You may tell me—I ken ye've seen him as weel."

Jenny resisted for some time, keeping her head averted. At length, when she could struggle no longer, she fell into a little burst of sobbing. "I never would have telled ye. I didna come to make you desolate—but I canna tell a lee. I saw him in the dark last night, just ae moment, glancing in at the window—and when I gaed to the door, he was gane."

Half an hour after, very drearily Jenny took her way down the hill—and looking back as the early twilight began to darken on her path, she saw Miss Janet's wistful face commanding the way. The twilight came down heavily—the clouds dipt upon the hill—drizzling rains began to fall, carrying down with them light dropping showers of half-detached and dying leaves—but still Miss Janet leaned upon the dyke, and turned her anxious eyes to the hilly footpath, watching, with many a sob and shiver, for Randall—in the flesh or in the spirit. Surely, if he revealed himself to strangers, he might come to her.

CHAPTER XXXVII

After this there fell some very still and quiet days upon Mrs Laurie's cottage. Every thing went on languidly; there was no heart to the work which Menie touched with dreamy fingers; there was something subdued and spiritless in her mother's looks and movements; and even Jenny's foot rang less briskly upon her earthen floor. They did not know what ailed them, nor what it was they looked for; but with a brooding stillness of expectation, they waited for something, if it were tempest, earthquake, or only a new glow of sunshine out of the kindly skies.

Was it a spirit? Asking so often, you make your cheek pale, Menie Laurie; you make your eyelids droop heavy and leaden over your dim eyes. Few people come here to break the solitude, and we all dwell with our own thoughts, through these still days, alone.

"Menie, you are injuring yourself; we will take a long walk, and see some people to-day," said Mrs Laurie. "Come, it is quite mild—it will do us both good; we will go to the manse to see Miss Johnston, and then to Woodlands and Burnside. Put up your papers—we will take a holiday to-day."

Menie's heavy eyes said faintly that she cared nothing about Miss Johnston, about Woodlands or Burnside; but Menie put aside her papers slowly, and prepared for the walk. They went out together, not saying much, though each sought out, with labour and difficulty, something to say. "I wonder what ails us?" said Menie, with a sigh. Her mother made no answer. It was not easy to tell; and speaking of it would do more harm than good.

A hazy day—the sky one faint unvaried colour, enveloped in a uniform livery of cloud; a faint white mist spread upon the hills; small invisible rain in the air, and the withered leaves heavily falling down upon the sodden soil.

"This will not raise our spirits, mother," said Menie, with a faint smile; "better within doors, and at work, on a day like this."

But why, with such a start and tremble, do you hear those steps upon the path? Why be struck with such wild curiosity about them, although you would not turn your head for a king's ransom? Anybody may be coming—the shepherd's wife from Whinnyrig yonder, the poor crofter from the edge of the peat-moss, or little Jessie's mother bound for the universal rural shop at the Brigend. We are drawing near to the Brigend—already the aromatic flavour of the peats warms the chill air with word of household fires, and we see smoke rise beyond the ash trees—the smoke of our old family home, the kind hearth of Burnside.

Hush! whether it were hope or fear, is no matter; the steps have ceased; vain this breathless listening to hear them again; go on through the ash trees, Menie Laurie—on through the simple gateway of this humble rural world. By the fireside—in the cottage—with such simple joy as friendly words and voices of children can give you—this is your life.

And only one—only one—this your mother—to watch your looks and gestures—the falling and the rising of your tired heart. Wistful eyes she turns upon you—tender cares. Look up to repay her, Menie; smile for her comfort; you are all that remains to her, and she is all that remains to you.

Look up; see how solemnly the ash trees lift their old bleached arms to heaven. Look up, Menie Laurie; but here, at our very ear, these bewildering steps again!

Do not shrink; here has come the ordeal you have looked for many a day. Well said your prophetic heart, that it drew near in the hush and silence of this fated time. They stand there, arched and canopied, under these familiar trees, the hamlet's quiet houses receding behind them—Burnside yonder, the limit of the scene, and the burn, the kindly country voice, singing a quiet measure to keep them calm. An old man and a young, learned with experiences of life: the elder, fresh and noble, daring to meet the world with open face, aware of all the greatest truths and mysteries of the wonderful existence which we call common life, but nothing more; the younger trained in a more painful school, with his lesson of self-forgetting newly conned, with knowledge sadder than his father's, with a heart and conscience quivering still with self-inflicted wounds—they stand there bareheaded under the cloudy sky—not with the salutation of common respect, which might permit them to pass on. A courtly natural grace about them both, makes their attitude all the more remarkable. With blanched cheeks and failing eyes, Menie Laurie's face droops; she dares not look up, but waits, trembling so greatly that she can scarcely stand, for what has to be said.

Mrs Laurie, with a sudden impulse of protection, draws her child's arm within her own—moves forward steadily, all her pride of mother and of woman coming to her aid; bows to her right hand and her left; says she is glad to see that this is really Mr Randall, and not the wraith her simple

Jenny had supposed; and, speaking thus in a voice which is but a murmur of inarticulate sound to Menie, bows again, and would pass on.

But John Home of Crofthill lays his hand upon her sleeve. "You and me have no outcast to settle. Leave the bairns to themselves."

With a startled glance Mrs Laurie looks round her, at the old man's face of anxious friendliness, at the deep flush on Randall's brow, and at her own Menie's drooping head. "Shall I leave you, Menie?" Menie makes no answer—as pale and as cold as marble, with a giddy pain in her forehead, unable to raise her swimming eyes—but she makes a great effort to support herself, as her mother gradually looses her hand from her arm.

Passive, silent, her whole mind absorbed with the pain it takes to keep herself erect, and guide her faltering steps along the road; but Randall is by Menie's side once more.

Father and mother have gone on, back towards the cottage; silently, without a word, these parted hearts follow them side by side. If she had any power left but what is wanted for her own support, she would wonder why Randall does not speak. She does wonder, indeed, faintly, even through her pain. With downcast eyes like hers, he walks beside her, through this chill dewy air, between these rustling hedges, in a conscious silence, which every moment becomes more overpowering, more strange.

"Menie!" With a sudden start she acknowledges her name; but there is nothing more.

"I said, when we parted, that you were disloyal to me and to Nature," said Randall, after another pause. "Menie, I have learned many a thing since then. It was I that was disloyal to Nature—but never to you."

Still no answer; this giddiness grows upon her, though she does not miss a syllable of what he says.

"There is no question between us—none that does not fade like a vapour before the sunlight I see. Menie, can you trust me again?"

She cannot answer—she can do nothing but falter and stumble upon this darkening road. It grows like night to her. What is this she leans upon— the arm of Randall Home?

Miss Janet sits in her shawl of state in Jenny's kitchen—very curious and full of anxiety. "Eh, woman, such a sair heart I had," said Miss Janet, "when wha should come, as fast up the road as if he kent I was watching, but my ain bairn? He hasna been hame since July's wedding; ye wouldna think it o' a grand lad like our Randall, and him sae clever, and sae muckle thocht o' in the world—but when he gaed owre his father's door-stane again, the puir laddie grat like a bairn. Will you look if they're coming, Jenny—nae word o' them? Eh, woman, what can make Miss Menie sae ill at the like o' him?"

"The like o' him's nae such great things," said Jenny, with a little snort. "I wouldna say but what Miss Menie has had far better in her offer. She's a self-willed thing—she'll no take Jenny's word; but weel I wat, if she askit me——"

"Whisht, you're no to say a word," cried Miss Janet, coming in from the door. "I see them on the road—I see them coming hame. Jenny, you're no to speak. Miss Menie and my Randall, they're ae heart ance mair."

And so it was—one heart, but not a heart at ease; the love-renewed still owned a pang of terror. But day after day came out of the softening heavens— hour after hour preached and expounded of the mellowed nature—the soul which had learned to forget itself; other pictures rose under Menie's fingers—faces which looked you bravely in the face—eyes that forgot to doubt and criticise. The clouds cleared from her firmament in gusts and rapid evolutions, as before these brisk October winds. One fear followed another, falling like the autumn leaves; a warmer atmosphere crept into the cottage, a brighter sunshine filled its homely rooms. Day by day, advancing steadily, the son drew farther in, to his domestic place. The mother gave her welcome heartily; the daughter, saying nothing, felt the more; and no one said a word of grumbling, save perverse Jenny, who wept with joy the while, when another year and another life lighted up into natural gladness the sweet harmonious quiet of Menie Laurie's heart.